Love!

She had dreamed of
delight of being able
another human bein
and giving at the sa
cravings by his own
she'd woken, reality

returning to a dead world. Yet always her natural
resilience had survived. Her longing and secret
desire had persisted, and never so fiercely as in the
lonely moors, with the winds strong about her proud
form, her rich gleaming hair blown free in the salty
heather-scented air.

Also by Mary Williams
in Sphere Books:

Heronsmere
Castle Carnack
Merlake Towers
The Tregallis Inheritance
Trenhawk
The Granite King

The Mistress of Blackstone

Mary Williams

Sphere Books Limited

First published in Great Britain by
William Kimber & Co. Limited 1984

Published by Sphere Books Ltd 1987
27 Wrights Lane, London W8 5TZ

TRADE
MARK

Set in 10/11pt Linotron Baskerville

Printed and bound in Great Britain by
Cox & Wyman Ltd, Reading

For Mike
My love

1

1826

She could not bear to leave him. The night was misty and seductive, holding a thousand scents of flowers, heather, lush bluebells and ferns, mingled with the tang of brine from the sea. Her lips were soft and urgent under his – soft as the velvet evening enclosing them. Her lustrous dark auburn hair had half-fallen from its pins. His profile, clearly chiselled under a fine brow, drew back momentarily, his eyes staring hard into her black-lashed blue-green ones. How beautiful she was; one day he would paint her just as she appeared then – a siren of nature – mysterious, yet vibrantly real against the line of cliffs and breaking tide.

For a brief interlude it seemed to him the whole world waited. All was still; so very quiet – no sound even from the small town of St Kerrick, only half a mile away below a fold of the moor.

Suddenly he swept her into his arms again.

'Oh, Lydia – I do love you—'

'I know.'

'If only your father—'

The small determined chin above her slender, rounded throat took a stubborn thrust.

'He will. Dearest Charles, he *must*. I'll make him. Somehow I will, and if he won't agree we'll go ahead anyway. I'll marry you, so there!'

Her smile, through the dim light was brilliant, confident. She was eighteen years old, and wildly, madly in love with this young artist, Charles Clarke, who only a year ago had come to Cornwall and stayed.

Her father had disapproved of the friendship from the

start, considering the 'foreigner' from up country merely an improvident adventurer with nothing in his pockets and certainly lacking sufficient talent to bring him the slightest recognition. Being head of the village school, which was run under the auspices of the Church, he considered it his duty ruthlessly to discourage any such character from making advances to either of his daughters. He was a strict disciplinarian, of stern moral judgement, overbearing will, and ambitious.

His sister and housekeeper, Anne Teague, who had taken charge domestically since Joseph's wife Ellen's death, had gradually moulded herself and her standards of life to his. Following his loss, seventeen years before, when Lydia's sister Clara had been born, she had been at first shocked by Joseph's iron determination to vanquish at all costs any visible sign of grief, then gradually reconciled. If he wished his family to be ruled with a rod of iron, then so it would be. Except on rare occasions, there had been little laughter at Greyfriars, the family home, and only rare moments of rebellion when the determined Lydia had proudly defied unfair discipline and been punished for it.

Clara was a different matter. She was fair, like her late mother, but more beautiful – so exquisitely featured, so gentle-mannered and compliant that even Joseph's hard heart softened when he thought of her. The fact that she had a defective spine, giving her rounded shoulders an obvious stoop, only increased his passion for this one lovely child. She was the weak link in the arrogant armour of his character. Whatever she wished for, in reason, he saw that she had. In comparison, Lydia's strength secretly offended him. If she minded, she did her best not to show it. She had a deep compassion for all delicate defenceless creatures, and a strong bond between herself and her weaker sister was established. Clara, the idol of her father's affection, became the subtle pivot on which the household turned. If Clara expressed a wish for some mark of vanity further to enhance her beauty, such as a length of material for a new dress, she generally obtained it at Lydia's expense.

'Lydia is careless with her attire,' her father pointed out. 'She's strong and healthy, and forever wanting to roam the countryside. Poor Clara has no such advantages. It's little enough to ask to make her a fresh gown – something to enliven the child's sad existence.'

'The child', despite the sympathy and pity bestowed on her, thrived on the attention, and was not half so sad in spirit as her father believed. She had learned in early youth that a pleading glance from her wonderful violet eyes could work wonders. Her father, whose salary from teaching was only £25 a year, could only afford to spend a very limited amount on any favours asked. This she quite understood, and was careful not to demand too much. He marvelled at her modesty and thought for him, quite unaware of the shrewd mind beneath the fairy-like exterior. To Lydia he frequently said:

'Never forget your duty to your young sister. When it pleases God to take me – which I fervently hope will not be for many years – I should like to believe I leave her well-being in loving care. I hope I have your promise on that.'

'I'll do my best,' Lydia replied dutifully. 'She may get married of course. She's very pretty.'

'And handicapped. Never forget that.'

No one at Greyfriars ever did. It was impossible. There were times when Lydia chafed, fiercely resenting the word 'duty' and the chains it imposed – hours when she managed to escape unseen and climb the wild moorland hills above St Kerrick, staring beyond the rugged Cornish coast towards the foam-flecked sea, or across the shadowed valley towards the opposite skyline where the dark shapes of tin mines dotted the wind-blown heights. There, among the heather, great granite boulders and standing stones of a primitive bygone era, she felt free, with the blood coursing wild and warm through her veins. For a brief time she could be herself, Lydia Teague, with all the delights and wonders of living ahead. There was so much to sense and experience – so much to savour and desire and love.

Love!

She had dreamed of it so often – the sensation and delight

of being able to abandon herself utterly to another human being – a man capable of both taking and giving at the same time, of subduing her utmost cravings by his own overmastering passion. Sometimes, when asleep in her small bedroom at Greyfriars, a male figure had stirred her slumber – not clearly defined – but someone, a force she recognised, as though she'd known him all her life – an impact that set her pulses hammering and her whole being alight. She'd felt the sweetness of kisses on her lips and the throbbing of her body at his touch. When she'd woken, reality had been momentarily like returning to a dead world. Yet always her natural resilience had survived. Her longing and secret desire had persisted, and never so fiercely as in the lonely moments when she stood, unfettered in spirit, on the high moors, with the winds strong about her proud form, her rich gleaming hair blown free in the salty heather-scented air.

It was on such an occasion that Charles had first seen her. From a sheltered spot by a group of granite boulders, he'd watched her climbing the slope towards the tip of the ridge and been arrested and excited by the swirling of hair and skirts blown back from swinging, firmly rounded thighs. He'd also noted, as she drew nearer, the prideful lift of chin and profile, the tilted thrust of breasts, and rosy glow of windlashed cheeks.

At a propitious moment he stepped aside from the stones, and stood before her, smiling. The afternoon sunlight glinted on his fair hair and gleaming teeth. He was wearing black boots, fawn breeches, and an olive-green frac. The double-breasted cut-away coat was open, revealing a frilled cream shirt. But it was the stance – not the attire – the lively impish quality about him that had first attracted her attention. He could have been some figure from Shakespeare – a Ferdinand or Ariel sprung to life from the bushes and ancient stones. Although elegant in his own way, his slim form somehow defied convention and fashion.

There was an instant rapport between them.

'How handsome he is,' she'd thought, with her heart quickening, and his own reaction – 'What a beauty.'

'Who are you?' he demanded instantly. 'And where do you come from? Some spirit of the moor surely? But no. Spirits do not blush or catch the sunlight in their hair—'

'Aren't you being a little impertinent, sir?' she'd queried quickly, in the manner her father had imbued in her to deal with any gallant seeking her acquaintance without the necessary introduction.

He'd laughed in her face. 'Of course. Otherwise you'd be off and away before I had a good look at you. And I don't want just one, but many. Come on now. Don't pretend you're annoyed—'

The rose of her cheeks deepened. 'I—'

'You're quite beautiful, and you know it.' He'd seized her hand. 'I want to paint you.'

'Oh, goodness. So *that*'s it. You're an artist?'

He'd nodded, and indicated an open box and canvas, jutting out from behind a boulder. 'Does that explain things?'

She'd shrugged tantalisingly. 'No. Not really. To call me beautiful is silly. My sister's beautiful—' Her words died as the light shawl she wore was caught on a strong gust of wind and carried away. He'd sprung after it, caught it by a tangle of briar, and ran back to place it round her shoulders. His touch had been fire between them. Moments later his mouth was on hers, and she was responding to his ardour with all the frustrated longing of her nature. Then, remembering where she was, she'd explained breathlessly, 'Please – don't. You mustn't. *Please*—'

He'd released her, and noting her expression, the trembling lips, astonished rapture of her widely set green eyes, had known she was not angry – only excited, and perhaps a little afraid. Of what? Of whom?

In the days following he'd learned, during secret meetings, something of her background and her father's solid stern reputation in St Kerrick's social circle. A mean man, and a tyrant obviously. One who was obsessed by the plaintive pathetic beauty of the younger daughter, to the complete detriment of the vivid girl he, Charles, found so fascinating. 'I should like to meet Clara,' Charles had said more than once. 'She sounds such a paragon. Too good to be true.'

'Oh, she's real enough. And you'd probably fall in love with her.'

'With *you* about? Hardly. Still, as she's your sister we'll have to be introduced sometime. Because—' He'd hesitated before adding, 'I think you love me, Lydia and I want to marry you. So of course a meeting with your family's inevitable.'

The admission had been music in her ears.

It was only later that formidable doubts of her father's approval had registered. In fact there really were no doubts at all. Joseph Teague considered all artists and actors as little better than rogues and ne'er-do-wells, unless of course they happened to have wealth and recognised status. Charles Clarke had none.

Her inward prediction had proved to be true.

Following an awkward incident when Joseph had inadvertently met Lydia and the young man walking openly together down St Kerrick's main street towards the square, Lydia had later received a stern injunction from her father to sunder immediately any contact or friendship with Charles.

'He has no credentials, no known background, nothing at all in his pocket, I've heard, and is a regular frequenter of the Silver Goat on most evenings.'

'So is the vicar,' Lydia retorted recklessly. 'The inn has a good reputation. Even the squire—'

'Hold your tongue, miss. We are not discussing the vicar or Sir Godfrey. It is your reputation I'm concerned with, and I forbid you – absolutely *forbid*, do you hear? – that you should see him wittingly again. If you meet by chance in the street you will pass by with only an indication of a slight nod – better still, without appearing to recognise him. Now—' raising a hand in dismissal – 'there is an end to the matter. You will retire to your room now and reflect on what I have said. If you disobey—' his cold eye narrowed – 'you will certainly regret it. Discipline I *will* have in my own house, even if I have to enforce it. Do you understand?' His glance strayed briefly to a switch lying on his desk.

Lydia's face crimsoned. For once indignation replaced all fear in her.

'Don't threaten me, Father, I'm no longer a child or one of your pupils. If you raise a hand or whip to me I will make your name a disgrace in St Kerrick by running away with the gypsies or—' she lifted her chin scornfully – 'doing something much worse. And I mean it.'

Her bright green eyes were so wild and challenging, her manner so openly defiant, he was momentarily speechless. Then he said, in deadly precise tones. 'Go to your room. Later you will return and we will say a prayer to God asking forgiveness for your sins.'

'Sins!' Lydia thought scornfully, as she left the study, and walked proudly down the dark hall towards the stairs. There was no sin in loving and freedom, and wanting all the wild sweet wonder of the world. Charles Clarke was committing no crime in wanting her for his wife. If he was poor, she would stand by him and they would be poor together. She could look after him, and although she might not be brilliant at hemming sheets and darning, she could spin and weave. She could make pretty things to sell in shops and haberdashers maybe. Oh, there was nothing she wouldn't do for him, and in time – for Clara's sake – she would somehow become reconciled with Joseph. Because of his harshness she had never really been able to love him; but she loved Clara with all the compassion and tenderness of her warm heart. Poor Clara, who in spite of her lovely face was unable to enjoy stolen moments on the moors at early dawn or on moonlit nights when it was possible to escape from the grey walls, or to savour the sweetness of a lover's lips on her mouth.

Remembering such things, Lydia's rebellious mood gradually died. In future, she decided, waiting for her father's summons for her prayer of contrition, she would make a great effort to appear humble in his presence and willing to accept any scolding without impertinent response. Perhaps, with a more docile approach she could at least bring Joseph to *meeting* Charles. Then, as the days passed, softened by her apparent docility, he might even agree to have him to the house on the pretext of studying Joseph's fine collection of classic books and writings. Charles, except for poetry, was not really interested in reading – especially of the moral kind, she knew that – but with their happiness at stake he could surely make a pretence of it. Such deception wasn't commendable of course, but she didn't care a fig about that. All that mattered was her passion for Charles and his for her. There was no reason on earth why they shouldn't be married like other young couples in love.

It was not as though Charles was uneducated or not of good family. He had been to Eton and Oxford, where he had disgraced himself by neglecting his studies for lighter, more adventurous pursuits, and had eventually been sent down. His father, who had two elder worthier sons, had 'disinherited' him and dismissed him from the family home with only a small monthly allowance to keep him out of debt. Unfortunately debts still accrued. 'Managing money,' he had told Lydia, wasn't his 'strong point.' He had laughed, with that whimsical tilt of his lips that she found so engaging, and she had treated the matter as a joke, not realising how very considerably these debts were increasing. Any practical sense he possessed warned him that becoming involved with Lydia Teague was stupid on his part. There were so many beautiful women in the world – wealthy girls who could provide security and the chance for him to follow the one pursuit he wanted – painting. The trouble was that Lydia tantalised and at the moment completely obsessed him. He wanted her, and if her dreary ogre of a father couldn't be persuaded to give his blessing – dammit, he'd take her with or without marriage lines. Meanwhile he restrained himself and tried to believe she'd work the miracle. Lydia, in exuberant moments, was almost convinced she could do it. Joseph's temper seemed certainly more equable as the days passed. But so far he had firmly refused to allow the young upstart to darken his doors.

Upstart! Lydia had thought scornfully, and that pompous expression 'darkening of doors!' how old-fashioned and *smug*. As if Greyfriars' doors could be made any darker than they were! It was such a forbidding, unbeautiful, loveless sort of house. Secretly she hated it. And never more so than on that certain afternoon of her avowal to Charles that whatever happened she'd marry him – and somehow make her father agree.

Never had the heather and gorse smelled sweeter, as she started running down the hill after kissing her lover goodbye. Never had her mood been more confident or filled with such wild expectancy.

Over tumps of undergrowth and wind-blown furze she skipped, skirt held up by both hands, springing nimbly as a goat over any obstructing stone or ancient briar-covered mine-shaft. Charles watched her with a deepening sense of unpredictable unease, until her figure was obscured by a fold in the moor. He had no share in her optimism. That devil of a schoolmaster was more than a nuisance – he was formidable. A force the young man was already becoming tired of fighting. He doubted even that if it came to a show of fists he'd win. Mean, hard, narrow-minded, and strong as an ox – that was Joseph Teague, and the thought of the power the despicable schoolmaster had wielded over his lovely daughter through her younger days – the punishments and chastisement, followed by hypocritical prayers when she'd been forced to kneel, chastened and smarting, proffering a guilt she did not feel, filled him with revulsion.

He'd rescue her if he could. But was it possible? Sombrely he walked away to the cottage he'd taken for the summer, half a mile on the far side of St Kerrick. He did not see Lydia suddenly tumble and fall, had no view of an erect figure astride a cream stallion riding towards her from the opposite direction.

Lydia meanwhile, struggled to her feet, brushed strands of long silky hair from her face, and looked down ruefully at a rent in her gown.

Oh botheration. What a fuss there'd be – especially if Joseph got to know.

It was just then that the sound of hooves registered, followed by its abrupt cessation as the rider dismounted. Lydia attempted to straighten her skirt against a rounded thigh, lifted her jade eyes upwards to the stranger's face, with her own cheeks flaming.

'How silly of me,' she said ineffectually. 'I fell.'

'Yes.' His voice was warm and slightly amused, but there was no hint of a smile on his lips. The dark eyes staring down on her were narrowed and enigmatic. His thick black hair sprang back from a wide brow, gleaming with rich russet lights in the dying sunlight. He was richly clad in an olive velvet riding jacket, yellow breeches and fitting black boots. A gentleman obviously; not really young, but not old either.

After his one short comment on her plight, she pushed her tumbled hair back over her shoulders, drew herself to her full height which barely reached his shoulder, and said, 'I must be going. I'm late. It was ridiculous of me to rush like that—'

'It certainly was,' he interrupted. 'You could have hurt yourself.'

'I'm quite all right, thank you.' Even in her own ears her tones sounded stiff and formal, but she was irritated that this rather condescending stranger should have witnessed her in such an undignified situation. She attempted to pass. Still holding his horse by the bridle he touched her forearm with his free hand.

'Will you allow me to accompany you to your destination?'

'Why?'

'Because I'd be pleased to see you comfortably and safely off my land.'

She stared, arching her clearly defined brows above her arresting eyes.

'*Your* land?'

He nodded.

'I purchased the manor of Blackstone a month ago. This portion of moor is included in the property.'

'Oh. I see.'

'Don't worry,' he told her. 'I don't propose to forbid anyone walking here, so long as reasonable care is taken not to risk necks or meet an ugly end down a mine-shaft.'

Her lips softened slightly.

'I know this land like the – the—'

'The back of your hand,' he concluded. 'Well—' he took a kerchief from his pocket and handed it to her – 'Please use this to clean it.'

Mortified she glanced at her earth-stained fingers, and made a quick attempt to rub the soil away.

Then she pulled her shawl round her shoulders, handed the fabric back to him, and said politely, 'Thank you. And there's no need at all for you to accompany me.'

'Oh, but I don't agree. And I've certainly got the right to know the name of any trespasser crossing my path.'

'*Trespasser?*'

'Yes. That's what you are – however charming. Well, Miss—?'

'Teague,' she said coldly and clearly. 'Lydia Teague.'

'And I'm Richard Fearnley.'

'Goodbye then, Mr Fearnley.' Very pointedly she swept past him, chin held high.

He laughed, and instantly caught her arm. She wrenched herself free, almost stumbling again.

'Come now. No need to be on your dignity. I won't bite or rape you.'

Antagonism swept through her in a wave of temper.

'Don't touch me. Leave me alone. My father's a very strict man – head of St Kerrick's school. He'd—'

'Put you over his knee for daring to walk with the new squire of Blackstone?' The query had a taunt in it. 'If that's so, the pretty picture I had just now of an abandoned young woman in her lover's arms would have caused a considerable scene—' Unconsciously they had both been moving in the direction of St Kerrick, his horse still held on a slight rein.

She stood quite still with such outrage flooding her lovely face, her green eyes so wide and blazing, he knew in that single instant he must one day, sooner or later, possess her.

'You were spying on me then?' she said after the brief pause. 'You *saw*. That was contemptible of you.'

'You were both quite obvious to me,' he answered, 'and if your father's the frightening disciplinarian you say, I advise you to be more careful in the future.'

She bit her lip as he continued, 'Your young swain has one of my cottages, I believe.'

'*Your* cottage?'

'It's on my property. Rents it for next to nothing, if my agent's figures are correct.'

Her anger died suddenly into apprehension.

'He's an artist. Artists don't make much money unless they're very famous. Charles has to make his way yet, then he'll be able to pay more. Anyway the place is in a poor condition—'

'Exactly. With a new roof and other improvements it could be made profitable. And we don't know when, or if ever your young painter is going to have anything at all in his pocket to help expenses, do we?'

'Are you threatening me?' she demanded coldly.

'No, no. The matter's none of your concern. But I should warn you, Miss Teague, that as a landlord I have responsibilities, also that I intend to reopen that old mine Wheal Chance, in the not too far off future. It has an adit running a considerable way under the sea, so when Mr Charles's tenancy ends at the end of the year, it's unlikely it will be renewed. The cottage will be made fit for a working family near the site of the mine, or put to some other useful purpose. However—' his mouth took a wry twist, 'by then I expect your little romance will have come to its natural conclusion as such highly impractical affairs generally do. In the meantime—' though his voice was casual, his glance was not '—keep your wits about you. If what rumour says is true, that dashing young reprobate of a dabbler, if you will forgive the term, has a roving eye for any pretty woman. So don't bank on faithfulness.'

She brought a hand up smartly, and slapped his face hard.

His colour deepened.

'Never do that again, Miss Teague, or I will repay in a manner most undignified to your person, and to your father's approval, I'm sure. One day soon I hope to meet him.'

Lydia, without deigning to answer, swept ahead of him down the path that took an abrupt turn towards St Kerrick.

He stood motionless for a moment, staring at the swirl of skirts and burnished gloss of tumbled hair. Then he swung himself on to his horse and headed towards Blackstone.

His blood was fire in his veins, his loins hungered.

'What a virago,' he thought, as the freshening wind brought a sting of brine to his face. 'And what a beauty.' Never had a woman so stirred him. Have her he would, whatever obstacles had to be overcome. That pretty boy – the artist – in his derelict cottage, might possess the looks of a Galahad, but when it came to marriage he hadn't a penny. And if what rumour said about old Teague was true, he would jump at the chance of a wealthy son-in-law.

Love? Well, the young madam had shown her claws pretty fiercely at this first encounter. But claws could be trimmed and tempers cooled. Sweetness could replace anger, and gentleness win trust. What a wife she would make.

He had no doubts of his capacity to win her – eventually.

He knew women, and had all the expertise of a lover's art at his disposal. Many, in the past, had pleased him; on two occasions he'd been on the verge of matrimony, then at the end, commonsense had prevailed and he'd withdrawn not gracefully, but with a crude honesty that although hurtful at the time had proved completely effective. This time it would be different. His decision was made. And when Richard Fearnley set his mind on any particular course he was seldom diverted. His primary object in purchasing Blackstone had been the challenge of bringing abandoned earth and stone to life again, of turning dross into gold and salvaging precious ore from Cornwall's rugged landscape. The wealthy Devon estate inherited from his father had no need of reimbursement – generations before, mining and shipping, combined with secret lucrative slaving activities – had established the Fearnleys as one of the richest and most powerful families in the land. Politics also had played a certain part in enhancing the public and social image. In debate the Fearnley voice and influence had been strong, but subtly ambiguous, generally managing to sense the way the 'wind was blowing' through the House, and assess cunningly the reaction of both Whigs and Tories to industrial and social problems.

Richard possessed no interest whatever in such matters. From a colourful and strong-willed grandmother who had been a great beauty and actress in her day, he had inherited a zest for life that demanded physical rather than mental pursuits. He was twenty-nine years old, almost thirty, and avid for conquest of new spheres.

Now he had found what he sought.

Lydia.

The thought of failure never occurred to him. True, she had appeared passionately over-fond of her rustic charmer on the moor. But with his natural shrewd insight of men, Richard guessed that if necessary the pretty fellow could easily be bought off. From what he'd heard, Clarke was frivolous, vain, and badly in need of cash. With Charles out of the way he'd soon manage to bring Lydia to heel – or rather, to his arms.

So the process of wooing started, all unknown to Lydia.

In the days following, Fearnley made a point of establishing himself agreeably with the residents of St Kerrick – not an easy undertaking considering the deeply implanted mistrust of the Cornish to any invading 'furriner'. But with employment at low ebb due to the closure of two mines, and wages – if any – at a minimum, the news that the fresh master of Blackstone meant to set the workings open again and see that no family was without food for hungry bellies, and with a few new comforts into the bargain, soon made its impact. Nods of respect were given where before heads had been turned away. It was said in the bar of The Silver Goat and kiddleywinks of lesser repute, that 'the man might have a bit of good in him after all'.

Even Master Teague was reputed to be on good terms with the young squire, who had visited the schoolhouse twice.

'I know tes true,' one housewife said to another. ''Cos I watched an saw 'en. Can you imagine et? A dreary preachin' joy killer like Joseph Teague, an that theer lord Tom Noddy?'

'Mus' be sumthen behind et all,' came the dour answer.

'Ais. An' ef you ask me et's a woman. That girl Lydia. Real handsome she do look these days.' There was a sniff. 'An' not without reason so I've heard. Bin seen goin' up the moor more'n once lately. Joe Baaze, farmer James' shepherd, watched things goin' on theer you wouldn' believe. That young painter feller – Clarke edn' et? – He's the one.'

'Oh Gawd!'

'There'll be trouble, you mark my words. Real trouble when schoolmaster finds out.'

Joseph, however, being secretly flattered by the wealthy Richard Fearnley's obvious appreciation of his learning, did not find out for some time. Lydia, now comparatively docile, had ceased temporarily to worry him unduly, leaving him at ease to cultivate the young man's acquaintance. However holy a facade the domineering schoolmaster might display to the world, his shrewd covetous sense was strong beneath. Power and wealth were not to be sneered at. Many advantages might accrue from a friendship between the two of them. So on the first opportunity Richard was invited to an evening meal at Greyfriars, which was politely accepted.

The food was well served, Miss Anne proved herself a prim but well-mannered hostess, wearing her best black silk with jet ear-rings, necklace and brooch. The maid-of-all-work Ellen had been well primed beforehand to bob at opportune moments, and Lydia and Clara behaved with utmost decorum, only speaking when spoken to, and keeping their pretty heads otherwise averted from the bold gaze of Master Fearnley. They both looked charming; Clara in pale blue that emphasised her bright gold hair, delicate complexion and cornflower blue eyes, Lydia in dark red made especially for her by her aunt when the occasion had been broached.

'For once, Joseph,' she had told her brother, 'you should be generous to Lydia. She's behaved well lately, and the girl at present has nothing suitable.' So Joseph had agreed for Anne and his elder daughter to visit the haberdasher's in St Kerrick and purchase the length of maroon organdie. Over the wide neckline which would have exposed too much white shoulder for his taste, a small black lace mantilla was modestly arranged. Lydia, secretly irritated, knew, however, that Richard Fearnley was quite aware of the translucent skin and well rounded breasts beneath. At moments his glance was warm and appraising in her direction, and although she pretended to be unaware of the sensual desire every time he looked at her, she didn't fool him for one moment. Miss Lydia might profess disdain, but he had already penetrated her chilly armour. It was a beginning. The younger girl, so obviously the apple of her father's eye, was entrancingly beautiful, and Joseph was gratified by the numerous compliments thrown her way. Her curved spine had been as cleverly camouflaged as possible by frills of lace, but her fragile loveliness left Fearnley inwardly cold. His hot blood and heart clamoured only for Lydia, though he did his best not to show it during the meal.

Later, when the two men retreated to the library, their conversation was concerned at first with St Kerrick affairs – the need for a new roof for the church, of an extra assistant at the school, and a eulogy from Joseph on the essentials of a good education, which entailed chiefly arithmetic, religious teaching, a certain limited knowledge of the classics, but none of the flippant arty business.

Richard nodded thoughtfully, then said, 'What about sport, health, and a little enjoyment?'

'Enjoyment, sir?'

'Why not? A boy or young man with a sense of fun is surely far more likely to make a good worker. And I'm hoping to provide plenty of employment round here; mining mostly of course. Copper – tin – and now something else – cobalt. I've already bought up a large number of shares in the smelting company. So I shall have a considerable say in what goes on there in the future.'

Joseph was dubious. 'I thought *that* mine was a white elephant.'

'It happens to be practically the only one in the country that can supply a large quantity of such pure colour. Remember that in the past England has depended mostly on foreigners for cobalt. But now we have it here I propose to sink a tidy sum in ensuring we don't just let it run out.'

'Hm. I hope you're right, sir.'

'So do I. If I'm not I'll have to accept the loss. But I like a challenge—' His voice faded away; he was thinking – 'And not only in commodities, trade, and adventure, but in women. At least, just one. Your daughter, Lydia.'

Joseph at that moment would have been quite shocked had he the remotest idea of what was passing through Fearnley's mind. He'd been gratified by Richard's open admiration of Clara. This was understandable – to be expected. In a wild moment it had occurred to him that admiration *might* possibly develop into something more serious. If so – how very convenient and propitious. During a recent visit from the doctor Joseph had been informed that new treatment for spinal defects was now available for those who could afford it. Joseph was in no such position, which hurt him deeply. That his beautiful much-loved child should be deprived of any help simply because funds were lacking, seemed grossly unfair and – he had to admit to himself – an error on the part of the Almighty. But if Richard Fearnley developed serious intentions – how very different life could be for her.

From that moment all his concentration, his ambitions, were devoted to that one end.

And when on his second visit to Greyfriars Richard openly confided to the schoolmaster that he was anxious to take a wife and asked permission to pay court to his daughter, Joseph's gratification was hard to conceal by a calm veneer. There had been a plan in God's will after all, he thought, as he nodded, saying benignly,

'Of course, Mr Fearnley sir. I am quite delighted for you to pay your respects to Clara. She *is* very young of course, and not exactly robust. But with your devotion and care I'm sure—'

Then the bomb fell.

'I was not referring to Clara, sir. It was Lydia. I more than admire her – I want her for my wife. I hope you have no objections?'

Joseph was so shocked, so completely taken by surprise he became momentarily speechless. Lydia! that passionate wild girl with her tempers and wilful ways! – for any discerning male to have an eye for her when there was a choice of winning sweet Clara, for whom he could do so much, seemed incomprehensible.

'Well, sir?'

Still not understanding, Joseph managed to say slowly, 'Lydia! I'm afraid I jumped too quickly to conclusions. I never thought – I couldn't see—'

'How adequately we're suited? We may not be – yet. But as a schoolmaster you should know that with sufficient tact, courage – even discipline perhaps – most beautiful women can be moulded to a lover's desire. And I certainly desire her, Mr Teague – did so from the first moment we met on the moors weeks ago.'

Joseph's thick brows drew together in a frown.

'I didn't know you'd had a rendezvous there.'

'It was just a chance meeting. And a very lucky one I'd say.'

'Hm.' Joseph's first reaction of disappointment slowly evaporated into grudging acceptance of a situation which although rather different from what he'd hoped for, could nevertheless be put to good account. As a wife Clara would have had a right to the very best the Fearnley fortune could provide. Her health would have demanded prior claim. However, as Richard's sister-in-law and in his besotted state concerning Lydia it should be an easy matter to work the miracle. Clara would be 'family', with influence and sufficient wealth behind her for consultation and treatment from the best specialists in the land.

By the end of the meeting Joseph's spirits had risen to conviviality.

'Have no fear, sir,' he said to Fearnley before he left. 'I'll inform my daughter of your intentions at the earliest opportunity. Tomorrow if possible. I can assure you she'll be honoured and delighted – you need have no fears on that score at all.' Secretly he was not at all sure of Lydia's reaction. But come what may, he determined that whatever means had to be undertaken he would manage to bend her to his will, either by physical threats, coercion, or – and this would probably be the most effective course – by stirring her compassion on Clara's behalf. Yes, he was certain the latter weapon, which was a moral issue would be the most effective.

The following morning Joseph was unusually considerate and polite to his elder daughter, and when, in the afternoon, he called her into his study for a 'fatherly chat', she sensed immediately that he might be going to ask some impossible favour. Knowing of her recent misguided interest in the improvident young artist, Joseph had expected stubbornness at first, but her violent refusal took him unpleasantly aback.

'Marry *him*?' she demanded. 'That conceited overbearing man? Why – I hardly know him. I don't even like him. How could you let him think so for a moment?' She was breathing quickly. Warm rich colour had flooded her cheeks, bright golden sparks of anger lit her jade eyes to flaming brightest emerald.

'Lydia!' At the peremptory note in his voice her chin took a stubborn thrust. 'Control yourself. Mr Fearnley is paying you a great compliment. Do you realise he could have the pick of most eligible young women in London society? Do you consider yourself so desirable or beautiful that you can afford to refuse such a chance? If so, take a good look at yourself in the mirror! Richard Fearnley may be misguided enough to admire you, but most men wouldn't. You are hoydenish, wild, with an ungovernable temper which should have been curbed far more strictly when you were young—'

'By whippings and being locked in my room with only bread and water for two days at a time?' Lydia intervened fiercely. 'Stop it, Father. I'm not a slave any more. I will *not* marry any man I don't love whatever you do or say. Charles will be my husband, however you try to prevent it—'

'I think not. I forbid it. And what about your sister?'

'Clara?'

'Who else? Her future is completely in your hands.'

She stared. 'Whatever do you mean?'

Turning his back on her Joseph walked to the window, and with his hands clasped behind him, said, 'She needs treatment, Lydia. Attention from London specialists that I cannot possibly afford to give. If you marry Richard Fearnley years of life for her can be assured; without it I doubt she has very long to live.'

Lydia was stunned. At last she managed to say, 'How do you know?'

'I have recently been in correspondence with a friend, Harold Carnley, who has a knowledge of such things. Our own doctor endorsed his opinion.'

There was a portentous pause before Joseph turned and with his eyes hard on Lydia's face said, 'Do you wish to be responsible for Clara's death?'

The colour suddenly ebbed from the proud young countenance. The rich voice shook when she replied, 'Of *course* not. You're not being fair though. Why should *I* be sacrificed? Why—'

'Why should *you* be so favoured as to gain the attentions of a rich and handsome suitor when your poor lovely young sister is disregarded? Only the good Lord knows that. But then it is not our business to question the ways of God.'

There was silence for a few moments – a pause in which Lydia's thoughts surged wildly this way and that – from one possibility to another – of running away with Charles and leaving St Kerrick and the duties imposed there for ever, to the picture of Clara on her death-bed, the helpless victim of circumstance, and her own – Lydia's – selfishness. Intermixed with the confusion was the ever invading memory of Charles – her beloved's kisses, the pressure of his arms about her body, of her promise to him that they'd marry whatever happened. Then Fearnley! She shivered with a tumult of emotions quickening her heart. She didn't like him. He was cocksure, conceited, and even a little frightening. The idea of him ravishing her body suddenly angered her.

'I don't know,' she said clearly. 'Even for Clara you've no right to ask such a thing.' She turned to the door with a whirl of skirts. '*No*. You haven't Father,' repeating, 'not even for Clara.'

Joseph's lips twitched in a small secretive smile.

'Think about it,' he said complacently. 'In the morning when you've pondered over the problem I am quite sure you will have found guidance to come to the right conclusion. I shall pray for you.'

The door closed with a snap.

That evening Lydia met Charles at their usual place on the moor. As his lips sought hers, draining it seemed all the sweetness and passion from her being, tears of emotion, under the thick velvet lashes, flooded her eyes.

Sensing her distress, Charles, stroking the tumbled mass of silken dark hair, murmured, 'Lydia – my sweet, my darling – what is it? What's the matter?'

Haltingly, in a flood of broken words, she told him. He led her to a boulder beneath the ancient looming carn, and sat there thoughtfully, with her head resting on his shoulder. Only a thin film of watery moonlight lit the night sky. Their figures merged into the blurred landscape of rocks and furze like effigies from a bygone age. Seconds passed, until she whispered, 'What are we going to do? I *can't* marry that man. I won't. Charles – *dearest* Charles, you must take me away. I'll write to Clara – she'll understand. We'll get the money to help her – I *know* we can, somehow—' her voice broke.

When he spoke his voice was steady, the tones reasonable and somehow chilling.

'My darling,' he said, 'there's nothing in the world I want more. Nothing. I love you. You know that – but—' he hesitated.

'Yes?'

He removed his arm from her waist and stood up. Through the misted light his figure still had that theatrical quality, like some youthful character from Shakespeare. He opened his arms wide and said, 'How can we? We can't fight the world or your father, Lydia. At the beginning I made myself believe we could. But the odds are too heavy against us. You must understand. I own nothing – not a bean. How could we make a living? And how would you live with your conscience knowing your sister was suffering because of our – our passion—'

'Our *love* you mean?' Her voice had hardened.

'Love? Yes. But the kind we have – the passion for each other – might so easily die with poverty. And I'm an artist,

Lydia. To be tied down in miserable circumstances could stifle me. *You*'d be the sufferer. And do you think I could bear that?'

She got to her feet sensing his true character for the first time.

'No,' she answered coldly. 'I don't suppose you could. I should have known better than to expect it. Very well. I'll be commonsensical and practical, and sell myself to that bossy rich landowner, for *Clara's* sake—' her lip curled bitterly '—and for yours, Charles, because I think my fascination for you is already wearing decidedly thin.'

She turned to hurry across the moor. He tried to stop her, crying, 'I'll always love you Lydia – always – always—' but she appeared not to hear.

When she reached Greyfriars a mist of cloud had completely hidden the moon, and already thin rain was falling. Summer rain which mocked the agony of her own tears as she reached her bedroom and flung herself fully dressed on to the bed.

In the morning, Joseph who had learned that the back door had been found unlocked and guessed the reason, questioned his daughter about the escapade. A switch was already in his hand. But he did not have to use it. Instead gratification filled him when she told him he had been quite right after all about Charles. She had taken a midnight stroll, got matters into perspective, and was prepared after all to marry Richard Fearnley.

2

Clara Teague appeared delighted when she heard of her sister's impending marriage. Her violet eyes glowed, a faint flush of excitement gave added radiance to her pale delicate skin. 'Can I be bridesmaid?' she asked wistfully. 'Will we be able to afford it, Papa – if Lydia wants me?'

Joseph gazed at her dotingly. 'Of course, my love. Of course. Many beautiful things will be available for you now which, alas, I could not provide before. Lydia is marrying a wealthy man who I'm sure will wish to please her in every possible way, and her first consideration I've no doubt – apart from her duties to her husband – will be your happiness and well-being, my child.'

His voice sharpened as he queried quickly, turning to his elder daughter, 'Well, Lydia?'

'Naturally,' Lydia answered without enthusiasm.

'You don't sound very sure,' the younger girl remarked, pouting. 'Is it because of my – my back?'

Lydia, pulling herself to attention immediately softened. 'What an idea. How silly of you to suggest it. You've only a little stoop. You'll look lovely in something soft and lacy and with flowers in your hair.' She sighed. 'Far more beautiful than me, I'm sure.'

'Are you going to have a veil and everything? A train? Shall I be the only bridesmaid, or will there be others? Someone Mr Fearnley wants?'

'He'll have nothing to do with it,' Lydia almost snapped. 'And I don't want a whole lot of gurgling creatures following me up the aisle. In fact—' she bit her lip. She had been about to say, 'I don't want to marry Richard Fearnley at all,' but a warning glance from Joseph stopped her, as Aunt Teague interposed tactfully,

'Master Fearnley has already made it quite clear that he prefers a quiet wedding, so I don't think we need worry about Lydia's attendants. Except you, Clara dear. We must start planning your gown, and the bride's as soon as possible.'

Her calm but decisive manner temporarily put an end to the problem, and the following week Anne and her nieces were driven to Falmouth to choose materials and consult a dressmaker noted for her skill with the needle and her knowledge of up-to-date fashions as favoured by the famous Bertarelli.

Lydia was bored by the whole proceedings. What did it matter what she, the bride wore? This was a marriage of convenience. She didn't like Richard, she resented being the victim of her father's avarice and her love for her sister. Deep down she was still fretting and yearning for Charles. He had let her down, but what else could he have done under the circumstances? During the sad days following their parting she had realised grudgingly that what he'd said had been true; life together without any means would have been hard and tiring, and she would inevitably have become a burden round his neck.

She herself would gladly have led the existence of a gipsy or tinker, tramping the roads happily as long as they were together. But Charles was a true artist. Perhaps if he hadn't been, she might not have loved him so much. In him she still sensed genius, and visioned a time ahead when all the important galleries of England and Europe were clamouring for his work. They might meet then on equal terms – he the famous painter, she the rich wife of an influential man – Mrs Richard Fearnley. He would bow graciously, and perhaps brush her fingers with his lips. But these slim hands of hers would be elegant in white gloves, her mouth would have a polite condescending smile on it as she said, 'Good day to you, Mr Clarke sir. I hope you are well—' or 'I must congratulate you on your success.'

Would it ever be like that? Would time ever erase the

wanton sweetness of their stolen meetings on the moor? Ever completely still the wild beating of her heart caused by one glimpse of his tall form? Eventually she told herself ruthlessly, it must be so. Youthful passion and anguish could not last forever. In the meantime she would use what was offered, and what so soon would be her right – for her own ends. Clara should have all possible benefits from Richard's pocket, paid for by her own body and submission to a man she didn't love. For herself she would indulge in all possible extravagances, have the finest clothes and most expensive jewellery money could buy. She would flaunt her beauty throughout Cornwall's social circles, and insist on visiting both the Fearnley Devon estate and his London Belgravia mansion. If he wished to marry her following a few brief meetings, then she was obviously capable of winding him round her little finger when an opportune moment arose. Oh yes, life had many exciting possibilities. The longing for the scent of thyme and heather, the pounding of white foam – spindrift – against her native rugged coast – for the crying of gulls and thin rain driven over the moors – could be smothered and forgotten in the whirl of social life ahead.

One day perhaps she would forget, even, that Charles Clarke existed.

In the confusion of mixed emotions the possibility that Fearnley might have quite different plans for their future did not register. Before the wedding their private moments together were few, and mostly chaperoned. Occasionally, when his lips, quite decorously touched her – she was aware of an urgency, a pounding of desire beneath the facade that briefly disturbed – even slightly frightened her. The blood, then, would be hot in her cheeks, even though she suddenly disliked him and wanted to push him away. But she bore the contact stoically, and when she faced him again his expression would be controlled, his eyes narrowed and speculative, indicating no obvious trace of ardour or desire.

The wedding took place in late September at St Kerrick Church. Richard had offered to pay for the expenses, but being a strict observer of the conventions, Joseph had insisted upon filling the usual duties of the bride's father, delving into his own limited savings for the event, and guessing that he would doubtless reap the benefits later. Only a few guests attended, including Fearnley's one and only sister Miss Agatha – a handsome but starchy-looking figure ten years older than her brother. She had managed, and reigned as chatelaine over the Devon estate, since the death of her mother a year following that of the old squire. Doubtless, she'd thought, when she'd had to accept the news of Richard's impending marriage, she would continue in the same role. An unsophisticated country girl would prove no difficulty in handling. But one glance at Lydia's slim erect figure walking up the aisle on her father's arm to the altar where her future husband waited, filled her with brief doubt. The girl, in her simply cut yet tasteful gown looked quite beautiful, proud and almost regal, showing no sign of nerves, unlike her sister Clara, who though strikingly pretty, was obviously unduly excited, glancing at odd moments towards the guests, with the bright colour staining her cheeks. But what a lovely young creature she was. And how sad, that in spite of all efforts – all the frills and lace intended to hide her slight deformity, the exquisite head still drooped from the delicate shoulders.

Of the two sisters Richard might have been wiser to choose her, Agatha thought with a stab of jealousy. She could have been cosseted and cared for, and there would have been little danger of her interfering with the running of the Fearnley establishment. Whereas Lydia! She obviously had fire and character and would have to be dealt with tactfully. Still, as Richard had made it clear that his married life would be spent mostly at Blackstone, due to this new fad of his for mining, the Devon home would no doubt remain under her own, Agatha's, control. So there might be no real problem after all. She had anticipated that the honeymoon would be spent in France or somewhere equally popular on the continent, or perhaps even Brighton, which the Regent had made so fashionable. Richard's news that he and his bride were to go straight to Blackstone had been a surprise.

'It seems very odd to me, dear boy,' she said patronisingly. 'I had hoped to set your new home into some sort of proper order myself. Although you and Lydia have been over a few times and discussed things, there are surely certain matters that need more experienced attention. If your wife-to-be had consulted me on carpets and furnishing – for the main bedrooms and drawing room especially – I would have advised her to be a little more – discreet in her choice. When you showed me over the place the other day the whole effect *did* appear slightly flamboyant.'

Richard had grinned.

'A little colour and flamboyance hurt no one,' he'd said, with a flash of strong teeth. 'Lydia's quite a colourful character herself I can assure you.'

'I can believe it,' Agatha had snapped. 'I only hope you understand what you're taking on.'

'I don't – quite. But I soon shall,' Richard had answered. 'I think both Lydia and I have a pretty accurate idea of our own potentials.'

That might be true, Agatha thought as the marriage ceremony proceeded, but only partially. No two human beings could completely assess the other's characters in a matter of weeks or even a month or two. Lydia, to her, was something of an enigma, the passionate green eyes and full beautifully modelled sensual mouth at strange variance with the girl's outward composure of almost unnatural calm.

However, later, at the reception following the ceremony, which was held in the Assembly Room of St Kerrick's Town Hall, Lydia's mood softened under the influence of champagne, the toasting and good wishes that followed.

When at last bride and groom drove away in the Fearnley chaise for Blackstone, the new Mrs Richard

Fearnley was a radiant smiling figure throwing flowers from her bouquet to well-wishers lining the cobbled main street of the small town.

It was only when they reached the outskirts that she noticed a tall fair-haired figure standing at a corner by the lane leading to the moors.

Charles!

Lydia's excitement turned suddenly to wild despair. He had a bitter half-smile on his lips clearly and cruelly defined through the slanting rays of the sun.

Automatically her form stiffened. 'What's the matter?' Richard asked sharply, glancing instinctively through the window.

'Nothing. Nothing at all.'

But he had seen.

'See that it remains just nothing, my love,' her husband told her coolly. 'That ne'er-do-well has nothing to do with your life any more. But then if he had, you wouldn't have married me, of course.'

The assertion, though casually spoken, implied somehow an indirect threat. When his arm slipped round her waist she remained rigid and outwardly aloof. Only when his hand travelled gently downwards to the subtle curve of thigh and buttock under the thin gown, did she soften slightly in response – not from love, but forcing herself briefly to the illusion that it was Charles touching her – Charles who'd held her close in the bracken – with foxgloves and gorse bright about them, and the great stones – pagan relics of the old gods, standing sentinel against the wind-swept sky.

Blackstone Manor stood a mile out of the village itself, which was straggling and grey with one main street bordered mostly by miners' cottages, and overlooked by the Church on a rising tump of ground. Facing a patch of waste land referred to as The Square was an ancient inn, The Mariners' Rest, a popular meeting place for tinners and seamen. In a fold of the moor below, near the cliff, a kiddleywink of ill-repute provided rival amusement for those dabbling in deals of darker nature, such as smuggling and other adventurous pursuits. There was one main store, and a Methodist Chapel ruled over by a stern minister who was gravely at odds with the Anglican Rector, William Drake.

The incumbency of the Church had been for generations under supervision of the De Verrys family who had gradually let the old estate sink into decline. The last of the line, Franklyn, recently deceased, though a good-natured jovial figure, and popular with the natives had left a string of debts behind, and two mines on his lands, one of which was so impoverished it was soon due for closure.

In purchasing the great house and its surrounding acres Richard Fearnley had roused considerable conjecture through the district. The easy-going Vicar had been anxious to promote a newly enforced spiritual image of himself as benefactor and caretaker of the parish which had not fooled Richard in the least. Still, the miners had at first been suspicious of change, and unforthcoming, due to past months of anxiety. But when it was seen, by Fearnley's lavish spending on the half-derelict mansion and neglected grounds, that 'the furriner' from Devon indeed had gold to spread about, suspicion had gradually turned to cautious hope. Rumours from St Kerrick that Wheal Fancy was not on its last legs after all, and Wheal Chance was to reopen, soon took fire, and were proved true when engineers were brought down from the North.

The new squire's wedding to Master Teague's daughter, strange and a little ill-placed as it seemed – Joseph Teague after all was no gentry, merely a schoolmaster – nevertheless had a certain appeal. Knowing how ordinary people lived would be a help, possibly, in understanding the conditions of the poor, and if Master Fearnley was as besotted about her as folk said, she might be able to do a deal of good in persuading him to better miners' conditions.

The wedding therefore was an event for celebration. Bunting and decorations were hung, wrestling was arranged in the square, and toasting and merrymaking at the hostelry ended eventually in good-natured riotous behaviour. The Manor also had an air of festivity. Servants – including the late squire's housekeeper, one or two members of the previous staff, a new footman and a linen maid ensconced there by Miss Agatha Fearnley – were waiting in the hall to receive the newly-married couple.

There was a short scene of welcome and further toasting, then at last comparative quiet following Agatha's command of dismissal.

'No doubt you two will wish to retire now,' she told Richard and Lydia in practical tones, betraying no emotion whatever. 'I shall myself be relieved to have a little rest. However pleasant they may be to those concerned, weddings can be extremely exhausting.'

'True,' Richard answered, although he did not consider his sister looked in the least tired. Her erect figure, magnificently but modestly attired in stiff grey silk, with an embroidered beribboned hem and lace shoulder-shawl, towered majestically with the impressive dignity of a dowager-duchess over the retreating retinue of servants. She was staying at Blackstone for only one night, which was as well, Richard thought with a touch of irony. He could hardly visualise either Lydia or Agatha taking a subservient role in household affairs. His sister of course was well-used to such a role, but Lydia had already shown an aptitude for knowing exactly what she wanted in a home, and so far, obtaining it, which he knew wouldn't coincide with Agatha's taste. So it was as well she would spend her days mostly as she had before – as chatelaine of Greenfields in Devon – but without his company. On the rare future visits which he planned to make to his old home with his wife, he'd made it quite clear to Lydia beforehand that she was to show no criticism of his sister's routine or her rightful place there. Blackstone and Greenfields would be recognised as completely different territories, ruled over by two very different women.

So with everything settled so satisfactorily, and the marriage night ahead already stirring his heart to wild anticipation, he took Lydia's arm purposefully, and after bidding Agatha good night, firmly ushered his young wife upstairs. The main staircase was wide and thickly carpeted, taking an abrupt turn to the right under a tall stained-glass window, and from there continuing to the first landing, which appeared more of a picture gallery from certain angles than a bedroom corridor. Ancient portraits of bygone owners that had been purchased with a quantity of antique furniture at the sale, stared down imperiously from heavy frames. This main corridor divided in two directions at the top of the steps, running past closed doors to further stairs at either end. The servants' quarters were situated towards the left where access was provided from the kitchens. Smaller passages led off in more than one direction.

If Lydia had not suddenly felt tired she would have been quite bewildered. As it was, the strange flickering glow from lamps placed at intervals by corners and in recesses together with eerie blueish-green light streaking through Gothic windows of coloured glass, gave her the odd impression of being in some mysterious dream. Lean, long, shadowed shapes streaked across the floor. Old wood groaned. Outside the sudden cry of a bird startled her. Involuntarily she pulled herself sharply from Richard's grasp. In a second his hand was on hers.

'Nervous?' he said, not realising the warmth, the tremor of his voice. 'Don't be. You've no need to be. I'm here – your husband. You're in my care now. For always.'

She did not look at him, or reply, but she was thinking, 'always' – *always*. What a terrible word. Terrible because Richard had spoken it and not Charles. The sense of being a prisoner – owned by this handsome possessive stranger, filled her with deepening panic. Why had she done it? How could she have persuaded Joseph to force this unwelcome situation on her so regardless of her own feelings? Clara of course, and the Fearnley wealth. Clara! always the lovely Clara. If only Charles had dared to face the challenge of eloping with her! if only he'd given her a chance to forget other ties. But he hadn't – He'd not had the courage. How naive and foolish she'd been to expect it for a moment. Indignation stiffened and hardened in her.

When Richard held the door open for her to pass into the bedroom, her head was high, her mouth and chin set determinedly to 'do her duty' and please her husband in the manner expected of a young bride. And perhaps after all it was not going to be so difficult. A large fire was glowing from the marble grate on the far side of the room. Candles glinted on glass, velvet curtains and newly upholstered Louis Quinze furniture. She had seen the bedroom before of course, when Richard, to Anne's disapproval, had taken her over the house, asking for her opinion and choice of decoration. But she hadn't visualised quite such luxury. The great canopied bed with its rose-coloured hangings and silk coverlet appeared theatrical, almost regal. Hot-house flowers were arranged on a rosewood oval table, and on a low chest. Silver toilet accessories glinted on either side of the gilt framed mirror hanging at exactly the right angle above the dressing table. An ornate French clock supported by gilt baby angels, ticked rhythmically from the white marble mantelshelf. A subtle scent of roses permeated the air.

Lydia, bemused, walked slowly to the mirror, treading the rich thickly-piled carpet soundlessly. Her head reeled. Automatically she stared for some moments speechless at her own reflection, and saw a stranger there. A dark-haired vision lit to ethereal loveliness in the flickering ever-changing light of wall candles flaring from crystal chandeliers. The white gown fell in a foam of floating chiffon from her waist to the floor. Licked to golden-rose by a sudden spitting and flaring of logs from the fire, her beautifully modelled facial bones and graceful line of throat and shoulders reminiscent of some legendary queen brought to life from a bygone era.

But this was no legend. And Lydia was no ghost from

the past. Unwillingly, dormant passion – a sensual awareness – stirred her blood as the reflection at her back clarified and drew near. She felt a touch on her arm, and the brush of male lips against a temple. Her heart seemed to stop beating for a second as a hand enclosed a breast, then travelled downwards, tracing the line of slim waist to rounded thigh. Angry at her own reaction, she stiffened. What right had this stranger to plumb deep dark emotions she had not known she possessed? It wasn't love she felt – but something far wilder and more primitive. Something that said, 'Give in – don't fight – you're his. He owns you—'

But he didn't. How could he, so quickly following her broken romance? If Richard Fearnley wanted her affection and esteem, he should woo her gently with a show of gallantry. She made an effort to release herself, knowing with a lurch of nerves that it would be no use. Fight him she might, but she would never win, simply because he was already master not only of the whole situation, but of her body, as his legal right.

'What's the matter?' she heard him say against her cheek. 'Come now, darling, not going to be shy, are you?' He loosened her bodice at the neck, tore it down the front, and swept her up into his arms. His eyes burned darkly into her own, holding something – a fire, a message – that excited yet troubled her with secret bewildered fear.

'Please—' she said, 'not yet, I can't—'

He laughed, though the strong brows met in a frown.

'Don't quibble, Lydia,' he told her as desire flamed into a spurt of irritation. 'We're married, remember? And I love you.'

'Love?' The faint contempt in her voice goaded him.

'Yes. And sooner or later you'll respond. Even now—' his voice shook slightly, 'it's not indifference makes you tremble so.' He parted the thin underwear, then loosened the petticoats and drew them gently down over her hips and thighs. The sight of her near naked form – the perfection of beauty and exquisitely proportioned limbs quickened his resolve to teach her this first night, what a strong man's passion meant. In minutes she was divested of any constricting frills or furbelows. Her body, satin smooth, was lying beneath his, kindling his ardour into searing flame. She closed her eyes as the first wild pain of his ravishing ultimately changed to a throbbing burst of fulfilment. His lips seemed everywhere then, on mouth, breast, thighs and most secret recesses of womanhood.

More than once he took her that night, erasing memory into a vortex of swirling light and shade – of breathless excitement through which her being drowned, caught on the timeless journey of nature's union.

When it was over they lay at last silent and at peace, bodies quietened and nerves relaxed. One arm lay over her stomach. His head was slightly turned towards her, and when she opened her eyes, she thought how young he looked, divested of all pretence and fine clothes. His body, strong and lean, glowed under the light. No repulsion stirred her, no shame. Joseph had taught her to avert her eyes always from any picture revealing a suggestion of male anatomy.

'Disgraceful,' he'd called even great works of art. 'Obscene. Degrading for a young girl to see.'

Well, she didn't find Richard Fearnley in the least degrading, although embarrassment caused her to look swiftly away.

He laughed, swung a leg out of bed and jumped out, as she drew the silk coverlet to her chin. He leaned forward, and pulled it down. 'Sit up,' he said, 'and come here.'

He stood with his arms out, waiting to receive her. Knowing it would be futile to refuse, she obeyed; together they stood facing each other, interlocked with their bodies very close, flesh against flesh; then he released her and holding both her hands, remarked, 'You're very beautiful Lydia. Perhaps we should celebrate.'

He went to a chest, took out a bottle of wine and two glasses.

'Again? So late?'

'It's almost morning,' he told her. 'Still, perhaps you're right. Tea will arrive presently. Here—' he threw her a wrap. 'Much as I hate to say so, you should be covered when the maid pops in.'

'Good gracious!' She blushed and drew the flimsy creation hastily round her.

He surveyed her assessingly. 'Not bad,' he remarked. 'Provided no admiring footman has a glimpse of you.'

Sensing the possessive note underlying the casual banter, she rushed to the dressing table and sat down before the mirror so only the firm lines of her back were defined through the thin material. She attempted to tidy the cloud of dark lustrous hair, coiling and pinning it on the top of her small head.

Five minutes later a servant appeared at the door. She was carrying a tray containing a silver tea-pot, jug, fine bone-china cups, cream, and two biscuits.

Despite Lydia's bewilderment and amours of the night, she was hungry, and avidly ate a biscuit after loading her tea with sugar.

In half an hour breakfast came, and by then Richard was already dressed and ready to ride to Wheal Chance and Wheal Fancy for an inspection of the mines.

Lydia dressed languidly, and a little later took a stroll through the Manor's neglected gardens. The autumn day was quiet and golden, her mood thoughtful and reflective. As she followed newly weeded paths, wandered along terraces, passing several small pools overhung with water-plants, she found it hard to believe it was really herself who had so passionately responded to Richard Fearnley's wild love-making. Love? So strange a word for such abandonment. There had been no sentiment in the experience – none of the sweet words so lavishly bestowed on her by Charles.

Involuntarily she sighed. How complex life was. And how difficult to understand her inner-self. Picture after picture of the last few months passed dreamily through her mind – stolen moments of young summer when she and Charles had lain close in the shade of ancient boulder or windswept tree, vowing that nothing would ever part them. Her trust had been complete. But it had been betrayed. The memory could still hurt like a knife-thrust. Fate, and Clara's health had outwitted her. Docile, delicate, lovely Clara.

At one point Lydia had briefly hated her sister for spoiling her future with Charles. Afterwards, reaction from such wickedness had swept through her in a tide of remorse. She loved Clara. From childhood comparison had become a habit, which now had to be paid for. Still, as she strolled under a pergola of roses, newly trimmed into shape following years of neglect, she had to admit there were compensations. The developing grandeur of her new surroundings and existence was exciting in its way. Her pulses still leaped sending a quick rush of warm blood to her cheeks when she recalled certain events of the night.

Had her father and late mother ever experienced such intimacies? Could Joseph ever have abandoned himself so completely to any woman, even his wife? Unconsciously she shivered slightly, as she touched the petals of a late blossom. Perhaps.

Perhaps her death had changed him into the thwarted domineering character he'd become. It was necessary for him to have someone to possess utterly. Clara. Clara probably was merely the vehicle for frustrated passion. *Poor* Clara! But *was* she?

At moments Lydia had glimpsed a certain knowing look in the beautiful eyes – a secret gentle smile on the flower lips which suggested, 'Don't pity me. One day I shall have all I want.' And perhaps she would. There had always been a quiet mysterious quality about Clara that Lydia had never really understood, and the day would probably come sometime when Joseph would lose his beloved child to an eligible suitor. *Then* how would he react? By sinking into dark melancholy, or taking it out on the helpless children he ruled over with the cane?

'I may be a strict man, but I always try to be fair,' she had heard him say to Aunt more than once. 'A beating, when necessary, chastens the body, but it is essential for the soul.'

Such observations had always filled Lydia's free spirit with disgust. It was at these times as a child she'd frequently managed to escape to the moors where badger and fox and all wild creatures were free to go their own ways through heather and gorse, and by the moorland streams trickling to the valley. She'd even occasionally seen an otter there. And once when she'd approached a shining pool under a drooping willow, it hadn't fled in fear, but sat up, front paw and head raised enquiringly, sleek and beautiful in the sunlight. A moment or two later it had dived leaving a circle of glittering water behind.

When she'd returned home her dress had been muddied and ripped at the hem. Aunt Anne had scolded her, and in the middle of the lecture Joseph had come in unexpectedly. His eyes had glowed like burning coals in his dark face as he'd forced her over a chair and thrashed her. When eventually he'd released her she'd jumped down and cried, 'I hate you – *hate* you. I always will.'

And to a certain extent this had proved true.

Now she was free; of Joseph anyway; and mistress of this great house and estate.

From the pergola she took a turn up a few steps, and on the edge of a wide lawn stared towards the great house. It was picturesque, but had become a conglomeration of different architectural periods through the centuries. The original building had been Elizabethan, of which only a small part now remained. The larger portion had been added during the newly revived Gothic phase when the fashion was for turrets, towers and the fanciful arches, so favoured by Horace Walpole. Ornamental sculpted plaster designs decorated mullioned windows and doorways.

There was an imitation ruin, a 'folly', standing on a rising mound of hill and giving the impression of an ancient hunting lodge. Plaster statues reminiscent of legendary Greek figures stood at corners of walls and by grottoes. Some of the invading weeds and undergrowth had not yet been cleared away, but the effect, as a whole, to Lydia's unsophisticated eyes was grand, if a little unreal. Whatever money was spent on the place, the manor and its surrounding terrain could never be entirely in harmony. The ornate Gothic towers of the house seemed to mock the smaller gables of the overshadowed Elizabethan wing. The Georgian portico overlooking the steps and terraces at the front appeared aloof and a little pretentious. She sensed that Charles would deride her new home, considering it ostentatious and perhaps vulgar.

Well, let him, she thought rebelliously. As Richard had pointed out, he was nothing to her now.

Nothing.

She shut his image away firmly, but in the far recesses of her being – a fleeting haunting memory stirred and as quickly died, with the poignancy of perfume caught on a spring wind – glint of a bird's wings through flashing sunlight, or note of a sad sweet song recaptured in a second's nostalgia, then lost.

Quite suddenly Lydia decided she must take a sharp walk. A feeling of being trapped and smothered seized her. There was nothing to do in the house. No father to defy, or Clara to cosset – no Aunt Anne in her lace cap and fussy apron to demand services in housework or cooking. Blackstone was full of activity with servants busy about their various tasks. But she – Lydia Teague – now Lydia Fearnley – was lonely.

So she cut out through a side door leading from the high granite walls of the gardens to the moor. Then she started walking towards a wood in a hollow eastwards, where she knew some gypsies camped. Below a ridge of moorland hills smoke curled upwards from tin mines which would now continue working, through Fearnley's interest and financial backing. Against the sky pumping rods rose rhythmically. Small grey clob cottages – the homes of tinners – dotted the landscape. Lydia pictured the bal maidens working at surface there, and even small children, following their brief education at a dame's or Church school. Only rarely was a miner's child considered worthy to attend Master Teague's classes at St Kerrick, and Lydia pitied these more than the many who had to go to work at seven years old.

Still, she ruminated, every young boy and girl should have the right to certain learning, and perhaps she could persuade Richard to change conditions at mines where he had influence. Perhaps even he might raise the age at which children were employed. If she pleaded or asked him very nicely, he might even be cajoled into allowing her to give a few lessons at Blackstone. Was he that type of man? She had just no inkling at all. All she knew was that he desired her madly, and a man so besotted might possibly be prevailed upon to place philanthropy for once before hard commonsense.

Optimism rose in her. She wandered on, drawing the rich earthy autumn scents deep into her lungs. The bracken now was browning, but gorse still flamed, and heather was purple among the tangled undergrowth. By a clump thorn suddenly, she became conscious of eyes watching from a dark face. She paused, then sighed with relief as the lithe figure of a young man stepped from the shadows directly into her path.

'Athern!' she exclaimed, placing her hand above her heart. 'You startled me.'

He was no stranger to her; they had met several times by chance on her stolen moorland jaunts when she'd escaped her father's vigilance. His family were gypsies who generally pitched camp either in the nearby thicket or some other sheltered spot closer to St Kerrick. They made a livelihood from making pegs and brooms, which they sold in available small towns and villages, and in the summer bunching wild daffodils, cowslips, and primroses. Their headquarters varied according to the season of the year, and localities where fairs were held.

His white teeth flashed as he said, 'Greetings, dordi! Very fine you look in all them fancy cloes. Pinched 'em have thee?'

She lifted her hand and slapped his face smartly. 'I haven't your ways, Athern. My husband is a very fine, rich man. In the future I shall never be seen except in proper attire.'

The dark brows rose over the light eyes.

'Oh, Married be thee?' He made a mock bow – 'To some dook perhaps? Or a king?'

He stuck a grass between his lips and performed a little jig, singing a lilting light song in a strange tongue. Then he bowed again, lower this time, and kissed the hem of her silk gown. Her irritation which had been in reality more of embarrassment because of her unsuitable attire on that wild stretch of land, turned quickly to amusement. She smiled.

He sobered instantly. The narrow glowing eyes became velvet dark; dark as a starless night.

'Whoever thy rich man is, may he bring thee joy, dordi. But the beauty and glory, the sadness and sunlight, the tears and the loving, come only from Del, the Great One, who knows where the fox hides and the badger has its lair – the drawing near of winter, and the whisper of spring in the cool winds and the brook's song. This is the true magic, rackli; keep a little in thy heart for the day of emptiness instead of gold – when thine own hunger is for other things than riches—'

His words died on a creeping shiver of wind. The next moment he had turned away quickly, and with the speed of a wild thing had cut towards the wood. Lydia watched his receding figure until it disappeared into the clustered shadows of tree-trunks and a thin veil of spiralling smoke. All was silent, except for the flapping of wings as a bird rose from the undergrowth flying against the clear sky towards the sea. Athern's predictions had bemused and vaguely disturbed her. She was brought to herself again by the approaching thud of horses' hooves and the sight of a mounted figure astride a horse galloping towards her from the ridge.

Richard.

She stood quite still as he reined close by, and strode towards her, leading his mount by the bridle. She smiled. 'I thought you were at the mine.'

'I was, but business was quick, and I had a sudden urge to be with my lady wife. Which was perhaps as well.' There was no sign of welcome on his lips. He was frowning. His lips were set in a tight line.

'What do you mean?'

'I witnessed quite a pretty scene just now, my darling. Do you generally have a liking for assignations with tinkers and gypsies?'

So he was jealous. She laughed, throwing her head back in amusement. The muscles of her throat rippled. She could have been some princess from a fairy tale standing there in her cape and yellow gown sprigged with tiny daisies, against the brown moor. Her hair was partly loosened and faintly filmed with a thin rising mist. Never had she looked more desirable.

'Athern?' she questioned. 'So you saw me with Athern? But *assignation*; how funny – how really funny. Everyone knows him round here. He wanders around a lot; you could meet him anywhere. He's like a rabbit popping up in unexpected places—' She broke off, intimidated by the lingering sternness of his face.

'Being a comparative newcomer to Blackstone,' he said, 'I've not heard of the fellow, neither do I wish to. And you should have more sense of decorum, Lydia, than to allow any shabby vagrant to touch your hand or sully the hem of your gown with his grimy lips.'

She gasped.

'*Sully?* Grimy? But Athern's not like that. And I didn't meet him on purpose. *Surely* you believe me—?'

Her shocked surprise was so genuine, he relented.

'Yes, I think I do – *this* time,' he agreed grudgingly. 'But—'

'You *think*?' A spurt of temper seized her. 'After last night – after – after—' Speech failed her.

He put out a hand and pulled her to him. 'All right, I *do* believe you. But it mustn't happen again, and that's a warning. Understand?'

She pouted. 'Not quite.'

'Well, be quick about it and learn, or there'll be trouble. And now my lady – up with you.'

He swung her on to the horse's back, then followed, and with one hand on the reins, the other arm round her waist, they broke into a canter down the slope towards the Manor.

3

During the first few months following Lydia's marriage, Joseph was careful not to raise the matter of finance to Richard. Meetings between the two men were rare; they had nothing in common except Lydia herself, although the schoolmaster was determined to bring up the question of Clara's health sooner or later. Meanwhile when any opportune occasion arose Joseph forced himself to listen stoically to Fearnley's plans for bettering conditions socially and educationally in mining areas where he had any interest and power. Outwardly Joseph agreed. Privately he considered Richard's notions new-fangled and impractical, and had a shrewd idea that his wilful daughter was partially, at least, responsible. However, for Clara's sake he did not argue, but commended Fearnley's suggestions as 'truly Christian'.

In November he and Clara were invited for the first time to the Manor to lunch. His sister was also to accompany them and Joseph informed Anne she might visit a costumier's establishment in Falmouth to procure a new cape and gown for his beloved daughter.

Anne at first protested. 'But, Joseph, do you realise what you're doing? The child had a great deal spent on her for the wedding. You're not a rich man, as you so often point out. Where is the money coming from?'

A secretive almost obsequious smile curved his thin lips. 'Now don't argue or fluster yourself, Anne. I have a tidy little sum put away for a rainy day—'

'And when the rainy day comes? What then?' Anne interupted quickly.

His jaws hardened. 'That's none of your affair. Your place is not to question my wisdom. Should such a sorry plight ever overtake us, the good Lord will provide. Now do as I say, make arrangements with Master Hunkin to pick you up in his van tomorrow morning. I know he is driving to Falmouth and will return in the afternoon; he'll be agreeable, *most* pleased in fact, to have two such worthy lady passengers.'

'If there is room, Joseph,' Anne snapped. 'He may be fully booked up already, and his vehicle is not particularly comfortable. To be overcrowded and with only those two ageing horses to pull it along the rough road, could make the journey extremely tiring.'

'Say no more,' Joseph commanded with his lean face reddening. 'I have said the last word on the subject. And another thing – make good use of the money I shall trust you with. My dear Clara must look her very best when we visit that great place. Indeed—' his voice lowered to a smug tone, 'her beauty alone will outshine any tawdry grandeur of the Fearnley establishment. She must appear what she is – a magnificent jewel beyond price, needing only a little extra care to make her presence unforgettable.'

Anne's eyes narrowed shrewdly. 'What are you up to, Joseph?'

Joseph braced his shoulders, his face once more expressionless. Then he said, 'You forget yourself, woman. Go away now. I have business to attend to.'

Shrugging her shoulders Anne left the study, deciding that her brother was becoming quite fanatical over his younger daughter. The situation wasn't good for either of them. Clara was showing signs of selfishness, and day by day was becoming increasingly vain. There was a veiled look in her violet eyes sometimes, a certain secret triumph denoting she was fully aware of her power over her father. And when they kissed good night before the girl went to bed, there had been latterly something so excessively doting in her father's glance and the manner in which he stroked her hair, that the older woman had felt faintly nauseated.

Still, perhaps she was imagining things, Anne told herself practically. The truth was probably that Lydia's presence was being missed more than was admitted. One interesting fact had emerged from that short conversation: Joseph obviously was not *quite* so limited money-wise as she and Lydia had been made to believe. Just sufficiently mean to hoard a little nest-egg away, so he could use it for his own devious purpose when he desired.

The next morning was grey, but fine, which was a mercy, Miss Teague thought, as they boarded Mr Hunkin's van, setting off at nine o'clock from St Kerrick Square. Four other passengers were already seated in the cramped interior and if the curtains had had to be drawn over the two small windows the atmosphere would have been exceedingly stuffy.

Clara's delicate beauty and frail form instantly impelled a male traveller to offer his seat which was in a position where her back could be more comfortable. Clara smiled winningly and accepted. He gave a polite little bow and moved his portly middle-aged presence to the other end of the vehicle so the two ladies could sit side by side. It was generally so, on such rare occasions. Clara's slight physical weakness combined with her looks invariably gave her precedence over more ordinarily endowed individuals.

The journey took two hours. When they finally reached Falmouth the vehicle stopped at an inn yard near the centre of town. Passengers alighted, and Anne and Clara first had refreshments at a coffee house before starting on their shopping expedition. Then Anne delivered a few preliminary instructions to her niece, before escorting her down a cobbled road not far from the great harbour, which led directly to the costumier's. The premises were known to be patronised by respectable families with an eye to fashion, yet demanding value for money.

'Now don't be extravagant,' Anne said. 'Your father is certainly being *extremely* generous, but remember his pocket is limited. Good taste matters more than fine feathers and frills. He wishes you above all things to appear ladylike.'

Clara smiled sweetly. 'I don't think so,' she contradicted in musical gentle tones. 'He wants to impress Richard Fearnley – make him feel he'd do anything in the world for me.'

Anne was shocked; her hand closed firmly on Clara's wrist and gave her a shake. 'Nothing of the sort. You're growing far too conceited these days, Clara. He simply wishes you to prove that the Teague background is a cultured one, with a sense of propriety and manners.'

'Of course, Aunt,' Clara answered demurely.

When it came to choosing her outfit however, as Anne had feared, Clara insisted on having one costing all that Joseph had given her to pay, and a little from Miss Teague's reticule as well. The gown was of pale lilac silk, and the cape rich purple velvet that emphasised the ethereal golden hair and long-lashed violet eyes. The girl indeed looked a dream in it, Anne confessed to herself grudgingly, and gave in with as good a grace as she could muster.

'We shall need some ribbon and a few more etceteras,' she told Clara while the assistant was packing the articles between layers of tissue paper. 'Some needles and silk to sew with. There's bound to be a stitch needed here and there—'

'I'll go and have a look,' Clara interrupted. 'You can join me, Aunt.' She had noticed between two draped curtains, a haberdashery department dealing with all manner of odds and ends – lace, thread, tapestries for embroidering, frames, and even water-colour paints. There was also something – or rather – someone else; a slender lithe young man with a poetic profile and rich shining hair, who appeared to be selecting tubes of colours and brushes.

Charles Clarke, Lydia's erstwhile lover.

Lifting her skirts gracefully by the tips of both hands, Clara moved softly, almost sliding, through the curtains.

A stream of winter sunlight fell full on her face from a window at the far end of the store, giving her the look of some fairy creature strayed from Shakespeare's *A Midsummer Night's Dream* into the real world.

Charles looked up and was momentarily struck by the effect.

She moved forward; he gave a short inclination of his head, a slight bow, and smiled.

'Hullo,' he said, 'Good morning—'

'It's almost afternoon,' she said. 'We came by van. Shopping. I'm Lydia's sister. You do know me, don't you?'

He nodded. 'By sight only, unfortunately. Your father, I'm afraid, doesn't approve of rogues and vagabonds.'

Her laugh of amusement rang with the tinkle of tiny bells on the air.

'Oh, Papa was always very strict with Lydia. I'm different. She doesn't know how to handle him.'

'Oh? And you do?'

'I don't have to try. You see he's always so *sorry* for me.'

'*Sorry?* For *you?*'

She nodded.

'Because of this—' indicating the curve under her cloak – 'my spine. He thinks I'm always to be cosseted and cared for and given in to. Poor Papa. It was when I was born my Mama died you see. Anyway, don't let's talk about me. Are you buying paints?'

'What I can afford.'

She sighed. 'Money can be an awful nuisance. Lydia told me you were very clever and could be famous one day. If *I*'d been her—' she paused.

'Yes?'

'I don't think I'd have given you up just because some rich land-owner came along with a great house and lots of money. But Lydia was always impulsive. She should have been cleverer. Still, I expect she'll be happy in her own way. She was always rather – kind of wild and theatrical, you know. Anything she wanted she went for like mad and got it.'

Yes, Charles knew. He didn't need to be reminded. The

trouble had been that with him she'd wanted too much, body and soul, career as well. Everything. But then this girl, too, was hungry for something; he could feel it, sensed that beneath the innocent exterior was a craving for attention – love, perhaps, which she was afraid might pass her by. Did she envy her sister? Was it unconscious jealousy of Lydia's marriage that made her anxious to impress, somehow to steer the conversation into emotional channels?

'Ah well,' he said lightly, 'that's a quality some women possess. A gift.'

'What?'

'Getting her way. You were talking about your sister Lydia.'

'Yes.' He watched a shadow cloud her eyes. She was certainly very lovely, and from an artist's point of view extremely paintable. She intrigued him, but roused no ardour. Still, he could not help feeling gratified at having caught the interest of Joseph Teague's younger daughter. She was attracted by him – he was sufficiently versed in the ways of women to know that. It would not be too difficult probably to see more of her in the future – somehow contrive to 'bump into her' at a convenient place and time. The mean old tyrant couldn't have his eye on her every moment of the day. School occupied him most of the morning. There'd be considerable satisfaction in gaining Clara's affection, if only to pay out the bullying schoolmaster for his treatment of Lydia and contempt of himself.

His half-formed plan was made all the easier by Clara saying a little wistfully, 'Lydia told me you used oil paints sometimes. I wish I could. But I'm only allowed to do tiny water-colour things of flowers and birds you know—' Her words drifted away.

'So *you* paint?'

'As I said – just a little. I go to Heather Vale – just up the slope you know – not very far from our house. Papa doesn't mind. It's sheltered there, and there are so many butterflies to watch.'

'I know the place. Picturesque, and as you say private.'

'Of course it's too cold now to stay long or do any drawing. But sometimes, when it's fine, I go just for a breath of air, and to see the trees. They look so delicate without their leaves against the sky, in the frost especially, like silver network.'

'I thought of going that way next Tuesday,' he said casually, 'just to do a quick winter sketch. It would be about eleven in the morning. So we *might* see each other.'

His smile made her decide instantly that they would.

'You never know,' she replied meaningfully.

Just at that moment Miss Teague appeared. Her thin figure stiffened when she saw the couple in conversation. For *that* young man – the 'arty scoundrel' as Joseph referred to him – to be *here* in Falmouth on this day of all days, and having the impertinence to address Clara! It was really *too* much. Joseph would be affronted and very angry indeed.

She gave a slight jerk of her head, and through thin tightened lips said sharply. 'Clara, we've already spent too much time and money here. Your father certainly wouldn't wish you to play about with such – such unnecessary frivolities. Have you looked at the thread and needles?'

With slight hauteur which Anne considered impertinent, Clara answered, 'Dear Aunt Anne, I've hardly had time. Charles and I were merely saying good day to each other. You *do* know him – Charles Clarke – don't you? The artist, Lydia's friend?'

'I recognise the young man, but we're not acquainted,' Anne replied coldly. 'Now, Clara—'

'Oh but you are now,' Clara's quick smile held a glint of mischief. 'Charles—'

Charles held a hand, which Miss Teague for the sake of good manners could not refuse. The contact was brief.

Clara sighed.

'There. Now we can really be at ease.' She turned her gaze on Charles once more. 'Are you returning to St Kerrick today, Mr Clarke?'

'No,' he told her. 'I'm spending the evening with a friend of mine. We were at Oxford together. I shall be back tomorrow.'

'Indeed!' Anne's comment was prim. She had already heard rumours of the young man's expulsion from university, and was wholly in agreement with her brother's attitude to the young reprobate. Certainly no acceptable acquaintance for a well brought-up girl, although she could understand his attraction for the opposite sex. He was handsome, and not ill-mannered. There was a sunny quality about him that made her suddenly feel old and out of things.

'Dangerous,' she thought. 'He could be a dangerous influence.'

She ended the short conversation by saying abruptly, 'Come, Clara. On second thoughts I've decided new thread will not be necessary. I'd quite forgotten a collection of silks I had put away in my chest. We must hurry. I have a few other errands on my list. And before our journey home we must have a little more refreshment—'

'Perhaps Charles would like to join us—' Clara interrupted.

'I'm sure Mr Clarke has other matters to attend to,' Anne stated stiffly. 'Neither would it be quite seemly, in your father's absence for us to eat with a comparative stranger.'

Clara shrugged.

'How stuffy that sounds.'

'Respectability generally is,' Charles retorted with a secret wink, unobserved by Anne. 'But I'm sure Miss Teague is behaving with utmost decorum.' He gave another of his characteristic short bows. 'Adieu, then, until we meet again.'

'What an impudent character he is,' Anne said coldly when she'd escorted her niece from the premises. 'And it's extremely forward and unladylike of you to have called him by his first name. If your father knew—'

'But he won't, will he?' Clara said cajolingly. 'You wouldn't want Papa to know that you'd been so careless as to let us meet.'

Her astuteness shocked Anne into realising what a shrewd mind lay behind the pretty head.

'We'll try and forget this unfortunate incident,' Anne stated in her usual clipped tones. 'To upset your father is quite the last thing I wish to do. But in future Clara remember your place, and behave accordingly.'

'Of course, Aunt dear,' Clara agreed demurely. But she was thinking, 'Why should I always have to be the one to behave, as she calls it, and do as I'm told? Lydia didn't, and look how luckily things have worked out for her.'

Although she didn't acknowledge it, even to herself, she was jealous. Jealous of Lydia's ability to have won such a rich and colourful husband, however domineering and possessive he might be – jealous of her sister's new status and fine house, and how cleverly she'd escaped the dull miserable existence at Greyfriars under the strict supervision of two such dull elderly individuals. Jealous also – not of Lydia's beauty – she knew she, herself, was far lovelier in her own frail way – but that her sister should have been born with no physical imperfection, in contrast to her own curved shoulders.

From that moment an idea which gradually emerged into a definite plan took root in Clara's mind.

Two days later, following a dress-making session with her aunt which involved a good deal of snipping and pinning the new lilac gown into exact shape, Clara slipped out of the house unseen wearing her light woollen hooded cape over her everyday blue gown. The morning was warm for the time of the year, with hazy sunlight penetrating the veil of thin cloud which spread a silver mist over the landscape.

Hidden under the cape was her small box of water-colours and a sketching pad. Not that she *really* intended to use them that day – there would hardly be time. At twelve-thirty Joseph would be back for his meal, and would certainly be annoyed if she was not punctual. Grace had to be said while she and her aunt bowed their heads piously. Then Papa would straighten his back purposefully, and with a self-satisfied air – especially if he had had excuse to cane a pupil for some minor misdeed – attack his food with relish.

Oh, those horrible boring meals of boiled mutton or stew, Clara thought distastefully, as she made her way to Heather Vale. Sometimes when her appetite was really poor Joseph would notice and force her to take a glass of porter, or share wine with him. She had to pretend gratitude or risk his displeasure. And this she was wise enough to avoid.

The path she took up towards the fringe of the moor narrowed gradually into almost nothing as it dipped suddenly down into a small dell sheltered by sloes, thorn trees, and a twisted gorse that still showed a few late yellow blooms. This one secret place was completely out of view of the house below, and Charles was already there, leaning against a bent trunk of a tree holding a pencil and pad, ostensibly to start on preliminary sketches for a later painting. He stopped any pretence of working when he saw Clara and went forward to meet her.

'Hullo and good morning, Miss Teague,' he said. 'How odd we should chance to meet in such a place at such a time.'

She dimpled.

'Don't be silly. You knew I'd come.'

He grinned. 'I rather thought so. And how is the dragon?'

'The dragon?'

'Your estimable aunt.'

'My aunt is very well, thank you. Extremely busy fiddling with the new gown we'd bought for me in Falmouth. She's so *fussy*!' Clara gave a moué of impatience. 'Of course I have to look my very best for *the* occasion.'

'And what is that?'

'Tomorrow we've been invited to have a meal at Blackstone. Imagine it. Personally—' she shrugged '—I think considering Lydia's my sister – the invitation's been rather long in arriving. But I expect that's because of her husband. I'm sure he's a very dogmatic man and won't want to be troubled much with such a humble family as ours – a mere schoolmaster and his daughter. That's why Papa's so anxious for me to make a sensation – to win Mr Fearnley's interest so he'll help with my health bills.'

'What health bills?'

Clara sighed. 'Oh, some new treatment from a specialist in London, for my back. It would be expensive, even just an examination. And I don't believe in it for one moment. I've just got to put up with the stupid weakness for good, I'm sure.'

'It isn't noticeable,' Charles said. 'Many beautiful things droop slightly – flowers, harebells, bluebells, and snowdrops. It's the graceful feature that adds to beauty such as yours—' The statement sounded so poetic that Clara blushed.

'I like you, Charles. You say such nice things.' She drew her cloak a little closer at the neck and gave a slight shiver. 'It's not *really* warm, is it? I thought it was mild when I came out, but Aunt Anne always says winter's treacherous, and I expect she's right. I'd brought my paints along, but I won't use them today. In any case, I oughtn't to stay – she'll probably want another quick fitting or something. May I look at what you're doing before I go?'

Charles showed her the pad where he'd already outlined a quick impression of the landscape with a drooping tree in front. There was a faint fragrance about her of lavender, which reminded him of his mother's chest and wardrobe when he'd been young. Just for an instant regret for a few of the lost elegancies he'd sacrificed, touched him with a strange gentleness. Although this lovely girl could raise no fire in him he had a desire to take her delicate hand in his and hold it for a second, in acknowledgement of her beauty, and even his own admiration. He touched her fingers tentatively.

'This isn't much,' indicating the drawing. 'I came here just to see you. And that's the truth.'

Her smile was shy under the bonnet.

'I know. So did I. Hoping we'd meet, I mean.'

Charles realised with a sharp shock that it would take very little effort on his part completely to woo and win Clara Teague – that whatever opposition her father might have, she'd defy him if he, Charles Clarke, insisted. Or was he too sure of himself? But no. Obtaining a husband was probably the one object Clara had secretly set her heart on. The very possibility created a challenge in his mind, a perverse picture of flaunting such a situation in Lydia's face.

Lydia! how angry she'd be, and what sweet revenge for him. To humble the wild wilful girl by taking her sister as his wife. Joseph too. Joseph of course would kick up a hell of a row, but serve the mean old tyrant right. He'd have to provide what he had to assist his beloved Clara's security. His love for this one child was obviously fanatical, and Charles, as her husband, would eventually have to be accepted.

Swift as lightning the thoughts raced through his head, and only abated temporarily when he heard Clara saying wistfully, 'Goodbye for the moment then, Charles. I hope we – I hope—'

'We shall see each other again, and often,' Charles interrupted. 'We'll have to be careful at first of course. But—'

'Yes?'

'Well,' he forced himself to reply with a spurt of confidence, 'elopements are in vogue now, I believe. Let us say tomorrow is another day, and many days to come, holding lots of surprise, I think, for one or two people.'

At first she couldn't speak. Was he really suggesting what she thought? *Elopement?* Did he mean that? Or was he teasing her?

The violet eyes narrowed. Her underlip drooped.

'You're teasing me. I'd rather you didn't.'

He shook his head.

'No, I certainly wasn't. I'd never do that to you, Clara. It was a true thought I was putting to you. But only a thought so far. We must think very hard.'

They did. Charles was intoxicated by the idea of paying Lydia out and turning Joseph's world upside down, and Clara by proving she could win such a handsome lover who in spite of her back was sufficiently entranced by her beauty as to offer her marriage. Apart from that, the suggestion of elopement titillated her enormously, completely obliterating any practical sense she possessed.

The next day when Joseph, Anne and Clara arrived at Blackstone, Lydia was not only impressed anew by her sister's loveliness which was enhanced by the violet gown, but also mildly puzzled. There was something different about her – a radiant vitality and secret inner glow that gave warmth and colour to the porcelain skin and luxuriant fair hair. In every way she acted decorously and in the refined manner Joseph expected of her. She was a credit to him he decided proudly, which in his eyes Lydia certainly was not. His elder daughter, wearing a dress of scarlet silk cut far too low on the shoulders for good taste and at the front disgracefully revealing the shadowed curves of her full white bosom, had the appearance more of an actress or fashionable courtesan than the strictly brought up daughter of a respectable scholar and follower of the Church. And the way she held her haughty head when she greeted him, the suspicion of a faint supercilious smile about her red lips – it was indecent; quite vulgar. If he had been her husband he would have torn the offending dress off her back, and put her over his knee, then seen she was properly clad before allowing her to appear before guests, especially her innocent young sister and father, in such guise.

But Richard quite clearly saw nothing wrong in her attire. His glance, when it fell on his young wife, was positively admiring. Fearnley himself of course, looked somewhat theatrical. In contrast to Joseph Teague's sombre puritanical black, he wore a smart waisted and tailed claret coat, cream silk shirt and ruffled high collar. His fine fawn cloth trousers were fashionably cut and very long, reaching over the ankles to the tips of his black, pointed shoes. His hair carefully waved back from a wide brow.

'A Beau Brummel,' Joseph decided with a stab of distaste. And probably with no religion at all, except for his curious notions of education and social reform. A powerful-looking figure for all that, and one he had to cultivate for Clara's sake. The thrust of strong jaw suggested formidable will-power. Well, it was to be hoped that some time in the future he'd learn to wield a little over Lydia.

The visit socially, if a little stiff and guarded under the polite façade, proved satisfying to Joseph. As they drove away in the Fearnley chaise, Clara felt her father's hand pat her slender gloved one.

'I am very proud of you, my dear,' he said portentously. 'You behaved decorously and put your sister completely in the shade.'

'Oh, Papa!' Clara remonstrated. 'You flatter me too much, you know.' She sighed. 'Lydia always looks so colourful and exciting, and that red dress was absolutely theatrical, so vivid against her dark hair.'

'Scarlet!' Joseph commented coldly. 'And that's what she appeared – a scarlet woman. There was no taste in her attire, and I'm surprised Richard Fearnley allowed her to appear like that in public.'

'Her own family?'

'Her family especially. She was flaunting herself – before *me*.'

Clara made no comment to Joseph's criticism. Her enjoyment of the visit was gradually turning to depression. How she secretly envied Lydia! How dreary it was having to live with such dry-as-dust guardians as Papa and Aunt Anne. Miss Teague had been quieter than usual during the family gathering. She had been aware of the hardness in her brother's eyes every time they alighted on his elder daughter and was a little concerned. The fanatical resentment held a violent quality that she considered was certainly not deserved. Lydia had always been vivacious and strong-willed of course, but warm-hearted and affectionate when she was allowed to be. Joseph had never been fair to her. It was as though he was determined to make her the scapegoat of his own thwarted nature. Several times when Lydia had made some harmless comment, his lean face had flushed a dark red, his hand had shaken, and there had been a tightening of the jaw that was not natural.

For Lydia's sake Anne was thankful she'd escaped his growing fanaticism through her marriage to Mr Fearnley. She only hoped that her niece had a true affection for him and had not acted on the rebound from the unfortunate entanglement with Charles Clarke which had ended so suddenly. Thinking of Charles took her mind back to Clara's encounter with him in Falmouth. She had wisely said nothing of it to Joseph, and there were moments of slight uneasiness when she recalled the girl's winsome, almost coquettish air – the brightening of the lovely eyes under her fluttering dark lashes, and the interested response of the young man. It must not happen again, Anne decided, as the carriage wheels rattled to the clippety-clop of horses' hooves along the rough road. She would do all in her power to see they did not meet again.

But she could not keep vigilant every moment of the day, and Clara had done nothing for her to be kept a prisoner in the house. Joseph completely trusted her. If he happened to be about when his beloved daughter returned from a short sharp walk, or appeared carrying her small sketching pad on a fine frosty morning, he was indulgent, and complimentary about any small drawing she had made.

'Just be careful you don't catch cold, my darling,' he said dotingly, 'and always take your muff with you and wear your fur bonnet.'

'Of course, Papa,' Clara answered demurely. 'I'm never cold, I promise you.'

This was true. How could she feel the slightest chill with Charles's arms round her, and his lips so warm against her cheek and mouth. She may not have loved him with passion. Their natures were so different. Clara's feelings were almost all emotional. But beneath the emotion, knowledge, and triumph in her conquest was gradually stirring. And Charles well knew how to fan feminine ambition. Above everything else Clara's deepening need was the desire – almost obsession – to have equal status with Lydia as a married woman. To remain the delicate, unfortunate Miss Teague, the treasured, beautiful, but weakling daughter of St Kerrick's schoolmaster, was a vision hard to contemplate, an affront to her femininity. Joseph of course would fly into a terrible rage or one of his deadly cold furies, if he even guessed what was going on between Charles and herself. So she was cunningly careful to see that he didn't.

When she and Charles were married – she was determined this should be – Joseph would probably come round after the first explosion. If he didn't – well, she had a rich sister. She was sure Lydia and Richard would see they were never in want of the necessities of life, or of a roof over their heads. She was so certain of it that Charles believed her, and went along with her all the way. Clara as the sister-in-law of the wealthy Richard Fearnley would be a very different proposition in marriage to the wayward, penniless Lydia.

He, Charles, would not necessarily be tied at home or in one place all the time. There would be periods when she could stay at Blackstone while he took off for a week or two on his work. He would be free to travel to exhibitions and have short terms of vagabond existence. When he returned there would be joy in reunion. She was, after all, a beautiful young creature. He was fond of her, and in marrying her would cause haughty Madam Lydia considerable anger and humiliation, and throw Joseph

Teague into a fit probably, which wouldn't worry him in the least.

So the secret meetings continued, with the imp of mischief and revenge spurring Charles towards his goal.

At the end of January 1827 it happened.

Clara Teague married Charles Clarke secretly at Helston, by a special licence stating her age to be twenty-one, two and a half years older than she actually was. When she had not returned to Greyfriars from a stroll for the midday meal, Joseph was at first irritated, then angry. He sent Anne to search for her, unsuccessfully. At three o'clock pandemonium raged through the house. Joseph's annoyance by then had turned to acute worry. His stress became panic.

'She must have fallen,' he shouted, 'broken an ankle or something – or perhaps been abducted. Something terrible indeed must have happened to my darling child. And it's your fault, Anne – yours! *yours!*' he was shrieking, with his eyes bulging prominently, his sallow face unnaturally purple. 'You should never have allowed her to go walking on her own. Never *never*. You know how delicate she is – how trusting. I shall inform the authorities – an organised search must be made immediately. How dare you do this to me, woman? How *dare* you?' he was breathing heavily. He clutched his sister by the neck of her bodice, shaking it so heavily she gasped, nearly choking.

'Joseph! Joseph! Calm yourself – you're ill – please—'

Realising abruptly that he was almost strangling her, he desisted, freed her, and flung himself into a chair, putting his hands over his eyes. When he looked up again his face was ashen.

'Get me the brandy, Anne.'

As she poured him a full glass, she said calmly, in spite of her racing heart, 'You need a doctor. I'll get him—'

Joseph sprang up again. 'No. Nonsense. All I need is to find Clara. Until then I've no intention of seeing anyone.'

He strode to the door and out into the hall where he grabbed his coat and stove hat. He was shaking, but strode wildly out of the front door, in spite of Anne's protestations. Where he went she never knew, but when two hours later he returned, he had a further shock.

Clara, with Charles beside her was waiting for him in the parlour. She was wearing her everyday dark blue woollen cape and a small bonnet perched to the back of her fair curls. Her pale skin glowed, and her eyes were alight with excitement tinged with apprehension when she glanced at Joseph's face.

Anne was standing close to the young bride, slightly behind. There was a redness round her eyes that suggested she might have been crying. She stood tensely rolling her handkerchief in her hand, as Joseph after a dead silence bellowed, 'What is this? How *dare* this – this mountebank – come to my house with my daughter. Speak, sir, speak—' He strode forward intending to grab Charles by his neckcloth.

Clara made a pleading gesture, 'Papa, don't look like that. I – I'm happy. Please, *please* believe me, I—'

Anne, too, tried to reason.

'Control yourself, Joseph. Anger will do no good now. It's too late. For all our sakes we must—'

'Too *late*? What do you mean, too late?' Foam gathered round Joseph's lips. He started shouting. 'I *demand* the truth.'

'Clara and I are married,' Charles said coolly. 'I have the lines in my pocket to prove it. I'm sorry we had to do it this way. But both of us knew you would never have given your consent.'

He waited. The short silence that followed was electric. Joseph's countenance from purple with a greenish tinge, turned a frightening yellow-grey. He grasped an arm of a chair to steady a fit of shaking. Then he muttered through teeth from which his upper lip was raised in contempt. 'You – you blackguard – you despicable cur. I'll have you – I'll have you—' his words died suddenly into a gasp. Clutching his throat, he staggered and fell, toppling the chair over.

Clara ran forward and flung herself down beside him, followed by Anne.

'Papa – Papa—' Clara cried. 'It's all right, don't look like that. What's the matter? Don't – *don't*—' She shuddered and put both hands before her face.

Anne eased her away and took a look herself at the writhing figure on the floor. Breath came from his lungs in tortured gasps that ended with a grating sound. His pale eyes opened wide, staring wildly for a second at Clara; then after a moment it was over. His head fell back, the twisted face was still.

Joseph Teague, the tyrant many had feared and some respected, but none had loved, was dead.

4

An air of grim depression hung over the dreary front parlour of Greyfriars, when, following the funeral, Joseph Teague's will was read, in the presence of Lydia, Clara, Anne Teague and the two husbands, Richard Fearnley and Charles Clarke.

Lydia, in full black, as decorum and convention demanded, appeared aloof, dignified and completely in control of herself. There was no sign of grief on her face. Anne considered she must be extremely hard of heart. This was not strictly true. Once, as a young girl, she would have wept. But affection for her father had been worn so thin by years of cruel discipline and rejection, she had no intention now of pretending emotion she didn't feel. Clara, looking ethereal as some fragile ghost in her dark skirts and veiling allowed a film of tears to cloud her lovely eyes, to her sister's considerable annoyance.

Lydia was shocked by the marriage. How could Charles have done such a thing? The curl of her lips, the flash of her eyes when she glanced at the man to whom she would once so gladly have given everything, told him she still had a hankering for him, and this gave him fleeting ironic pleasure. The will, too, was something of a triumph, considering all Joseph possessed, except for a meagre legacy to Anne, was left to Clara, which meant, according to the law, that he would benefit.

Unfortunately for both Charles and Clara, when Joseph's affairs were examined and finally settled a fortnight later, it was discovered that except for a few paltry guineas all of Master Teague's small capital was swallowed up by debts. The house itself yielded nothing, as it was Church property. The furniture at a sale might fetch a little – but certainly not more than a hundred pounds.

'I'm extremely sorry,' the solicitor announced when the sordid details had been revealed. 'However—' turning to the tragic bereft young wife of Charles Clarke, 'your sister and brother-in-law, I'm sure, will see that you are never in want, my dear. Things could be worse.'

Could they indeed? Charles thought bitterly. Richard Fearnley so far had not behaved in at all a friendly manner, and the devil of it was that he, Charles – had now become burdened with a delicate wife who'd no doubt demand his presence as much as possible at her side. Any thought he'd had of taking off somewhere in the near future for a week's painting and enjoyment, leaving Clara safely secure at Blackstone, quickly faded. Old man Teague's death had effectively put paid to such a prospect. If he was to become accepted by Lydia and her rich husband he had to observe the proprieties following a bereavement.

There was also the question of whether Fearnley would accept a couple of paupers willingly into his household. *Paupers*. That's what they were, and the thought infuriated him. Still, they had been allowed a month at Greyfriars while the young husband, supposedly, was to find somewhere else to live. The idea of returning to the cottage occurred to him, but Richard had refused to renew the rent.

So what?

'Don't worry, darling,' Clara pleaded that night, as she lay beside him in the bed Lydia and she had shared before her sister's marriage. 'It will be all right, I *know* it will. Something will turn up. You're so clever—' she sighed. 'And anyway Richard will have to find premises for us. It would make him look so brutal to everyone if he didn't. Don't you understand?'

She snuggled nearer. Her slender body smelled fragrantly of lavender or lily-of-the-valley – the refreshing perfumes she always used held an old-fashioned sweetness that roused no fire in him – only an awareness of her youth and lack of sophistication. Yet her lips resting against his cheek like the soft brush of butterflies' wings demanded response. In her own way he knew she needed him. His arm tightened round the slender waist, while the other hand stroked the satin-smooth contours of her body. Then, for a moment or two, he was perfectly still, before drawing her close.

She stared up at him. The look in her eyes startled him. It was not innocent at all, but hypnotic, almost feline. If only he could love her. Love her from the bottom of his heart with fire and desire; if only somewhere about her was the bitter-sweet tang of heather, the pride and challenge of a wilder more passionate demand.

Lydia.

Curse her, he thought savagely. Why should she intrude on his marriage? All she'd proved to be was worthless – a rich man's whore who'd sold herself to the highest bidder without a tinge of regret. Reinforcing and driving his bitterness to believe what he knew was not really true, he had taken Clara, with a hardness and hunger that made her wince and cringe, moaning as he thrust into her. Her first shock and show of rejection was only momentary. Knowing he expected it, she quickly assumed a façade of pleasure and gratification. He was further astonished. A look of complete, almost smug satisfaction hovered about the flower-like lips and in the violet eyes.

Then she had said in a cool light voice, 'Now I'm really yours, aren't I, Charles? We *belong*. You and Lydia never did, did you?'

Anger shook him.

'Lydia? What the—'

'Oh, I know all about it,' she said, 'you wanted her more than me. But she couldn't keep you, could she? Well – *I* shall. Because I'm your wife, and being your wife will be a help, Charles. I'm not – a fool you know.'

'I—'

She put a finger to his lips. 'Sh-sh. Don't fuss, don't be

angry. I'm clever. Richard will see we're all right, and one day what you want will come true. You'll be a great painter, and your name will go down in the history of art.'

She half closed her eyes, and lay dreamily staring up at the ceiling from the flood of her spilling, shining, gold hair.

Released from sexual tension, bewildered by the astuteness of the strange young girl he'd married, Charles's faint annoyance changed abruptly to wry amusement, holding even a tinge of gratification. His vanity flowered again, titillated by her flattery. After all, he'd taken on no pig-in-the-poke. Looking back reflectively he had to admit to himself that all along he'd considered she could eventually prove to be a good bargain. And he'd been right.

Impulsively he put his lips on hers again, but Clara's remained cool, and unresponsive. She opened her eyes wide, staring at him, then smiled engagingly.

'I must have a wash, darling,' she said. 'Do you mind?'

Her evasion, so prettily put, started a pattern to their marriage, which, although he did not recognise it then, was to be sustained fairly accurately during their life together.

Lydia's first shock over Clara's marriage gradually turned to a confusion of mixed emotions; resentment, combined with anxiety on her sister's behalf, bewilderment, hope for her happiness and apprehension for the future of them all – especially now that Charles had been welded into so integral a part of the family. He – Lydia's brother-in-law. The fact seemed not only ridiculous but embarrassing, causing a stab of secret unpleasant jealousy. She had never been jealous of Clara before. But now she was, in spite of the passionate experience of her physical response to her own husband. The latter had been and was, satisfying in a certain way. But sentiment – the dream and the romance – were lacking.

It was not Clara's fault of course. Clara had had nothing to do with the break-up of her romance with

Charles. The fact remained that she visioned every future meeting with her former lover as a hurtful humiliation. Playing the grand lady would be no help in easing the inner bitterness. Charles would only smile to himself because he well knew she was no such thing. He would picture her always, probably, as the wild free girl of the moor, running with torn skirts to meet him. Unless, of course, he had become so besotted with Clara that he did not bother to think back at all, and accepted her just as part and parcel of the household – Mrs Richard Fearnley, mistress of Blackstone.

Well, perhaps that would be best, Lydia told herself reasoningly. The probability was that unless Charles could somehow provide a suitable home for his young wife, they would have to be allowed an apartment in the Fearnley establishment; so calm acceptance of the situation had to be aimed for. She could never see Clara homeless or living in sordid poverty-stricken conditions. This would be quite unforgivable. She was sure Richard would see the point.

He did. But not in the way she'd anticipated.

'No,' he said bluntly, when Lydia broached the matter. 'I won't have that improvident fortune-hunting Romeo under my roof. I'm sorry, but your sister's married him, and—'

'She has made her own bed and must lie on it?' Lydia interrupted sharply. 'That's what you were going to say, isn't it?'

'Something like it. And it happens to be true. I've a notion the young lady isn't half so innocent and defenceless as you seem to think.'

'What do you mean?'

Richard shrugged. 'Just what I've said.'

Realising there was no point in pressing the matter just then, Lydia, adjusting a dark curl that had fallen loose from a ribbon over her eyes, said. 'Their notice to leave Greyfriars is very short. You'd have thought following Papa's death the Church could have been more charitable.'

'If you want charity, my love,' Richard told her, 'look in another direction.'

Grasping the opportunity, Lydia smiled sweetly.

'Yes. You're so right. It's just occurred to me – if they *don't* find anywhere in time, what about the Dower House?'

The Dower House was a neglected granite dwelling less than a mile away from Blackstone Manor situated in a dip of overgrown land lush with undergrowth, straggling stunted trees and bushes. It had last been occupied five years previously by the old sister of the late squire. Following her death there had been little use for it, except for storage purposes and workers on the estate. Most of the old furniture remained; the main rooms were kept locked, with contents under dust sheets. At the best of times its dark granite face, twisted chimneys, and slits of windows gave an impression of haunting, or being haunted. The curving nearby lane was overgrown by clustered sycamore, sloes, briars, willow and glossy-leaved rhododendrons which in the summer blossomed with rich crimson flowers. Shadows lurked and encompassed the landscape for most of the day. Little could be seen from there of the wide moorland hills beyond, glint of the sea, or distant mine-works. It was three miles to the west that cobalt was found, at the side of a narrow valley starkly bordered by the mineral rock.

'The *Dower* House?' Richard echoed. 'That derelict place?'

'It needn't be derelict. It could soon be put in order.'

'At my expense, I suppose.'

Lydia's cheeks reddened. 'Couldn't you afford it?'

'That's not the point. In the first place I consider it too close to Blackstone. More important – to you, surely – is the health issue. I thought Clara had to have special treatment. Fresh air's surely one of the primary considerations.'

'The gardens could be tidied and the trees cut,' Lydia persisted. '*That* would make a difference, and add value to your property too. I don't suppose Clara and – and Charles – would want to stay forever—' her voice softened, became pleading and seductive. 'Oh Richard – *please.*'

He stared deep into her glowing eyes which in the slanting rays of the sunlight were lit from flecks of gold into varying shades of blue, jade, and deepest amber. Brilliant unfathomable eyes holding depths he couldn't yet reach. His emotion was so strong, so overwhelming, all that mattered for an instant was to take her, and somehow eradicate every moment of the past from her memory, so that she was completely his. His alone.

But he steeled himself to tear his gaze from hers; they were standing at the window of the large sitting room which overlooked the garden. The sky was clear, lit to brief splendour before the sun slipped behind the trees fringing the moor beyond.

Then he asked bluntly, clasping both hands firmly behind his back. 'Just tell me this. Are you thinking of Clara? Or – *Charles*?'

'What?' The direct question took her completely unaware. She hadn't really considered her own feelings on such an issue.

'You heard what I said. Don't prevaricate.'

'Clara, of course,' she replied shortly.

'Hm.' Still not looking at her he walked to the door.

'Well?' Her voice had become hesitant. Obviously he was not going to comply as easily as she'd thought.

'I'll think about it,' he told her. 'The house is too near Blackstone for my liking. And as I've already pointed out, Lydia, I will *not* have that sly lady-killer on my premises. Wheal Chance is only a few miles away. I shall be going backwards and forwards quite a bit – we're bound to run into each other from time to time, which could be decidedly unpleasant. And how am I to know that your scheming young sister won't lure him into my home one day when I'm not there?'

She laughed and ran after him, clutching his arms which were rigid and hard.

'Oh, Richard, I believe you're jealous.' He turned then, and looked down on her again.

'Jealous? Damn right I am. And why the devil shouldn't I be? Only a few months ago, or is it weeks – you were lying in that arty buccaneer's arms trying to tempt him into matrimony. That's right isn't it? I saw enough to imagine the rest. You weren't playacting, my darling. You were doing all you could to seduce him. Well, that's in the past. But I warn you, Lydia, if I ever discover you practising your charms on him again, you'll regret it.'

'I won't be threatened,' she said, with her cheeks whitening.

'Lydia! I'm *telling* you. It's obviously high time we learned more of each other's potential and where we stand. A little advance education is all to the good I'd say, and could save a deal of trouble later.'

She was vainly trying to think of a suitably tart reply when he turned on his heel. There was the snap of a latch, and he had gone.

Although mortified by Richard's unseemly attitude, Lydia had a feeling she had won concerning the question of Clara.

And she was right.

The following day he informed her that if the newly married couple could find nowhere else to live, they could have the Dower House, taking Miss Teague with them, providing they vacated it when any more suitable accommodation was found.

'In the meantime,' he said. 'I expect that young mountebank to pull his weight with getting the place into order. He'll have to forget his dabbling for a bit, and come down to earth.'

'Oh he will, he will,' Lydia promised recklessly. Her face was radiant. 'I'll tell her as soon as possible—' she broke off breathlessly.

'You'll do nothing of the sort, my love. I'll do the telling, and I'll see Charles Clarke has no false illusions about the situation.'

With this Lydia had to be content.

Richard rode over to Greyfriars that same week. As he'd

expected, Charles had achieved nothing in finding a home. He was confident 'something would turn up'. In the meantime he was quite prepared to visit a friend in Plymouth for a time – a man who dealt in property and might have a suggestion to offer.

'I take it you wouldn't mind putting up Clara for a bit,' he said calmly. 'Being Lydia's sister they'd probably be pleased to have a week or so alone together.'

'Hardly alone,' Richard said drily. 'Lydia has a husband now: myself – remember? And I would mind very much having a third party forced on us at the moment – even the beautiful Clara.' He paused, adding almost immediately, 'And I'm sure *she* wouldn't appreciate being so speedily abandoned.'

'*Abandoned?*'

'Oh, don't try and fool me, young man. You're quite an adept at making plans, as you've already proved.'

For a second Charles's eyes blazed. 'I don't *quite* take in what you're getting at, Fearnley, and it's perhaps as well. But in case you're under any misapprehensions, let me inform you I wouldn't be such a fool as to try and get a foothold in your mansion – *or* thrust Clara on your charity. Money's important though, as you've obviously discovered. But I happen to have a career that matters, however puerile it may appear to you. I'm an artist, and one day society will accept it. It may be a struggle at the beginning, I've faced that. There'll be times when I have to leave Cornwall, and I'd hoped you'd provide – a refuge – maybe – for Lydia's sister. Perhaps you'll put it to her, will you? I'd be interested to know her reply.

'Another thing—' he waited while Fearnley eyed him curiously, '—this cobalt business. I know certain things about it. Before my Oxford fiasco I learned a few facts from an uncle who was an expert mining engineer. Thénard's blue, which is an aluminate, is the one used in oil paints. I doubt very much that Wheal Chance will produce the large quantity you're counting on. Do you know what it looks like in its pure state? – silver white.

And it's hard. Harder than iron. Brand first discovered it in 1733. At first Central European miners considered it false ore because it yielded no copper. I've had a stroll down that dark valley of yours – ugly, but dramatic. From the look of it – and a feeling I have for such things, I'd guess the area was more rich with tin than cobalt. Still,' he shrugged, 'that's your problem.'

'Thank you for the information. What's it in aid of?'

Charles smiled ambiguously, then, with a hint of mischief in his eyes he replied, 'Nothing. Probably just an excuse to show I'm not *quite* an ignoramus in the ways of work, men, women, and the old earth itself. Believe me – they can all be unpredictable at the most unexpected moments.'

A devious dangerous character, for all his artistic appearance, Richard decided. But in spite of his instinctive dislike of the man – a defensiveness because of Lydia – he felt a grudging admiration for the manner in which he'd steered the conversation to his own advantage.

The interview following Charles's little oration on cobalt, was short and businesslike. Fearnley's offer was accepted, with a generous undertaking on Richard's part that he would foot any expense for putting the house in order, providing Charles was on the spot to supervise and give any necessary help.

When Fearnley had gone Clara rushed into the hall from the parlour.

'Well? What did he say?' she asked, gasping prettily. 'Will he agree? Can we have an apartment at Blackstone?'

Charles shook his head.

'Not exactly. But—'

'But what? Oh do *tell* me—' Her eyes widened pleadingly. She looked so lovely, so vulnerable and young, that Charles felt tenderness rising in him. In a queer way, he thought, trying to ease his own conscience for marrying her without physical desire, he could love her. Perhaps in time, when she was more mature, the bond between them would strengthen into something deeper. He outlined

Richard's suggestion, and after a pang of disappointment, she agreed later to inspect the premises. Her reaction when Charles took her over to see the proposed new home was at first doubtful.

Although by then a man and a boy, assisted by Charles himself at periods, had done a good deal of hacking away weeds, undergrowth and tenacious ivy that seemed everywhere – the Dower House still appeared depressingly derelict and uninviting. Except for wild flowers and occasional patches of white thorn blossom the vista was one of grey-shadowed wilderness.

She shivered involuntarily, exclaiming, 'But there's no proper drive; it looks – looks so *lonely*, Charles. And the windows are small. There'll be no sun – no proper garden, and inside it's sure to be damp—' She broke off, frowning helplessly.

'There's no sunshine anywhere today,' Charles affirmed stoutly. 'In a week or two everything'll be different. In fact I can imagine doing quite a bit of gardening here.'

'Can you? I can't.'

'I'm afraid you'll have to try and make the best of things,' he said with a hint of impatience. 'Fearnley could have seen us without a roof over our heads if he'd wanted—'

'What? I'm Lydia's sister. And he *likes* me.' Her tones were petulant.

'He likes himself and Lydia,' Charles retorted bluntly. 'And you'd better get it into your head once and for all, Clara, that any intrusion into life at Blackstone – even by such a pretty little sister-in-law as yourself – is going to mean trouble. So cheer up, wipe the gloom off your face, my love, and try and be grateful for what you have.'

'*This* place?'

'For *me*,' he told her. 'You've got a husband now – quite a good bargain don't you think? – under the circumstances.'

She winced.

'Because of my back, you mean.'

'No,' he answered firmly. 'I was thinking in terms of dowry; material assets. Most girls have something of the sort when they go to the altar. But your preaching prig of a father left nothing but debts on your behalf. You should thank your lucky stars for Richard Fearnley's Dower House. So should your dragon of an aunt. Presumably the estimable Miss Teague has nothing to her name?'

'She's a few savings, I believe; but I still think if you'd tried harder – been more tactful – he'd have agreed to an apartment at Blackstone.'

'With *me* around, to tempt the luscious Lydia's attention again?'

Clara's expression changed, became colder, more speculative. For seconds there was silence between them, then she asked with her eyes staring unblinkingly at his face, 'Does she still attract you, Charles? Are you afraid of being near her?'

A dull red suffused his face. He could have slapped her. But instead, after a quick pause, he pulled himself together, laughed shortly, took his young wife by the shoulders and said, 'Now aren't you a ninny to ask? What man in his senses would give a second thought to a black-haired virago like Lydia with such a beautiful creature as you available.'

She was partially mollified by the reply, but realised later that he had not really answered her question. Resentment gnawed her. Her bright mind told her that circumstances, in her case, might have been far worse. She might have been dismissed to some institution or other where they cared for the sick and penniless, or thrown on the mercy of the parish. But then Lydia would never have allowed it. Lydia somehow would have taken care of her, because she was that kind of person, with a terribly strong conscience where she, Clara, was concerned.

All the same it was humiliating and had been frequently irritating to her in the past having to live so much under the dominance of her father's smothering care, and her sister's overshadowing vitality. *That*, at least, thank heaven, was over. By her own charm and devious means she had won a husband – the man Lydia loved so wildly, and maybe still did. Her status as a married woman and mistress of the Dower House – however drab and dreary it appeared at the moment – was assured. Miss Teague would merely be resident in her niece's home, and unable to order her about; domestically of course she would have a role to play, because Clara disliked household duties, and in any case was not strong enough to shoulder physical tasks, nor ever would be.

Lydia had informed her that Richard Fearnley was arranging an appointment with a specialist from London to see her. He was arriving shortly at Blackstone where he would stay for two nights, and examine her for himself.

His treatment, Lydia had said, had been most effective in certain spinal cases. If he thought Clara's condition could be improved by a period at his own hospital in London, Richard would pay all expenses for a stay there. But Clara had little faith in the prospect. And her opinion proved to be correct, the verdict being that what she most needed was complete rest, freedom from anxiety, country air, and daily doses from bottles of patent tonics and medicines prescribed to strengthen tissue and bones. The price demanded for such concoctions seemed exorbitant, even to Fearnley. But he paid without argument, anxious only to get the pompous medico off his premises as soon as possible. The man might be genuine in his belief, but he was a great bore, and had appeared interested only in himself and his own theories and long words, except during one brief meeting with Lydia when his curiously light eyes had lingered upon her for a moment appreciatively under his heavy lids.

'So that's it,' Richard said after the brougham had rattled away through the gates of Blackstone. 'Waste of money, if you ask me.'

'It may not be,' Lydia asserted. 'We'll have to wait and see.'

Clara, who unknown to them had approached the door

and heard, smiled sweetly and said, 'I think Richard's right. But thank you for doing so much for me. Papa would have been grateful too.'

She looked so frail and winsome, so very delicate and utterly beautiful standing there, that Richard's senses softened.

'I don't want gratitude, Clara. It's my pleasure and duty to do all I can for my own wife's sister.'

Lydia!

Always Lydia, Clara thought.

When Joseph was alive it was the other way around. *Now* – in spite of the Dower House and Fearnley's generosity, everything once more seemed to revolve round her elder sister. *Everything*.

Except Charles.

Charles belonged to Clara now, and she would see in future that Lydia recognised it, and even suffered a little. It wouldn't be too difficult. Having won Richard's interest in her well-being she would contrive somehow to get a footing in Blackstone. Fearnley, then, would hardly be able to forbid Charles, her husband, to cross the threshold, especially considering the cobalt enterprise. There would be fun in witnessing the reaction between the two men – and Lydia. Clara was only half conscious of her devious planning. She had for so long lived under Joseph's dominance, that the thought of creating drama and colourful situations went to her head like wine.

So during the weeks of restoring and making the Dower House habitable again, Clara became so sweetly compliant and gentle that her aunt was mildly concerned. Poor child, she thought, she was suffering more from the shock of her father's death than anyone had known. Still, she would recover; she was young, and although their future home was too isolated for her liking, it had possibilities. Mr Fearnley was allowing them a small carriage and paying for the services of a man to drive them to St Kerrick or further whenever they desired. He would also assist with the gardening, helped by a youth.

Then there would be a girl employed in the house. Anne, at Richard's request, interviewed several and decided on the daughter of a farmer – a smallholder who had a difficult task in making both ends meet. His wife was frail through childbearing and hard work, his land poor, and his moral principles strict, based on the teachings of John Wesley, though without Wesley's inherent compassion. Of his five children only two had survived – a son Thomas and a daughter.

'A good influence in the house,' Anne Teague had decided, noting approvingly the girl's modest air of inclining her head and eyes downwards, her neat blue print dress, and shining brown hair pushed primly under a mob cap. No frivolity – no slight indication of wilfulness or ill-mannered coarseness. She could be well trained in the duties and made into a capable servant. She was sixteen years old. Her name was Jess. During that first interview Anne had not perceived that despite her plain countrified appearance, Jess Treen had full red lips above a slightly receding chin, and that her eyes, when she lifted them, were palest blue-grey, a little prominent, but with strange darting lights in them, betraying a capacity to absorb and make use of anything that was to her advantage.

So Jess was given the post, and was told by Anne that she could expect to move to the Dower House at the end of March.

When the day came, the sun was shining, allowing maximum light to penetrate the newly cleaned glass of the small windows. Furniture which had remained and been used intermittently at periods through the years, had been cleaned and polished to Miss Teague's satisfaction. Most of it was of solid mahogany, including the round table, chairs and sideboard of the dining room. But the drawing room proved a pleasant surprise for Clara. From time to time pieces had become intermingled from different periods; yet all seemed in harmony. Rosewood and walnut gave an air of gentility to the pale pink upholstery and faded cream and pink carpets which in the past must have been costly to install. A circular crystal chandelier hung from the ornately embossed cream ceiling. A gilt china clock, probably French, was the centrepiece of the marble mantelpiece.

Clara clasped her hands delightedly. She stood for a moment before moving forward and touching it with a finger.

'Please make it tick,' she exclaimed to Charles who was standing slightly behind her. Charles examined the clock, discovered a small key lying nearby, and wound it. Almost immediately there was the tinkle of a short merry tune.

Clara turned round abruptly and cried to the stern-faced Miss Anne, 'This will be *my* room. I shall do my tapestries here, and my paintings, small ones, so that they can be added to those miniatures on the walls—' she broke off breathlessly, as Miss Teague interrupted:

'Not in a *drawing* room. To paint in such a room would be ridiculous.'

'If I want to be ridiculous I will be,' Clara said stubbornly, 'in my own home.'

'Yes, why not?'

All three of them looked quickly towards the door, and saw with astonishment, Lydia standing there. She was wearing an outfit of dark green velvet that turned her jade eyes to brilliant emerald jewels through a dancing glint of golden sunlight. No one had expected her. Richard had expressly forbidden her to be on the premises when Charles and his wife arrived. But he had been summoned away unexpectedly to a meeting of the smelting company in Mount Caerion, and Lydia had rashly decided to ignore his wishes. After all, to greet her sister was surely a duty!

She waited, smiling faintly, until Clara went forward, lifted her arms, and felt Lydia's lips brush her forehead. Clara could not see the cold condemning look on her sister's face as Lydia lifted her head, staring straight at Charles. Neither was she aware of the tightening twist of his lips which could have been bitterness, or a secret devious triumph.

The brief pause was shattered quickly by Miss Teague saying a trifle shrilly, 'Everything so far appears quite satisfactory, Lydia. I did not expect to see you here.'

'I didn't mean to come yet. But Richard has gone off on another meeting about that cobalt business – Wheal Chance, the mine. Something to do with smelting.' She paused, then added, 'He offered to take me – just for the drive, to Mount Caerion. But it's such a dreary village, and the valley's worse. It always depresses me – so dark and forbidding and narrow – as though nothing lived there—' She made a little moué of distaste.

'Probably nothing does,' Charles said bluntly. 'Or very little. Not healthy. I wouldn't wonder if the soil wasn't riddled with arsenic. You get that sometimes, mixed up with the remains of copper, especially where there's cobalt. Not that I believe there's much of *that* there, as I've told your ambitious spouse more than once. The broken-down huts and desolation are just relics of life gone sour.' While he was speaking his eyes were still on Lydia's face. 'Of course you can never tell. If I had a sovereign or two to risk I *might* – just *might* put a bit of capital into the company, not because of what I'd hope to get back on it, but because of the interest – the pristine beauty of colour – its use to an artist's brush—'

'That doesn't sound very practical,' Anne remarked critically.

'No. And I don't believe Richard Fearnley will find the project practical either. But that's his funeral.'

Lydia sighed. 'Richard's willing to take the risk. He's that type of person. If the whole thing fails he'll accept it and find another outlet I'm sure.'

'Naturally.' Charles' tones were acerbic, his glance cold with condemnation. 'He can afford to. Not all of us are in the same position, able to risk what we haven't got, if you understand me—?'

Yes. Lydia understood. Charles was taunting her with his refusal to marry her when she'd so wildly wanted it – attempting to exonerate himself from rejecting the responsibility. And yet he had married Clara. Why? For his own advancement of course. To gain a foothold in the Fearnley establishment he now possessed. A faint curve of contempt momentarily touched her lips. Yet even now, she couldn't wholly dislike him; she recalled with a stab of nostalgia and against her will – the wild delight of moments spent in his arms on the moor, when she'd believed so passionately in their future together, never doubting anything could tear them apart.

Trying to force the memory away she heard her aunt saying briskly, 'Well, now you're here, Lydia, you may as well stay for a little. I'm sure there is still a certain amount of rearranging to do – you may be of help. And I, for one, will be glad of a little refreshment before we start. Will you join us over a dish of tea?'

'Well – yes, thank you, but I won't be able to stay long,' Lydia answered doubtfully. 'I came in the carriage, and the man knows I have to be back soon—'

'At Master Fearnley's command, I suppose,' Charles' voice was supercilious.

'Master Fearnley, as you call him – my husband – will be away quite a time,' Lydia answered, with angry colour flooding her cheeks. 'And I certainly don't have to ask his permission to leave home for an airing. I was thinking of the horses—'

'The horses! of course. We must certainly not detain the horses from their nose-bags!'

'Oh don't argue,' Clara snapped. 'Just when I was loving this room you two have to start bickering. It's not fair.' Tears blurred her lovely eyes.

In a wave of contrition Lydia stepped towards her, and took her hand.

'Sorry, darling. It's all due to this stupid cobalt business. To be honest, it bores me as much as it must you. *Please* smile, Clara. This *is* such an important day for you—'

'I'm glad you realise it,' Anne interrupted tartly. 'Now, Lydia, come to the kitchen. As you're here and the girl doesn't come till tomorrow, you may as well lend me a hand.'

'In this?' Lydia stared at her green velvet gown ruefully.

'Why not? I've not asked you to scrub the floor.'

Controlling her temper, Lydia followed her aunt out of the room, leaving Charles and Clara together.

Charles went straight over to his young wife and kissed her.

'You mustn't bother about Lydia's moods. You know what she is—'

'Yes, *And* you, Charles. I can't forget that you once – that you loved her—' She dabbed an eye with a dainty lace-edged handkerchief.

'Now, now, my sweet, what a stupid thing to say—'

'Is it?' Her expression changed, became defiant and sharp.

He hesitated for a moment, then replied, 'I think so. There's no point in delving into the past. If I'd *really* loved Lydia I'd hardly have married you, would I?'

She turned away.

'I'm not sure. Men do funny things.'

'And what do you know about men?' His voice was teasing.

'Oh, more than you think.'

'Well, then—' He caught her by the shoulder, and with a finger under her chin, turned her face up to his. 'You'd better forget it, I'm not having my own wife think back on her stream of other suitors.'

She was just going to blurt out that there had never been any other suitors – none but him, but wisely thought the better of it. Instead she rested her fair head against Charles' breast and murmured with apparent docility, 'Oh, Charles darling, forgive me for being so silly. It's just that I love you so very much – and Lydia can be so terribly sort of forceful and overbearing when she wants to be.'

'I agree,' Charles said lightly. 'And for once I think she's met her match in Master Richard Fearnley. Serve her right.'

His statement proved to be correct.

When Lydia arrived back at Blackstone considerably later than she'd intended, Richard came out of his study to greet her as she appeared from the front entrance. Her cheeks were faintly flushed, her jade eyes brighter than usual. There was a breathless quality about her that he found disturbing.

'Where have you been, Lydia?'

'Oh I—' she hesitated for a moment or two before saying, 'You said you'd be away a considerable time, and I was bored, so I ordered the carriage, and went to see my sister settled at the Dower House. She was there. *And* Aunt Anne, of course.'

His grey eyes darkened, searching her face.

'And Charles Clarke?'

'Naturally.'

Richard took her hand and led her to the study.

'I'd told you expressly to keep away from that bounder. Then why didn't you? Couldn't you bear the thought of being away from him in my absence, just for one short hour or two?'

'I *told* you it was my sister.'

His grip tightened on her shoulder, 'Don't lie to me, Lydia. And don't ever – *ever* dare to steal off to that godforsaken place again, or I'll—'

Two vivid spots of colour stained her high cheekbones.

'Or I'll regret it. I suppose you'll put me over your knee and spank me like a naughty girl,' she finished for him. 'I know. You've already told me.'

'There'll be no telling next time. I'll do it, and damn thoroughly. Meanwhile, my darling—' He lifted her up suddenly in his arms and held her close, before carrying her upstairs. Her heart was pounding wildly as she struggled, not with fear, but rebellion. Rebellion at the power this one man seemed to have over her.

Once in the bedroom he deliberately locked the door, laid her on the bed and took her to him with an expertise of masterly passion that left her bewildered and wondering how she could so easily have responded and succumbed. If she'd been in love with him – but she wasn't, not truly. How could she be? Love meant romance and gentle words – gallantry and adoration; something she'd once found in Charles – or thought so, until he shattered the illusion.

She could never feel romantic about Richard – *never*. He was so down to earth and realistic. So completely domineering and sure of himself.

Nevertheless, even when the true facts registered, the pulses of her body were still leaping as though a raging fire seared her veins.

Life, indeed, was very difficult to understand – and most of all herself – Lydia Fearnley.

5

After Clara's first delight in arranging and rearranging the drawing room at the Dower House to her own satisfaction, she began to find life in her own home slightly tedious. Charles no longer seemed interested in her dainty attempts at painting, and was frequently away from home finding new scope and subjects for his own work. Without saying so openly she resented anything that diverted his attention from herself. If they had had more money, allowing her to travel in the carriage further afield than the St Kerrick district – Falmouth perhaps, where there were fashionable shops to patronise and sufficient in her purse to squander on vanity, the days could have been more exciting. As it was the Dower House, during that early summer, became oppressive to her. Now she'd obtained security nothing remained there for her to do. Anne Teague took charge of the domestic routine as she had done before, and with Jess and the man in attendance Clara was left very much to her own resources.

At the beginning she had secretly hoped and planned to inveigle herself into the Blackstone menage. Lydia *had* invited her to tea twice, but that was all, and on each occasion Richard had not been there to work her charms on. She had returned the second time to The Hollies – the official name of the Dower House – thwarted and irritable, venting her ill humour on her husband, if by chance he was on the scene when she got back. He happened to be in the bedroom that day as she went in.

'Lydia seems so awfully smug,' she told Charles, removing her best beflowered headgear, with the other hand fluffing out her golden curls on either side of her face. 'She sails about like a duchess, and is *so* condescending. "You look so pretty, darling. Are you tired Clara? How are things going with you and Charles? You *are* happy, aren't you?" – *Happy!* imagine it! when we're treated like pariahs!'

Charles laughed and attempted to soothe her.

'My dear love. What an expression. On the whole Fearnley hasn't behaved badly—'

'It's all right for you to say that,' she snapped. 'But he's my brother-in-law, we should have had some proper invitation to the house; *both* of us.'

'Ah well! Under the circumstances—'

'*What* circumstances?' Clara demanded petulantly. 'You mean because of you and Lydia?'

Charles' face hardened.

'For Heaven's sake get that bee out of your bonnet, Clara. I thought the subject was over. To tell you the truth your jealousy's getting damned boring.'

She stared. '*Jealousy? Me?*'

His jaws tightened. 'Yes. You've got *me*, haven't you? Why have you forever to be dwelling on the past? And why can't you ignore what Richard Fearnley does or doesn't do?'

'Because you're out a lot, and this place depresses me.'

'You're not exactly an enlivening influence yourself, are you?' He frowned, regarding her assessingly. 'Perhaps that's the trouble—'

'What?'

He pulled her to him more firmly than usual.

'You haven't *given* anything lately, Clara. Isn't it about time we came to grips with things?'

'What do you mean?'

'This. The husband and wife business. The love, Clara.'

'Love?' Her voice was a bewildered whisper. 'I don't know—'

'No. Exactly. You don't seem to know a damn thing of what a man expects from the woman he's married to.'

She managed to extricate herself from his grasp.

'Please don't,' she said. 'It's so *hot*.'

Ignoring the remark he caught her again, picked her up in his arms and laid her on the bed. She stared at him half in anger, half fear. Very deliberately he prepared himself, disrobed her, and forced himself upon her. She struggled at first, endeavouring to keep her thighs tightly pressed together. It was no use; he was too strong for her. Some moments later it was over. She was still moaning with pain. Her eyes, though blurred with tears, were hard. She hated intercourse now. At first, having lured him into marriage she'd borne it with a certain satisfaction. But slowly warmth between them had died.

He jumped up quickly, tidied his clothes as speedily as possible, then bracing himself into a jaunty stance walked to the door, paused, turned, gave a little mock bow, and said icily, 'Thank you, madam, thank you – for nothing.'

There was the click of a latch and he had gone.

Neither he nor Clara had the faintest inkling that Jess, the servant, had heard most of their revealing discussion, standing close to the door, with a duster in her hand. At the right moment she'd disappeared down the narrow landing to the linen room.

A curious, secretive little smile curved her sensuous lips.

Life wasn't going to be so dull after all, she thought smugly. Men! They were all the same – except that this one was a bit above the rest of them – more exciting than others she'd known.

Lydia was confused. Resentment at Richard's possessive attitude and obvious jealousy of Charles, conflicted with a sense of gratification that she had the power to rouse such strong emotions in her husband. All the same, she told herself rebelliously, he'd no right to try and make her a prisoner, or change her from the wild wilful creature she was at heart, into some gentle 'yes woman', the conventional well-bred wife content to remain compliant to his slightest wish and word of command. There was little for her to do at Blackstone except supervise the servants if necessary, and this seldom – if ever – occurred. The housekeeper was in complete control. Everything was quite well-ordered and satisfactory.

'I can't just sit here doing needlework or twiddling my thumbs forever,' she told herself. 'Driving round in a carriage gives me no exercise at all. There's no fun any more in showing myself off to St Kerrick people. I've just got to have some kind of activity.'

So she asked Richard about a horse.

'I'd like to ride,' she said, 'I shall get fat and lumpy and more bored every day, doing nothing. Can't you understand, Richard? I'm not a lazy person!'

An odd smile of amusement twitched his lips.

'I never thought you were, or I wouldn't have fallen in love with you.' He paused, then continued, 'What about gardening? There are still patches in the grounds needing flowers. I'm sure Peters would give you a hand. You could study books on the subject; there's a new one just come out – I forget what it's called, but I can find out – something like *Floral Tips for the Gentlewoman with Green Fingers*—?'

The title sounded so ridiculous Lydia burst into laughter.

'Oh goodness! Richard – *really!* Can you see me pottering about in gloves, with a trowel in my hand following instructions from a little book written for *ladies*—?'

Her laughter was so infectious he joined in.

'No, quite honestly I can't. But you like the out-of-doors—'

'Yes. To smell it and *feel* it, and have the wind against my face. To get a glimpse of the sea, and go for a canter over the moors when I want to—' She broke off restlessly.

He frowned.

'The moors are treacherous.'

'Not everywhere. Anyway, I could keep to the lanes. Anyone in my position – as your wife, Richard – should be able to handle a horse. If we'd had the money when my father was alive, a horse was the first thing I'd have wanted—'

'And the one thing Mr Joseph Teague would have forbidden, I'm sure,' Richard pointed out.

'Maybe,' she frowned, then moved towards him, lifted her face and smiled radiantly, with the brilliance of sunlight breaking through cloud.

'But you're *not* my father,' she said, with her breasts rising and falling quickly. '*Please* – don't deny me a little excitement – I can't live completely cooped up. And I'd promise to be very careful. You could get one of the grooms – Carne perhaps – to teach me. You say he's a wonder with animals, and if you told him I wasn't to ride out alone on my own until I was absolutely safe – he'd be very careful to do just as you said I'm sure.'

'He'd *try*,' Richard answered ironically. 'Whether he'd succeed or not is a different matter.'

'Oh, he would, and you know it. Anyway my word should be enough.' She leaned closer, and touched his chin with the tip of one finger. 'Well?'

He stared into her strange lovely eyes before replying huskily, 'You play the devil with commonsense, and all I've got tells me I'm a fool to give in—'

'Then be a fool,' she begged. 'It can be fun sometimes.'

He sighed heavily, shook his head slowly, then suddenly his lips were on hers, as an arm encircled her so tightly she could hardly breathe. When he released her, his heart was pumping heavily against his ribs; the desire in him was urgent. If it hadn't been for a subtle coy certainty in her eyes – the knowing sensual awareness – he would have picked her up, taken her to their bed, and made love with all the fire of his being. But an inherent caution, stiffened with the resolution never to allow her to cajole him or think she had the upper hand, made him turn away.

'Very well,' he said slowly, no longer looking at her. 'I'll see about a mare for you, and have a few words with Carne. Just one thing though—' He glanced back briefly. 'You'll not ride in the vicinity of the Dower House, or attempt in any way to run into Charles Clarke. Is that understood?'

She nodded and smiled, despite her chagrin at so summary a dismissal. She'd expected the interlude to end differently. Already her senses were alight and yearning for him. Yet she managed to answer coolly, 'If you say so, Richard, of course.'

'Good.'

He went out, shutting the door with a sharp snap.

She stood for a few moments, depressed and deflated, feeling she had in some way failed. Then, gradually, her natural resilience returned. She'd got what she'd wanted after all – the promise of a horse. When she'd learned to ride well she'd go where she chose, providing she was skilful enough not to cut directly towards Clara's home. Richard would not be able to keep strict watch on her – especially as he was so occupied with his stupid cobalt business.

As for Charles! Well, Charles wasn't important any more. His romantic words had proved false and he was Clara's husband. Richard had no cause to doubt her; with a flash of sudden knowledge she knew he never would have. Strange as it seemed, however much she defied and bickered with him, he mattered. Without him, she'd be lost. The unpredictable thing had happened. She was falling in love. Not romantically, with a dream figure out of a fairytale – but with a flesh and blood mate. Someone she could both passionately desire and hate at the same time – as integral a part of her being as the sharp moorland winds blown from the sea, and the thunderous breaking of waves against the grim Cornish cliffs. And more than that – much much more.

In those first moments of knowledge she knew she had never properly lived before. Sexual fulfilment had been complete, but now another dimension had been added. It was not only his strength and power that counted – but the humanity and warmth of him. *If* he could be made to understand – what a wife she would be. He *wanted* her – she knew that, but there must be giving too, as trust and complete faith in her, so that a bond could be wielded between them stronger than any trick of circumstance as petty misunderstanding.

Instinctively, she smiled. For a moment magic seemed to flood the world. Against the summer sky blossom foamed, the nostalgic subtle scent of bluebells crept from the lanes and lush hedgerows to the garden, mingling with that of roses and other growing things.

She sighed deeply, then, still in a dream, wandered down the hall and out into the grounds of Blackstone.

True to his word Richard spoke to Carne about choosing a suitable mount for his wife, and a week later Lydia, having acquired an olive green riding habit, had her first lesson on horseback.

Richard left her alone with Carne on the first occasion, but the next day stood watching as she cantered round the paddock on a well-bred velvet-eyed chestnut mare, Melody – 'easy to manage, quiet, Melody is,' Carne had assured him, 'placid and trustworthy. Nothing temperamental about her, though she can take a fence as good as any.'

One glance told Fearnley that Lydia was an apt pupil, and a born rider. Her assurance even mildly discomfited him. No doubt, he thought, she would be taking the fences referred to by the groom more quickly than he'd anticipated. He could just imagine her galloping off when the mood took her simply for the fun and excitement of it. Still, so long as she kept well away from the Dower House and heeded his instruction to take care, he didn't grudge her the pleasure. How erectly she sat; how proud and beautiful she looked in her plumed hat, waisted coat and velvet skirt gently drifting in folds against the animal's sleek and shining flanks. The true aristocrat, he decided in a wave of admiration. 'My Lady Fearnley'. The suggestion titillated him oddly. Sometime perhaps this might well be true. He was not unduly concerned over his own material aspirations, but the possibility of one day being acclaimed as something more than *Mr* Richard Fearnley wasn't to be sneered at. He was no opportunist out to *buy* a title. But dammit, he believed in fair play and honest recognition, and if he was prepared to use his business sense and considerable capital in providing work for poor families as well as his own gain and satisfaction, a little public acclaim would be justified.

Instinct told him that Lydia, also, would enjoy an appendage to her name. In spite of her wild spirit she'd revel in the chance to queen it a little over other women. And why not? There was no harm in natural feminine vanity – especially in one who'd had hers so ruthlessly thwarted in the past by the despicable cruel tyrant who'd sired her.

Thinking of Joseph brought Richard's mind to Clara. There was something odd and secretive about his sister-in-law that despite her beauty, disturbed and puzzled him. He doubted that she had any profound affection for her husband, but had laid an emotional trap to ensnare him, at the beginning perhaps even half believing herself that she cared. At heart she was cold though, and wily. He didn't blame her for wanting security and a wedding ring on her finger. But there was more to Clara than that. Much more – as one day the arty Charles would discover.

Well, the fellow had asked for it. And between them they'd pulled off quite a bargain. Richard was mildly chagrined when he had to accept how carelessly he'd played into their hands. If he'd given in to Lydia's plea to allow Charles to stay at the cottage, it would have saved him considerable expense. They could have made the best of the confined space and let the starchy Miss Anne fend for herself. As it was, according to Lydia, there was still much to be done at the Dower House to make it really comfortable. And the trouble was, Richard was finding it increasingly hard to resist his wayward lovely wife when she asked for anything.

In spite of himself, he smiled. He loved her. And love such as his had a devilish capacity for making a man soft when he could otherwise have been hard. So he had to accept that Clara, now, had become a liability and something of a trespasser into what should have been a straightforward beginning to his married life. However, if things became difficult or too complicated, he'd have them out of the Dower House, and settle them somewhere else further away, which would mean delving into his pocket again for the sake of peace and quiet. It wouldn't hurt him to do so, but he'd be annoyed – damned annoyed. By degrees a small fortune could be swallowed up in such a way. Another niggling fact that irritated him was the cobalt business. According to a recent highly qualified opinion on the mine's future, Charles could easily be right. The yield showed signs of fading. If it did, what his own instincts had told him would be proved wrong – something very rare in his life before.

Not that he'd let the men suffer. Wheal Chance would be in a position to take more workers on. There was another mine, too, that needed development – a new shaft sinking. Endowing it with the necessary capital meant he became principal shareholder and ultimately owner, capable of producing very profitable copper. So viewed objectively, he was not going to fret unduly over the cobalt project. Life was too short to waste energy flogging a dead horse.

During the weeks following, Richard was forced to admit that though the 'horse' in question was not yet dead, it *did* appear more than ever to be in a very shaky state – a fact already accepted by the smelting company.

Indeed, the whole narrow valley had a stark derelict aspect. The very quality which in the beginning had challenged and inspired him to drag life from it and stir something that had once been there into action again, was now becoming increasingly depressing.

Moodily, one late afternoon in April, he mounted his horse, and rode to the site. The sun was already obscured behind a rising belt of cloud and the mountainous dark thrust of grim land on either side of the narrow lane. Derelict huts, now no more than ruined symbols of past human hopes and efforts, loomed occasionally against the shadowed rocky soil. It was as though he had entered a dead world where nothing moved or lived. Due to the arsenic, probably, he reminded himself as he cantered ahead. The knowledge was depressing. Even his mount betrayed a certain unease and disinclination to go further. Richard patted the sleek neck comfortingly.

'It's all right, Flash,' he said. 'Nothing to harm you here—'

That was just it; nothing. Nothing to stir or shatter the extreme silence except the hollow sound of animal hooves echoing over the chilly stones.

At a turn of the road where the dusty earth rose slightly, he reined and stared at the end of the track where the shadows lifted revealing widening ground and a faint glimmer of sea beyond. The works, including the smelting house, were silhouetted briefly in a sudden transient beam of light. But there was still no sign of movement, no sound of activity or men moving.

Then Richard recalled it was the weekend. Workers there had probably left early as was customary on a Saturday. Well, he'd no inclination to go further. He turned, jerked the reins and kicked Flash to a sharp canter that quickly became a gallop. Once the open landscape was visible, he allowed himself to relax, and settled his mind to more practical matters. He didn't blame the men for not being at their work, the region was dreary enough to dampen anyone's enthusiasm. But they were on full pay which didn't allow for slackers or early quitting, even on a Saturday, and it had yet to be proved that the quantity of cobalt available wasn't worth toiling and sweating for. His mood, from depression, was lifting to annoyance, when something startled him – the cry of a bird – a raven was it? Or a large crow – as it flew from the blackened stump of a tree and with black wings flapping dived and rose again only a few yards before the horse's nose.

Flash jibbed, reared slightly, and almost before he knew it, Richard had slipped sideways from the saddle. He didn't fall, and quickly got the steed under control again. As he rode on cursing quietly, he noticed movement to his right. A figure stood by a thorn tree, watching – lean, dark, wearing shabby gipsy clothes, with a bundle hanging from one hand, and a look of amusement on his brown face, which was unmistakable in the clouded summer night.

Athern.

Richard ignored him, but when horse and rider passed the youth cried. 'That's bad land maister – mochardi. Athern knows. Have no truck with it, Mus, or ol' Bengh'll have thee. Take care now, for the sake o'thy rawnie – thy rackli wife. Kushti she be, maister, have a care—'

Richard neither heard completely, nor understood the jargon.

It was only later when he discovered that Lydia, too, had been out riding, that the little incident returned to disconcert him. When he asked if she'd seen Athern she looked puzzled.

'*Seen* him? Today? No, why should I?'

'You know each other. He was hanging about when I returned from the smelt house.'

She shrugged.

'Athern's generally about somewhere. You know he's a wanderer. Why are you worried? He does no harm.'

'He's a damned odd fellow,' was Richard's only comment.

She smiled and lifted her lips to his. 'So am I odd. So are you, in your own determined way. We all are, aren't we? Individuals, with our own peculiarities.'

'That's a profound thought for a young wife – a bride.'

She was thinking of how to reply when the necessity was avoided. His kiss was warm, more hungry than usual, a need to which Lydia gladly gave response.

6

For the next three weeks time passed comparatively peacefully both at Blackstone and the Dower House. Lydia was careful not to transgress over the boundaries set by Richard for her riding, and Clara, at The Hollies, did her best not to show irritation at Fearnley's determination to exclude Charles from the family circle. When she visited her sister she was driven there in the carriage, alone, bearing inward resentment under a façade of nonchalance. Only Anne Teague sensed Clara's chafing, and one day brought the subject into the open by saying abruptly, 'What's the matter with you this morning, Clara? You seem so edgy, and you frown more often than not these days. It doesn't suit you. Is it anything to do with Lydia? Or what—?'

'Of course it is,' Clara answered sharply. 'Charles and I have been married for months now, and still Richard forbids him to set foot in my sister's home. It's so humiliating. Just as though I've married a – beggar or something. Charles is more of a gentleman than Richard. His family's more aristocratic, and he's clever. It's not fair we should have to be so isolated just because Richard can't appreciate him—'

She broke off with underlip thrust out a little, making her appear a petulant child.

Anne sighed.

'The two men dislike each other, and that, really, is the end of the matter,' Anne told her niece firmly. 'And if you were wise, Clara, you'd stop worrying over Blackstone and give your attention elsewhere, to your own home and husband.'

There was a warning significant note in her voice that

made Clara turn and ask sharply, 'What do you mean? Has Charles complained about anything? Criticised me in anyway?'

'Oh no, my dear. But I've noticed a certain – disregard in your manner to him lately, that suggested you were not so infatuated as you used to be.'

'How silly! What a stupid thing to say.'

'Is it?' Anne's glance was shrewd. 'Men of Charles' type need all the attention possible from a wife. And if they don't get it they'll go elsewhere for satisfaction.'

Clara's large violet eyes widened in disbelief. She was aghast. 'You mean you're really *suggesting* that my husband would – would *look* at another woman?'

'*Looking*, as you put it, would be merely the beginning,' Anne said bluntly. 'He's a romantic.'

'But there are no women here to tempt him, and – and—' Clara broke off helplessly.

'He's out quite a deal,' Anne pointed out, 'painting – and if I were you, my dear, I'd see that when he's absent from home for a few hours, your image remains sufficiently charming in his mind to keep his heart from straying.'

Clara was too astonished, indignant and angry to reply. But after the brief conversation, in spite of all her denials and refusal to accept the possibility of what Anne suggested ever happening, she became suspicious and watchful, under a veneer of renewed affection for Charles.

She felt affronted one day, when after a show of undue ardour, before Charles went out of the house, presumably to inspect a new site for a painting, he disengaged himself irritably from her embrace and said, 'Don't smother me, Clara. Look what you've done—' His cravat was loosened, faint pink from her lips tinged one cheek. He tidied the cravat and drew a hand over his face.

Clara appeared downcast.

'Don't you love me any more?'

'Oh, Clara!' he bent to kiss her, more from duty and a niggling sense of guilt than desire. 'What a stupid question. Of course I do, you little silly.'

'You never say so now. Why don't you?'

'My dear love.' Exasperation filled him, because he would probably be late for a certain assignation ahead. 'I rather think you've been the chilly one lately.'

'*Me?*' How innocently the word came out.

'Well—' he paused before continuing assessingly, 'it may be not your fault. But ordering that single bed a fortnight ago wasn't calculated to fan passion, was it?'

'It was because of my back, and you know it. Even Aunt Anne said I should have proper sleep, and – and—' She faltered on the fringe of an emotional outburst.

'Of *course*. And she was quite right,' Charles agreed quickly. 'Now get all silly nonsense out of your head, and tonight I'll prove how I love you.'

'When will you be back?'

'In two hours at the latest.'

'Then shall I come with you? I could bring my stool, and a cushion.'

'No.' The refusal sounded more abrupt than he'd meant it to. 'You'd get muddied and tired out. The climb would exhaust you.'

'Climb? Where?'

'Oh—' Momentarily taken aback, he gave a careless indication of the slope of moor at the side of the house. 'Over the ridge. And there are adders there. You know how dangerous they can be, and how they frighten you.'

'Very well.' She sounded cool and compliant but her heart was racing. He was hiding something, she decided, recalling Anne's words, and she wouldn't be treated in such a way, she just *wouldn't*.

Clara waited twenty minutes before leaving the house wearing trim boots under a blue gown half covered by a thin cape. Over her fair curls she had placed a shred of veiling to make her fragile form less conspicuous. She took the same path Charles had used when he set off with his paints and easel.

Anne, busy in the kitchen, because Jess had been given the afternoon off to collect eggs and butter from a farm a mile away, did not notice her niece slip out, and was quite unaware of the tumultuous effect caused by her warning of a few days ago.

Clara walked lightly, stepping carefully over stones and clumps of hill turf, trying to avoid catching her shawl on any protruding undergrowth or stunted tree. At intervals she paused to regain her breath. The hill steepened after the first hundred yards, and at one point she almost turned back, thinking perhaps it was indeed stupid to traipse after her husband in such a wild manner. Then his disregard for her, his obvious objection to her company when she'd suggested it, spurred her on again. She thought she knew where he'd be. Once, after they were first married, he'd shown her the locality – carrying her half of the way.

The spot was a glade in the centre of a small copse which would be lush with bluebells and ferns now. Charles had made previous quick sketches when branches of the trees were leafless, giving a view of the landscape beyond. Now the scene would be one of dappled light and shade, inspiring him to experiment in an impressionistic manner with his brush. If he was not there he might have gone further, to a distant menhir near the moorland ridge. It was wild open country, with only rocks entangled in briars, and perhaps a few early foxgloves. She hoped he hadn't gone so far. She was already tired.

He hadn't.

When she reached the copse, something – a muted sound of voices – followed by ripples of low-throated laughter and male murmurings, caught her attention. She stood perfectly still for a moment, listening, then pushed ahead. There was a crackling, a breaking of small twigs as she passed a twisted sycamore. Then her senses froze. Her throat constricted followed by a cry of horror and disgust. Confronting her were two recumbent half-naked figures lying on the ground.

White female thighs became disentangled from the male body on top. Both sat up, hastily endeavouring to cover themselves. The woman – or girl – tried ineffectually to look at ease, stroking her hair from her forehead and saying stupidly, 'Had a fall I did – silly of me. He was just trying to pick me up—'

Clara gazed at her with contempt. Jess. The servant girl Anne had taken on in such faith in her domestic abilities. And Clara's own husband – Charles. How filthy of them. How completely obscene. If Clara had had the strength she'd have taken a stick to her and kicked the dirty creature with her boot – or else half strangled her. But her heart was beating so violently she found it at first impossible to move. When she could, Charles was already buttoning his trousers and moving towards her.

'Clara love—' There was a placating note in his voice. 'Don't misunderstand. It's nothing. Honest, I—'

He stopped abruptly, shocked by the wild white face confronting him.

'Don't touch me,' she shrieked. 'You beast! You complete beast. And *you*—' turning to Jess, 'get out, do you hear? – before I *kill* you.'

She raised an arm. The girl, taken aback by the shrill voice and blazing eyes, scrambled for her skirt, pulled it round her, and with one hand clutching her bodice turned and blundered through the trees – grazing her face as she did so – in the direction of the Dower House.

Clara and Charles, both breathing heavily, stood still as statues for a moment or two facing each other. Then at last, Charles said, forcing a calmness he didn't feel into his voice, 'I don't expect you to properly understand, Clara. I'm sorry to have – distressed you. It was just—'

'Just that you wanted a tumble or two with that creature,' Clara interrupted. 'Something I couldn't give. Oh I understand. I understand perfectly. And I'll never forgive you – *never*. But it's not a matter of forgiveness, is it? It's what you *are* – cheap – nasty—' Suddenly she started to cry. Heavy thick sobbing that went on and on.

He attempted to comfort her, but with both hands she

pushed him away. He stood helplessly watching her and waiting for her to recover.

When at last the crying stopped he handed her a kerchief and said, 'Dry your eyes. We'll stay here for a bit, and then go back. In the morning—'

'In the morning you'll be gone,' she managed to say. 'I won't live under the same roof as a – a—' Words failed her.

'In the morning we'll talk,' he told her emotionlessly. 'I shall still be there, and so will you. Come, Clara.'

Eventually she gave in, and when they reached the house Clara went straight up to their bedroom before Anne could notice anything was amiss.

Charles slept on a sofa in the parlour that night, and was woken in the early hours of morning by a hand clutching his shoulder, shaking him violently. He screwed his eyes up, blinked, and saw Clara's white face glaring down at him. The nails of her fingers dug into his flesh cruelly, her eyes were narrow slits of rage. Through the wan light of a candle on the table she had the appearance of an outraged ghost with her pale hair loose and flowing over her white night-shift.

'Get up,' she hissed. 'Get up you horrible thing – before Aunt Anne or that – that awful girl find you here. Or the man. I won't be sneered at or pitied. I haven't slept at all. Because of *you*—' She broke off as her voice threatened to rise.

He jumped up, still fully clothed, one hand smoothing the hair from his forehead, the other reaching for his cravat.

'You'd better get back to the bedroom yourself,' he said wearily. 'If anyone causes a commotion it will be you.'

'Don't worry – I'm going.'

She reached for the candle, but he pushed an arm in front of her and took it himself, saying quietly, 'Go on, Clara, don't trip, and for God's sake try to keep your mouth shut until we've talked things out. I shan't molest you; have no fear.'

He ushered her ahead of him through the door and up the stairs to their own room. There was an icy silence between them until he told her calmly and coldly, 'You'd better tidy yourself, and use a little powder perhaps. Your eyes are puffy, and tears don't suit you.'

'Because of *you*,' she stormed, half sobbing. 'Your unspeakable behaviour—'

'Oh shut up about my unspeakable behaviour, and try to be reasonable, can't you? I'm sorry I've offended you. I regret taking a little pleasure on the side since it distresses you so much. If you'd been a little more generous with your charms where I was concerned, it might not have happened. You were alluring enough at the beginning to catch me, Clara—'

'To catch you? What do you mean?' She jumped up from the bed where she had been sitting and faced him squarely, her expression still outraged, eyes cold, wide and condemning.

'Just that. You wanted a husband – if only to get even with Lydia.'

'How *dare* you?'

He laughed unpleasantly. 'Sh – sh! – unless you've changed your mind and want to make a scene. If so I'll inform the admirable Miss Teague myself. Oh, believe me, Clara, I've no wish to stay here on sufferance to be frowned on and dictated to like a naughty boy under probation. Last night you ordered me from the house – or should it be *our* house, according to the law? – anyway, I'm *quite* prepared to go just as soon as I've collected a few things, and informed the household why.'

Clara thought a moment. Then she said very sharply, '*No*.'

His features relaxed. 'I thought not. It would be rather humiliating, wouldn't it – for you? Too much of an affront to swallow. I'm glad you've realised it in time.'

For a long pause Clara was silent. Then she said, plaintively, with a catch in her throat. 'It's nothing to do with pride—'

He laughed softly. 'Don't deceive yourself. *Everything*'s a matter of pride with you. In a way—' his voice softened slightly – 'I can understand. But I'm not going to be tied to your pretty apron strings. Clara, and I'm not going to sleep back to back with you every night. When I want a little warmth and wifely satisfaction, I shall expect to get it, whenever I wish, and without begging, or as a favour. I *married* you, and if we remain together it must be on my terms—' He was taking a chance, a dangerous risk, in speaking to her like that, and he knew it. But when she didn't demur he continued ruthlessly, 'Well? What is it to be?'

She lifted her lovely head as high as possible, and replied, 'Very well. On one condition.'

'And what's that?'

'Jess goes.'

'Jess stays,' he contradicted her. 'I've had what I want of her, and you can rest assured it won't happen again. That's a promise.'

'I see. You just – seduced her – took her like a – a—'

'There was no seduction. It was very mutual. A pleasurable game, no more.'

'Like two – two animals—'

'Exactly.'

She turned and went to the window, wringing her hands over her breast. How *cruel* he was.

'I don't know that I could stand it—'

Seizing the advantage, he followed her quickly and planted a light kiss on her shoulder. 'Of course you can. You're strong underneath that pretty exterior of yours. And Jess is a good servant. Your Aunt Anne would want a feasible excuse for getting rid of her. Unless you tell the truth you haven't got one. So be sensible, my love.'

'Your *love*?' The last word had a bite in it.

'Well, does the word affront you? If you wish me to find a better no doubt I can—'

'I don't wish anything from you – except to be left alone and at peace—' Her temper crumbled suddenly into the threat of tears.

He shrugged, gave his characteristic mock bow and after a formal 'certainly', went to the door.

'Where are you going now?'

'To have a wash. The servants will be about. You'd better slip into bed and try and look rested when Jess comes in.'

'I don't want Jess.'

'Very well, I'll bring up your tea myself, in the manner of an extremely devoted husband fretting over his young wife's headache.'

There was a click as the door shut behind him. She listened until his footsteps had faded along the landing, then gave vent to a renewed fit of bitter sobbing. Jealousy, disappointment and outrage rose up again in a tide of emotional fury, consuming her. Her whole frame shook. How could she bear to live in such circumstances? Insulted, and knowing Charles at any time might find someone else to dance attendance on, and flatter, while she, his wife, was left on her own humiliated and despised.

Yes, he must despise her – he *must*, or he'd never have resorted to such a vulgar intrigue. There was only one thing to do – get advice, tell someone who'd understand and sympathise, and there was only one person she could turn to.

Lydia.

Lydia would help her. She'd always protected her in the past. She, too, had once been fond of Charles. His faithless nature must have driven them apart. The picture now, was quite clear in Clara's mind. So, with the Fearnley influence behind her she'd somehow manage to pay him out – make him toe the line. She'd get word to Blackstone as soon as possible, asking Lydia to come and see her.

Charles was in the attic at the top of the house – a place allotted to him as his studio, when Clara, having feverishly penned a note to her sister stating how distressed she was, and how badly she needed immediate advice, sought out the gardener's boy, with instructions to ride to Blackstone immediately and deliver the envelope personally.

The youth was at first dubious. 'I'm s'posed to be in stables, workin',' he said. 'How'll I do without – without someone seein'? Miss Teague, Ma'am, as I've—'

'It won't take long—' Clara said in flurried, hushed tones, 'across the moor you'll soon be out of sight. Anyway—' drawing herself up as erect as possible. 'I'm the mistress here. Go on, do as I say. If any questions are asked I'll know nothing, and you can make an excuse of wanting a blacksmith or something. Do you *understand*? Quick now—'

There was a quality so compelling about her, wild and tragic, that made him agree suddenly. 'All right, mistress, I'll go—'

'And see you speak to *Mrs* Fearnley. Not the Master.'

Grudgingly, wondering how he was going to do that, the youth nodded, and muttering something under his breath, left.

A few minutes later, from an upstairs window, Clara watched horse and rider galloping upwards to the high moor where they were soon obscured behind a dip in the land below a belt of wind-blown scrub.

7

Lydia was about to leave Blackstone for a ride down the valley, when a housemaid hurried up the hall from the kitchen with Clara's note in her hand.

'For you, ma'am,' she said, keeping her voice to a minimum. 'There's a young man – at the side door. Said he must see you personal – that's the word he used – personal.'

Frowning but curious, Lydia glanced down at the handwriting. There was no mistaking it; it was her sister's.

'Give it to me, Sarah.'

'Oh but – he *did* seem anxious, ma'am. A bit simple, if you ask me – wouldn't give it me at all, until I said you'd have an answer – and I told him unless I'd got it to show, he'd be sent off. Not to let it out of my hand, he said—'

'You forget yourself. I'm mistress here. Hand me that letter immediately.'

The girl thrust the envelope out. As Lydia took it, she said, 'Sorry, ma'am.'

'So you should be.'

After scanning Clara's spidery slanting scrawl, Lydia thought quickly, 'Tell the youth – no, I'd better write a few words – stay there,' she said, 'I'll just get a pen.' She darted with a swish of skirts into the parlour, took a feather pen from an ink pot, and wrote at the bottom of Clara's note, 'Don't worry. Coming presently. Lydia.' She pressed it face down on a sheet of blotting paper, and hurried back into the hall.

'There you are. And no dawdling. I want him out of sight when I start. Another thing – say nothing of this to *anyone*. Or there'll be trouble. You understand?'

The girl nodded and scurried back down the passage,

leaving Lydia standing for a few moments wondering what had happened. She guessed the matter concerned Charles, and indignation brought a rush of high wild colour to her cheeks. What had he been up to? Well she'd soon know, and see things were put right. The thought of any confrontation with Charles stimulated her. Luckily Richard was away for the day at St Austell, and would not be back until the evening, so she would be spared interference from him, and was satisfied that the housemaid would hold her tongue.

The gallop to Blackstone was exciting and gave zest to the meeting ahead. For the first time she experienced the old sense of freedom that had driven her in the old days to forbidden territory against her stern father's command. How ridiculous Richard had been, she thought, almost laughing aloud – to draw such strict boundaries, and deny her access to her favourite spots of heath and moor. There was no wind; the air was fragrant with the drift of bluebell scent and damp sweet earth, of thyme and heather, bracken and gorse. Melody, too, conveyed a sense of unfettered joy; together they rode easily, mounting the slope to the ridge without mishap or having to falter by stone or boggy pool. Just for a few moments, when they reached the highest point before cutting down the slope towards the sheltered valley where the Dower House crouched in its nest of trees, she reined, looking round at the wide expanse of land, sky, and glittering sea. Silhouetted in the distance, coils of thin smoke rose from working mines above huddled hamlets of grey granite cottages. At intervals sunlight glinted on pumping rods rising and falling rhythmically against the sky. Yet where she waited for those brief minutes, man had not yet put a stamp of industry or driven bird or beast from its natural habitat.

Even as her eye scanned the lonely acres a fox darted from the undergrowth and with burnished coat and tail flying, fled down the hill in the direction of St Kerrick. Small pools shone jewel-like from the green bracken, and she recalled with a quiver of delight how more than once she'd confronted the otter washing its whiskers by a stream. Oh lovely, lovely world! Instinctively she patted the mare's neck, then suddenly remembering the urgency of Clara's note, kicked her mount into a trot again, gathering speed as they headed down towards the shadows of The Hollies.

When she arrived at the house she found, as she'd expected, that the youth was already back. She handed Melody over to him, and walked briskly, half running, up the path leading along the building, and finding the door open, went in.

Anne Teague was in the hall, looking flurried and grim. She *would* be, Lydia thought resentfully.

'I don't know what's the matter with Clara,' Anne said. 'She has such moods these days. I asked her what was wrong. She wouldn't say. But it's clear it's something to do with *him*.'

'Who? Charles?'

Anne gave a short derisive laugh. 'Who else? They're not suited; they never were. But whatever the trouble is I don't put all the blame on him.' Her lips tightened significantly. 'She's become quite a little madam these days. I didn't know she'd sent for *you* though. I suppose it was that youth – Ben!'

'I heard,' Lydia answered ambiguously. 'It's possible she's just lonely or not well. After all – this house isn't exactly cheerful. There are too many trees still. I should have thought—' She bit her lip, recalling how hard she'd pleaded with Richard to allow Clara and their aunt to live there.

'We're lucky to have it,' Anne snapped. 'And as you've come, try and make her see sense.' There was a short pause before she added, 'Does your husband know?'

Lydia shook her head. 'Certainly not. And I don't want him to. He says the moor this way is – treacherous.'

'H'm! I'd have imagined it was something else, quite different, after the way you carried on in the past.'

Lydia's cheeks flamed.

'The past is over. Where's Clara?'

Anne's shoulders shrugged. She gave a wave of her hand indicating the drawing room. 'In there. She's been crying her eyes out; whether from self-pity or rage I don't know. She was quite hysterical with me when I enquired.'

Lydia, not waiting to hear more, swept past Anne and found Clara staring sullenly out of the window, with a handkerchief clutched in her hand. She turned when Lydia entered. Her lovely eyes were still dewy bright from distress, with smudged shadows beneath. She looked strained, and older than usual, but her ethereal beauty, though faintly dimmed, had taken on something else – the quality of a tragic muse.

She rushed towards Lydia and flung her arms round her neck.

'Oh, Lydia – Lydia – I've had such a terrible time—' and then, when Lydia assisted her to a couch, and they were both seated, the truth came out.

Lydia was horrified. 'You mean Charles was lying with that – that peasant girl? That ill-bred coarse farmer's daughter?'

Clara nodded, dabbing her eyes, with her chest heaving uncontrollably.

'And what did he say when you confronted him?'

Clara told her. 'And he won't even send her *away*. He refuses. He's simply determined to keep her here.'

Lydia's chin took a dangerous thrust. 'We'll see about that. You wait here.'

She stalked into the kitchen, only to find that the girl was upstairs cleaning the top landing where she slept.

Catching up her skirt by both hands, Lydia made her way up the two flights, and soon located Jess who was sweeping something from the floor of her own room.

Incensed with anger, Lydia confronted her. The girl's pale eyes widened, her full underlip dropped when a hand clutched her plump shoulder and a peremptory hard voice said, 'Do you sleep here? Are these your things?' She was pointing to clothes hanging over a chair.

'Yes they're mine. What's it to you?' Jess demanded, as truculence replaced shock and surprise.

'This is what,' Lydia strode in, picked up the bundle, and threw the garments at the girl. They tumbled and lay in disordered bits and pieces at her feet. 'There!' Lydia exclaimed. 'Pick them up, and get *out*. Immediately, do you hear? Or I'll take the whip to your back. Well—' She moved a step nearer the broad figure, with the riding crop held before her threateningly.

Jess, suddenly cowed, backed away. 'You haven't no right,' she muttered, 'no right at all to do this. Tedn' *your* house, an' them things is *mine*. Why sh'd I go? *Why?*' Her face had a sly look, her voice changed. 'I don't think as Master Fearnley'll think much of it, if I let on. A fair man, he is. He wouldn't like his proud madam of a wife attackin' a servant, I'd say. Oh, there'll be gossip enough if I go tellin', an' I will – you just *see*—' She broke off, breathing heavily.

Lydia's lips tightened. But her heart was beating quickly, painfully, in spite of her brave words. She knew that what Jess said was true. Richard would be exceedingly angry to know she'd been in such an unseemly brawl. But her determination didn't flag.

'Don't threaten me or be so insolent,' she remarked, gaining firmer control of herself. 'Pick up your things and leave. You're dismissed.'

'Not with nuthin' in my pocket I'm not. If you don't want trouble you'd better pay for it – *ma'am!*' She gave a contemptuous mockery of a curtsey. 'I'm not arriving home for a beltin' an nothing else, I can tell you. You act right or Mr high-'n-mighty-squire Fearnley'll get an earful of what you done– an' more,' she added spitefully after a second's pause.

With her mind whirling this way and that, Lydia acted on impulse, searched her pocket wildly, and discovered some coins there, pulled them out and thrust them recklessly at Jess.

'There you are then, that should spare you a belting,

but don't ever ask for more, and keep your mouth shut over this despicable affair, or I'll see my husband himself attends to you.'

The girl smirked, grabbed the gold, and languidly started picking her clothes up, while Lydia stood watching her, hands on hips.

A quarter of an hour later Jess, carrying a sack containing her belongings, was on her way back to the farm.

Satisfied in one way, but still angry and in a disturbing way apprehensive, Lydia returned to Clara and said, 'She's gone. Dry your eyes now, Clara, for heaven's sake, and I'll have to concoct some story to satisfy Aunt Anne. Then there's Charles. Where is he?'

Clara's violet eyes widened.

'Why do you want *him*?'

'Never mind. A word of warning's sure to do some good. I expect what he said was perfectly true, about the affair meaning nothing. But you must try and keep him faithful in future. It shouldn't be difficult you know – with your beauty.'

Clara was slightly mollified, and when Lydia questioned her a second time about Charles' whereabouts, replied, 'In his studio. At least I *think* so. But he may have gone out.'

'I'll have a word with him if he's available,' Lydia remarked casually.

'*Why?*' The question came out sharply, stimulated by a renewed stab of old jealousy.

'Because he needs a good telling off, and I'm going to give him one,' Lydia answered promptly. Then noticing the dubious expression on Clara's face added soothingly, patting her hand, 'Don't worry dear. I've no longer any liking *at all* for Mr Charles Clarke. But he happens to be my brother-in-law, and if I can put the fear of God into him, I'll do it.'

'How can you do that? – I'm not sure that I want it anyway. A husband who has to be threatened into being faithful isn't – isn't—' Clara's voice became choked again. 'Well – it's not much of a compliment to me.'

No, it wasn't, Lydia inwardly agreed, but all she said aloud was, 'You must take it as just a lapse of good sense and manners on his part, Clara. In London society—'

'The Hollies isn't London society,' Clara snapped.

'Let me finish. In the most fashionable circles more husbands than not have had the odd – flirtation, or moral lapse – I know this is true Clara, from magazines and books – and their wives either shut their eyes, or accept it. They have to. But I think it will be different with you. Charles won't be so stupid again. He has an easy life, a good home, and a beautiful wife he cares about. All the same he needs a jolt and a warning so he's not tempted into playing any more games. As Richard's wife I'm in the position to give it. Charles owes a lot to my husband, and it's right he should be reminded.' Lydia finished speaking feeling very much the elder sister in giving such worldly advice.

'Very well,' Clara agreed grudgingly. 'Are you coming back after you've seen him?'

'If he's in the studio, yes. But if he's out I may not have time. I may not even find him. Anyway—' Lydia took her sister by the arms and planted a light kiss on a cheek, 'don't you worry. Everything's going to be all right. Relax, Clara, and put a little salve on your lips – titivate yourself. Make him realise what an utter fool he's been, and he'll be besotted all over again.'

Minutes later, not finding Charles in the studio, Lydia was riding in the direction where she thought he was most likely to be.

She found him near a small pool close beneath the ridge of the moor. From there one of his favourite painting spots was visible. The locality was wild, dotted by wind-blown clumps of briar, gorse and heather. Occasionally small pools glinted, beneath massive boulders where twisted sloes shadowed the misted heads of thrusting bluebells. The ridge above rose bare, except for the stark granite shape of an ancient menhir. All on that summer day was a changing vista of light and shade – of gold, brown, deepest purple and the pale lemon green of young bracken brightening the taller, darker fronds of mature growth.

Charles, standing half hidden behind the bent branches of a thorn tree, saw Lydia's approach up the slope, and was ready to step from the shadowed branches into the full sunlight as she dismounted, and with one hand holding the bridle of her mare stared about her, blinking against the brilliant sky.

He moved, and ambled forward in the old characteristic way she remembered so well, sending a wave of nostalgic annoyance through her. She bit her lip, her blue-green eyes changing to fire-lit jade, her full sculptured mouth angrily set above the stubborn young chin. He noticed the cleft in it, its piquancy emphasised by the angle of light, and had a sudden desire to sweep her to him, to hold the exquisite seductive form close, feel once again the sensuous warmth of young breasts against his chest.

She had put on a little weight since her marriage, but the gentle rounding of her hips and thighs beneath the tightly cut riding jacket, only emphasised the narrow waist and beautifully proportioned figure. Desire, however, only stiffened to aggressive frustration, because as she drew close, leading the horse, he saw she was prepared for a fight. Well, blast her, if she wanted it that way, she could have it.

'Good afternoon, Lydia,' he said, 'how very surprising we should meet in this benighted spot. Or could it be that longing drove you?'

'There's no need to be insolent,' she said coldly. 'And I'm Mrs Fearnley to you.'

'Of *course*!' – with heavy sarcasm. He gave a mock bow. 'My dear madam, then to what reason do I owe this so charming interlude?'

'You know very well,' Lydia snapped, forgetting in her anger to tether the mare.

'Oh?' His eyebrows rose mockingly.

'You're insufferable,' Lydia cried, striding a foot or two nearer, so she could vent the full fury of her gaze upon him. 'A cad, Charles Clarke, to play such a disgusting trick on my sister – to betray her as though she was – she was—'

'What? Please enlighten me.'

'Just anyone – some light sophisticated girl content to accept low down behaviour from a husband she adored. Lying with that cheap slut! It was despicable of you.'

'Maybe. I fear cheap sluts are sometimes necessary to men with cold wives.'

His audacity stung her anew. For a moment there was complete silence, then Lydia said very coldly and clearly, 'I hate – despise you. I always will. But for Clara's sake—' She broke off as he stepped nearer, with a wry half-smile on his lips.

'No, you don't,' he said. 'It's not hate you feel, Madam Lydia Fearnley. Why—' he laughed in her face. 'I declare you're even jealous – lusting in your heart and luscious body for a taste of what Jess had.'

Her hand suddenly struck him forcibly against one cheek. He reeled for a second, then suddenly had his arms round her, and was holding her, struggling against him. His lips were hard on hers. Her head fell back, sending the plumed hat tumbling to the ground. The strengthening wind caught the tumbled glory of her molten hair, sending it in a rich stream through the air. In a fury of desperation her teeth caught his chin, staining his cravat with a thin stream of blood.

He let her go abruptly. 'You little demon,' he said, putting a hand to the wound. 'I only gave you what you wanted—' He paused before adding sneeringly, '*Clara!* – as if you came up here because of *her*. You're a hypocrite, Lydia. You always were. Brave in words, but a scheming liar if ever there was one, out to catch a rich man and get the other thing from someone else. Well – it's not quite worked out, has it? And it won't. I wouldn't touch you with a bargepole. Get that into your pretty head once and for all, and you can tell that sister of yours I'll lead my life just as I choose, and you stuck-up dull-as-ditch-water Teagues and Fearnleys can take it or leave it, or go to hell. I damn well don't care.'

He turned, and was walking away, when the approaching sound of galloping hooves halted him. He glanced back and saw to his astonishment the strong tall figure of Richard swing himself from his saddle after reining abruptly.

Blast him, Charles thought, he must have seen the whole episode and got quite the wrong idea.

Fearnley, appearing not to notice Lydia, lunged forward and dealt Charles such a blow that Clarke fell back into the bracken, narrowly escaping cracking his head on a stone.

'Now,' Fearnley said coldly, dragging him up by his collar, 'get out. Go back to that poor creature you married. I'll see you later.' Dazed, Charles stood for a few seconds facing Richard before turning away and retreating in a downwards direction towards the Dower House. 'As for *you*,' Fearnley said to Lydia, 'you realise I suppose that in your ardours you forgot your mare? Lucky perhaps, as she gave me a clue. On the other hand—'

He paused, jerked her towards him, held her for a moment, with her face close to his, not kissing her, but staring so hard into her eyes she winced. Then he slapped her sharply across a cheek, waited a strained few seconds, before pulling her down and deliberately forced her over his knee, pushing the velvet skirt up and giving her a smart spank or two with the hard flat palm of his hand. He didn't really hurt her, but she was shamed by the humiliation.

'Get up,' he said. 'Obviously your father was right. There's only one way to treat a wanton firebrand like you, although you deserved the riding crop.'

When she'd adjusted herself trying to assume a veneer of dignity, he picked her up and placed her on his own horse. The sun was lower in the sky. Long shadows were already streaking the moor. They galloped remorselessly, close, yet briefly hating each other – dark shapes against the deepening greyness.

When they were face to face again, in their bedroom at Blackstone, Lydia said, 'I loathe you, Richard Fearnley.'

'Yes, and I loathe you,' he answered, not adding, 'But I also love you, you little devil, and that's my misfortune, God help me.'

The next day Lydia learned that she was being sent off for a stay with Richard's sister at their Devonshire estate.

8

Greenfields was situated three miles from the Devon coast and four from Chestercoombe, which was the nearest shopping resort, and gradually becoming a holiday retreat for visitors from London wishing for a taste of the lush Devon countryside and fresh air.

The mansion had been partially rebuilt by Robert Adam, leaving the restored older wing at the back of the house, facing a courtyard and paddock. More recently John Nash had made attempts at glorifying the frontage, and the whole effect, though indefinite in period and style, was not inharmonious. Miss Agatha would have considered further embellishment vulgar and ostentatious. Dignity, like her person, was her first consideration. It was the same in literature. She despised such colourful and, in her opinion, licentious characters like the poets Byron and Shelley, while conceding that Miss Jane Austen might sometime take a modest place in the annals of literature.

Therefore, she was gratified by her brother's request to 'take over' his country-bred young wife, for a period in which she could be trained – hopefully – more in the manners of the gentry and family tradition.

> Lydia has been restless lately [he wrote]. The change from comparative penury to having exactly what she wants has obviously gone to her head. In a way I can understand. I'm very busy myself with the estate, and incapable at the moment of satisfying her craving for excitement and colour. I'm not asking you to be hard with her – just firm. And don't try to remodel her character – you wouldn't succeed, and it's the last thing I want. I find her quite adorable as she is – *except* for

sudden wild spurts of behaviour which sometimes are quite infuriating. I expect I get on her nerves too. So a change of scene and company will be a deal of good for both of us. I don't know what else to say. Our private life is our own concern. You may find her moods bewildering at first, but I'm sure in the end you'll like her. Anyway, for *my* sake try.

'Hm!' Miss Fearnley gave an ambiguous little cough after reading the letter, while her shrewd mind thought, 'It's not working. I wonder what the girl's been up to. Obviously Richard's most seriously put out. He should not have married her. Infatuation, that was it. Oh, poor, dear Richard. Never mind!' She replaced the letter firmly back into the envelope, and started planning for the weeks or perhaps even months ahead.

She was a woman of rigid habits, of which an hour and a half's rest in the afternoon was a priority. It was not that in any way she wished to represent a 'languid lily' image – indeed such an idea would have been highly offensive to her – but simply that her strong forthright exterior and figure belied her years, which were considerable. This hour and a half therefore were sacrosanct, in order to preserve her energy. All the servants were strictly observant of the rule, though secretly aware that despite Miss Agatha's pretence of having to attend to correspondence and certain personal affairs, she was in reality relaxing prone on her bed or chaise-longue, with her eyes shut and corsets loosened to give a blissful sense of peace.

Promptly at four-fifteen she appeared in the small lounge for tea, which was brought in by a servant on a silver tray, containing a small silver tea-service, exquisite bone-china cup and saucer, and finely cut sandwiches, preferably of tomato or cucumber. If she felt indulgent she also had one of her favourite queen cakes still warm from cook's oven. This dainty interim was generally the most pleasurable of her day – peaceful, without intrusion or argument, although on rare occasions she had the company of a privileged visitor such as the Vicar or Lady Mountcurran from Castle Varne eight miles away.

Lydia, she supposed a trifle ruefully, would in future have to join her. She hoped she wouldn't be too greedy, or take more than her share of the cream from the antique silver jug. Such habits – if apparent – would have to be ruthlessly displayed. Of course the girl might go to the other extreme so frequently displayed by the lower orders when wishing to impress – of crooking her little finger when she held a cup to her lips. So ridiculous and *obvious*! So indicative of the *middle-class*.

The last description Agatha Fearnley would have accorded to herself was that of being a snob. But deep down she was a snob – of the first order. While declaring outwardly that 'every human being in God's sight was equal—' – the Vicar's own words – quite clearly their positions in life were not. Individuals, she believed, were born to the place in society destined by the Deity. Richard, her brother, had foolishly taken upon himself the task of elevating the daughter of plebeian heredity to the ranks of a nobler lineage. So far the effort had quite clearly not succeeded, or he would not be sending the bride so soon to the ancestral home for tuition.

Well, she would do her best to instil a sense of proportion and good manners into the girl. It would be a challenge, and not entirely unpleasant. A grim little smile touched her firm, primped up lips, when she considered the prospect. Any trace of wildness would quickly be checked in Greenfields' well-ordered menage. She would keep a quick eye on the young woman at all times – except of course during the sacred blessed afternoons of peace and rest. Lydia at such times would be given tasks to occupy her – such as a certain amount of tapestry work – arranging the flowers, after taking Pom-pom the King Charles spaniel, for a walk on a lead round the grounds. Tiny Pipin, the ancient Pekinese, had his own fur-lined basket in Miss Agatha's room. He wore a blue bow round his neck, was old, and felt the cold. Not for the world would Richard's sister have trusted him to the care of a stranger, especially a robust wild girl like Lydia. Apart from Richard, Pipin secretly took prior place in her heart. All the latent frustrated gentleness and love in her starchy being flowered for him. And he, in his doggy way knew it, gazing at her with dark soulful eyes that were already slightly rheumy from his ten cosseted years of living.

When her practical mind had formulated a reasonable pattern of living for Lydia's enforced stay at Greenfields, Agatha conceded with a gratifying sense of inward generosity that naturally, after a period of initiation, a few rules might be relaxed on certain occasions.

She herself could take a brief respite after lunch and go by chaise to Chestercoombe perhaps, where they might take a dish of tea in a coffee house famed for its good name and clientele of gentry. Lydia would naturally want to do a little shopping. She was clearly vain – but then after her penurious strict upbringing this was to be expected, and must not be curtailed too rigidly. The important thing would be that Agatha's presence could be assured to direct her young sister-in-law in any purchases made. All should be in good taste, quietly fashionable, but subdued and ladylike, as befitting a connection of the Fearnleys, and new mistress of Blackstone.

Unfortunately for Agatha, matters did not work out according to plan. During Lydia's first week at Greenfields her strong will and personality became all too evident imbuing the hitherto well-ordered menage with a subtle restlessness, which against Agatha's preconceived determination not to appear ruffled, nevertheless did ruffle her.

There was no open rebellion to her wishes. Lydia had a maddening habit of saying, 'Yes, Agatha. Of course, Agatha,' or 'I'll do just as you wish,' while implying that she found the domestic lectures and instructions profoundly boring – as boring as Agatha herself.

Inwardly Lydia frequently fumed. On her apparently

docile walks with Pom-pom round the carefully kept gardens with their straight orderly paths, well-tended flower beds and clipped trees, her thoughts were far away on the Cornish moors – her heart half bursting with longing for the tangy sweet smell of brine and heather, and for a glimpse of Richard's strong form approaching – even though she hated him, and was determined one day to force an apology from him for his unwarranted behaviour. How long, she wondered, was she supposed to stand this dreary existence with Miss Fearnley? No punishment could have been more irksome. She did her best at the beginning to appear compliant, simply because she hoped in this way to be able to return to Cornwall in the minimum of time.

When after a fortnight there was no sign from her husband of wishing her back, frustration and temper drove her one afternoon in Agatha's rest time, to order the family chaise herself to take her into Chestercoombe.

The coachman, at first reluctant, eventually agreed, when Lydia complained very convincingly that she had a dreadful pain in a tooth and simply *had* to see an apothecary. Her distress and the tender woeful manner she placed a hand to a cheek, which she'd previously rubbed to give the skin a reddened look, dispersed his reluctance, and a quarter of an hour later they were off.

Chestercoombe, though a small market town set in a valley surrounded by hills and lush agricultural country, was gradually responding to the new age of travel that sent wealthy visitors from London and up country to explore its picturesque cobbled streets and ancient church. The square, on market days, held a fascination for visitors from Europe – even a few Americans anxious to trace forebears from the old country. During the summer months craft-workers displayed their wares on booths, and from the windows of tiny shops huddled in intriguing byways. There were two fashionable coaching houses, The Golden Fleece and The King's Head, two or three smaller less reputable hostelries, and a number of coffee houses which opened only during the season.

The shopping centre was limited in area, but select, catering for the feminine population with all manner of haberdashery, and materials made from hand-woven cloth. Antiques, many genuine ones and some of a more doubtful origin, also provided a lively interest, and scholars, both old and young, frequently visited the town simply to dig and delve into the annals of Church history. Many considered Chestercoombe should have been the county town – or even a city. St John's, indeed, would have made a magnificent cathedral, its oldest part dating back years before the Norman conquest.

The main street was busier than usual on that certain afternoon when the Fearnley chaise drew up outside the King's Head, by the corner of the main street.

'I shall wait here in the yard, ma'am,' the coachman told Lydia. 'There's an apothecary, where Miss Agatha gets her pills and potions just three doors round the corner. A good man they say, and he'll likely have something to ease the tooth. If you'd care for me to accompany you—'

'Oh no, no,' Lydia interrupted quickly. 'There's no need at all. Three doors you say?' She laughed. 'I can hardly be robbed or pounced on, or raped in such a short time.' Catching a fleeting look of shock or disapproval on the manservant's face she brought a hand up to her jaw sharply, grimacing as though from a stab of acute pain. He helped her step from the vehicle, waited a second or two watching, as she hurried the few yards and disappeared into the apothecary's porch, then took his seat again and turned the horses into the yard.

Lydia paused in the shadowed doorway until the rattle of wheels and hooves had died, then she slipped out, and holding the lower frills of her pink muslin gown by both hands to her delicate ankles, hurried fleetingly down the narrow street. Draped over her shoulders was a wide, lace trimmed silk shawl. A tiny bonnet-shaped beflowered hat was pushed to the back of her dark russet curls, which were fluffed out casually yet becomingly round her face.

She was fully aware of her slightly theatrical appearance, and conscious too, that Richard's starchy sister would be most offended. The knowledge itself was exhilarating. She had no idea in those first few moments of escape what she was going to buy, except that it would be something outrageous – something colourful and exciting to ease the bored frustration of life at Greenfields. Surely, she thought, she must soon find an interesting salon or haberdasher's catering for ladies of fashion.

She was not disappointed. Only a short distance from the apothecary's she came upon a small yet expensive looking millinery establishment where she quickly chose a most absurd yet highly elegant and coquettish item of headgear consisting mostly of chiffon veiling and flowers, with a tiny bird on top. The bird was not only a decoration. At a pressure from a thin cord it broke into an enticing whistle, at the same time emitting a fragrant waft of perfume.

What fun; Lydia felt quite delighted, although she had had to pay a considerable sum for it. Still, Richard, thank goodness, had never been mean with her over money, and she had brought a considerable amount with her, so there was no problem over cost.

Remembering the coachman waiting in the yard, her first instinct was to hurry back to the King's Head. Her intention was diverted however, by the window of an enticing bow-fronted coffee-shop, next door but one to the apothecary.

Happiness had made Lydia suddenly hungry, and her mouth watered at the sight of the home-made sweetmeats and cakes displayed.

She went in, and seated herself at a small table in an alcove not far from the door. Several customers – mostly gentry – were assembled there. And as she glanced up, after removing her gloves, she noticed a young man sitting nearby who obviously had his eye on her. He had a pointed, rather mischievous-looking face under fashionably styled fair hair, blue eyes, and was elegantly attired in a golden-brown velvet fitting jacket over pale blue breeches reaching almost to the tips of his toes. His neck scarf was frilled and high above the embroidered white shirt. He had no moustache, but his very narrow beard was carefully styled from the ears round the chin which had a deep cleft in it.

Lydia naturally did not absorb such details – only that he was quite clearly a young man of fashion – one of the type generally classed as 'dandies' at that period. Her heart quickened very slightly. It was pleasant being noticed and admired after the boring days at Greenfields. She glanced down provocatively, only looking up again when a serving maid appeared to take her order for coffee. After that things happened in what seemed at the time quite a normal and reasonable manner. She dropped her shred of handkerchief, and was about to pick it up, when a ringed hand below a frilled white cuff descended and did it for her. Lydia blushed charmingly, and saw the blue eyes crinkling above the lazy whimsical smile.

'Yours, I think, madam,' a cultured voice remarked. 'Allow me.' Conventional enough words, but somehow suggestive of coquetry and harmless flirtation on that summer day.

'Thank you,' Lydia said demurely.

He could of course, have gone back to his own table at that point, but instead was seated a minute later beside her, chatting in a most casual but titillating way about the weather, and charm of the locality which he said he visited from time to time for a stay with an elderly aunt. 'I'm very fond of her of course,' he said, 'but—' shrugging expressively, 'youth and age you know – do not always see eye to eye—' He broke off, giving Lydia the opportunity to agree heartily.

'I know,' she said. 'I understand exactly,' and went on to explain her drawn-out holiday with Agatha. 'She isn't *really*, so *old*—' she admitted with a sigh, 'but she seems so. I suppose it's not being married.'

'And you are?' The question was unnecessary, since he

had already noted the flashing diamond and ruby ring on the third finger of the left hand above the gold band. He'd been both impressed and relieved. A grass widow, and a rich one apparently, young and beautiful – bored, and ripe for flattery which could prove well worthwhile in more ways than one. Oh yes, Cedric Lyndsey was well versed in the whims and wiles of women, and seldom made an error concerning their potentials. Although a gentleman by birth, his career, after a disastrous period at University, had turned to more adventurous and heart-warming channels which had alienated him from his family, and driven him to exploitation of his personal charms which were considerable, and certainly commercially remunerative.

That short meeting, which was the first of others to follow, astonished Lydia when she reflected on the circumstances a little later. She hadn't remotely guessed at her capacity for such devious coquetry.

As she hurried to the spot where the chaise waited a tinge of guilt marred her excitement and pleasure – not on Agatha's, or Richard's account – but because of her deception towards the coachman – lying did not come easily to her – and, poor man, he had been quite deceived by her little act concerning the painful tooth and jaw. Later, also there would be Agatha to face. Oh dear! And she'd quite forgotten to make a purchase at the apothecary's. She turned quickly, took a few steps back to his premises, and bought a tiny bottle of balm advertised to eradicate pain magically, provided it was used as directed.

Miss Fearnley was waiting for her irately when the chaise deposited her outside the front entrance to Greenfields. Lydia walked up the terrace steps and found her sister-in-law with a set expression on her lean strong-boned face, two brilliant spots of crimson burning in her usually parchment countenance.

'How *could* you, Lydia?' she demanded, and her voice held genuine concern. 'You could at least have asked my permission, or for me to accompany you on – whatever mission you had concocted. If you wished to go for a drive you had only to tell me and—'

'But I didn't want to disturb your rest,' Lydia interrupted feeling relieved *this* at least was true. 'And as I'd heard there was a good apothecary in Chestercoombe, I thought I'd be there and back perhaps even before you woke up.'

'I don't always sleep,' sharply. 'And what do you mean by apothecary?' She glanced significantly at Lydia's slim form. 'You're not—'

'Oh no, *no*.' Lydia laughed convincingly, and retold her story about the tooth, soothing her conscience by the unspoken excuse that any tooth might start aching at any moment, and that it was most important to have a remedy near at hand.

Agatha grudgingly appeared to accept the explanation and for the next few days Lydia was particularly careful to be friendly and apparently docile to Richard's stern sister. Then frustration and boredom once more encompassed her. If Richard had visited or even written to her in a gentle way suggesting he was sorry about what had happened, or even that he was missing her and wanting her back, all might have been different. But his only note – delivered after she'd been away for a full fortnight – was almost impersonal, containing references to the opening of the new mine, her sister's health, which gave no cause for concern, and adjuring Lydia to behave herself, and try and give Agatha understanding and friendship. He ended by saying:

> but should you get any mad-cap notions into your head, or upset the household by mad pranks, you'll have me to deal with. When you return to Blackstone I hope things will be better between us.
>
> Your devoted husband
>
> Richard Fearnley.

Lydia tore the letter up impatiently, and threw the pieces into the wastepaper basket. Not a word of apology, or endearment; no indication that he missed her. Just commands and scoldings.

'Botheration,' she thought, 'He *shan't* do this to me. He may *think* he bought me, but he didn't. I hate him.'

That again was not strictly true. Sometimes her feelings and emotions were so inextricably mixed up she couldn't exactly define what she *did* feel towards the ruthless overbearing man she'd married – only that life was curiously flat without him, and that she'd rather have been fighting him than not seeing him at all.

His apparent indifference and warnings instead of subduing her, merely increased her seething desire for independent action. From that moment appearances for convention's sake were ignored. Agatha could not possibly keep watch on her all the time. Neither could she cause a scene by locking the wilful girl in her room. Roses were delivered at the door by her admirer of the coffee-house incident. Once he had the temerity to call at the house openly, and Agatha was forced to take his hand momentarily as he left.

'But don't you realise Cedric Lyndsey has a *reputation*?' she demanded of Lydia following his departure. 'And to think you met *unchaperoned* – *you*, the wife of my own brother, and therefore a connection of the Fearnleys – under such cheap and degrading circumstances.'

'Why cheap? Why degrading? He's amusing and kind. We only met by chance, when he was polite enough to pick up my handkerchief that I'd dropped.'

'On purpose, no doubt,' Agatha remarked coldly. 'It really can't go on, Lydia. You're making a spectacle of yourself and getting the family name into disrepute—'

Lydia shrugged.

'*Fiddlesticks!*'

'*What* did you say?'

'Fiddlesticks. And I meant it. Oh—' Lydia broke off for a moment, confused by her burst of temper. 'I'm sorry, Agatha, I don't – I didn't mean to be rude. But can't you understand? There's nothing in it. Cedric – Mr Lyndsey –

doesn't mean a thing to me. He's just an acquaintance. Please don't imagine something that isn't there.'

'Isn't it? How do I know? You steal off at any unexpected moment when I'm not at hand and the next I hear is that you've gone for a stroll, or hired a cab – yes, I heard about *that* episode from the vicar's wife – she *saw* it waiting round the corner of the lane below – the rectory has a good view you know – and was quite astonished when you appeared to step into it and be driven away. Where to *that* time, Lydia? And all the others?' She broke off, panting from indignation and anger. Lydia was momentarily disturbed by the quick breathing and mottled look of her complexion.

'Please, dear Agatha, don't get into such a state—'

'But I *am* in a state, and you're the cause of it. We can't go on in this way, we really can't.'

No, Lydia thought, that's certainly true.

Following her first burst of vanity, which had flowered from Cedric Lyndsey's attentions, his flattery was beginning to mildly irritate her. Stolen moments together had lost their excitement; she had exhausted her extravagant impulses for purchasing colourful, and sometimes quite unsuitable new clothes and accessories. Her inward frustrated longing for the wild sweetness of Cornish moors blown on heather-scented winds increased inwardly, making her so restless and moody that Agatha in desperation, wrote to her brother.

> . . . I'm extremely sorry, Richard, but I feel I'm accomplishing nothing constructive where your wife is concerned. I'm sorry to have to complain, but I find her wilful, capricious, and an upsetting influence on the household. I have done my very best, but you must remember that I am considerably older than you, and my health is not what it once was. I have been considering if you could not send her to some seminary or place of education where she could be trained in the duties of a respectful and respected wife? Obviously you

have been unable properly to discipline her, and I must admit I'm not wholly surprised. There is a wayward wild streak in her with which I simply cannot cope, so will you please make arrangements for her to leave Greenfields without undue delay?

Your devoted sister

Agatha Fearnley.

Richard frowned when he read the letter, and the following day sent a reply stating that Lydia could leave Devon the following week for Blackstone. He apologised for any trouble that had been caused, and assured Agatha that in future he would resume full control and responsibility for his wife's behaviour.

He wondered grimly what the chit had been up to, and in doing so made a decision he'd been contemplating for some time – a decision that took him to the Dower House the day after receiving his sister's note, for an interview with Charles Clarke.

He had known for some time that things were very wrong at The Hollies. From servants' gossip and words dropped here and there by workers on the estate, he'd gathered Clara and her husband were in constant conflict, and no longer slept together. He had also heard more recently that the girl Jess who'd worked there was expecting a child, and the inference was that Charles was responsible.

If so he guessed that the arty young reprobate would easily agree to his plan and although Richard was exceedingly angry at the thought of bribing Clarke to take himself off, it was better all round for him to dig into his pocket than to have the fellow lurking about when Lydia returned. Also – a quirk of amusement seized him when he saw how the outcome *might* bring Madam Lydia to her senses, in another way.

Charles was in the lane apparently about to start on a sketch when Richard cantered round a corner at a sharp pace, with the stance and expression on his face of a man bent on business.

He reined, and dismounted, recognising it was preferable the meeting should be away from the house rather than under the noses of Clara and her aunt.

Charles put his pad and easel down and waited, with an ironic smile on his lips, as his brother-in-law approached, leading his horse by the bridle.

'Quite a surprise seeing you here,' Charles drawled, when they were face to face. 'To what do I owe the pleasure – if it can be called a pleasure?'

'I can assure you it's no pleasure on my part,' Richard answered sharply, 'just a damned nuisance, and if I did what my temper's itching to – gave you a hiding with this—' holding out his crop '—I'll find it infernally more agreeable. However, for Clara's sake, and Lydia's, I have a proposition.'

'Oh yes?' Charles's tones were ambiguous, but his eyes had hardened. 'And what's that?'

Richard wasted no words. For a sum that made Charles's mind and heart leap, and Charles's signature to a statement agreeing never to contact or wittingly see Clara again, or to set foot within twenty miles of Blackstone, or The Hollies – the sum of money would be placed at a certain bank the following day, for the payee to collect at his earliest opportunity.

Fearnley waited, watching devious thoughts hesitate, change, and hover behind the surface of the calculating blue eyes. But he knew his offer had already, inwardly, been accepted, though at first there was slight badinage between the two.

'I see. So you are trying to bribe me to desert my own wife?'

'I would hardly call it a bribe, since you've done that already. There's also another reason I've heard, which would make an offer more than welcome. You're a blackguard of the worst kind, Clarke – the type of bastard that gives a bad smell to my nose every time I set eyes on you.' He had the satisfaction of seeing the other man flush, 'However, for the sake of all concerned I'm giving you this one chance to get out, with no more trouble to me or mine, and to be well paid for it into the bargain. But not a penny more; take it or leave it.'

'And if I don't?'

'Then, by God, you'll be sorry. But I don't think you're that kind of fool.'

Charles proved it, by eventually signing the paper, after which Richard placed it in his pocket and rode away.

Four days later, when it became obvious to Clara that Charles had left her, Richard once more visited the Dower House and produced the document proving it.

'He was only too willing to sell you for gold in his pocket,' he announced, 'so don't fret over a faithless ne'er-do-well who was only too pleased to get rid of you—'

'Richard, please—' Anne interrupted, distressed by the sudden flood of tears from Clara's eyes.

'It's true, Miss Teague, and Clara knows it.'

His eyes momentarily softened. He placed an arm round Clara's shoulders, took out his own kerchief, and dabbed the lovely eyes.

'Why the tears, Clara? You've discovered his true character for some time now, and I've no doubt that, with my influence, we can somehow get the marriage annulled. In the meantime I suggest you and your aunt leave this place as soon as possible, and join myself and Lydia at Blackstone. You can have your own apartments, and I'm sure your company – and Miss Teague's influence – will be very beneficial to my wife.'

A moment later Clara looked up. Her expression was radiant. She really was a very beautiful creature, Richard thought dispassionately. Sufficiently so even to cause a little jealousy on her sister's part, if he played his cards well.

Deviousness was not a natural ingredient of his character. But this time, maybe, he would resort to it, if necessary. As for Anne Teague – she had proved an efficient tyrant in Joseph Teague's household, and no doubt with a little encouragement, could be prevailed upon to use her stern influence once again over his erring wife.

And so things were arranged.

When Lydia returned the following week, it was to find her sister and aunt firmly entrenched as members of the Blackstone household.

9

'So you found it impossible to behave decently to my sister, even for such a brief time?' Richard enquired coldly when he and his wife once more faced each other in their bedroom at Blackstone. 'I suppose I should have expected that in some way you would make a spectacle of yourself.'

'I did a little shopping, bought some new clothes, and was daring enough to take a few outings on my own,' Lydia replied calmly enough, though inside she was tensed and quivering with nerves.

'Where you had assignations with young men and made a point of flirting outrageously. Haven't you any sense of decorum?'

Lydia shook her head. 'No. Not when I'm treated like a child and sent away to be ordered about by a starchy prim woman old enough to be my mother. I found Agatha horribly boring, and if you ever treat me in such a way again, Richard, I shall run away for good.'

She didn't notice the sudden flame of desire light his eyes, against his will, or sense the almost overmastering longing he had for this stubborn lovely young woman with whom he had become at such cross-purposes.

'You'll do nothing of the sort,' he told her. 'Miss Teague will see that there is plenty to occupy you here in your home, and you'll have Clara to sustain, and me to reckon with if I have complaints from either.'

Lydia, who had already been informed of the new domestic arrangements, shrugged.

'You're trying to tell me I'm no longer mistress in my own home?'

He smiled without humour. 'As my wife you have the prerogative – so long as you act in a manner deserving respect from the servants, and the neighbourhood. Otherwise, my darling—' he stepped forward, took her chin in one hand, tilted her face up to his, 'I'm afraid you're in for trouble.'

'Don't threaten me, Richard.'

His voice was slightly husky, when he said, 'I never threaten – only give orders when necessary. Now, my love, do you mind disrobing?'

Her lips parted. Quite unconsciously she gasped.

'What do you mean?'

He drew her a little closer, expertly located the fastening of her bodice and pulled it open, revealing the edging of broderie anglaise on her underwear and corset. The full curves of her creamy breasts were flushed pink from the rosy glow of sunlight filtering through the window. He touched her waist significantly with fingers that trembled. 'Take it off and those absurd creations you wear beneath. What favours you may have allowed your lusting admirers I'm in no position to judge, but—'

'How dare you suggest I'm that kind of woman?' Lydia interrupted, with blazing eyes, and her cheeks flaming.

'Sorry,' he said. 'I may be wrong in assessing such a possibility. I take your word you've observed certain limits. It's hardly feasible you'd flaunt yourself naked in a second rate coffee-house or hostelry.'

Lydia brought her hand up to slap his face, but wisely refrained, when she glimpsed the expression in his narrowed eyes.

'That's wise of you, Lydia,' he said. 'Now, are you going to oblige? Or shall I have to play nursemaid myself?'

Lydia bit her lip, was on the point of refusal, but realising the futility of doing so, unbuttoned the waist-band of her underskirts and petticoats, scrambling out of stays and chemise as quickly as possible. Then, mastering a fit of trembling, she forced her head high, and faced him.

How beautiful she was; how infinitely desirable and provocative, breasts upturned like pink buds of flowers above the exquisite tiny waist. Faint rings of deepened flesh showed where hooks and eyes and lacing had been lightly impressed. The gently rounded thighs below were ivory pale, tapering subtly to knees and shapely calves and ankles. If he'd imagined for one moment she really cared for him, he could have knelt in worship at her feet before taking her. The truth was though, that through her defiance, and his memory of her in Charles Clarke's arms outlined against the sky, only coquetry registered in his mind just then. Of any deep feelings in her, he could not be sure. To him she was a torment and enigma. The eternal Eve presenting a challenge to his manhood.

'Is that what you want?' he heard her ask with a show of bravado that he took as contempt and an insult.

'Yes, madam, that is exactly what I want.'

He picked her up, and flung her on the bed.

'Just wait,' he said, 'and don't you dare move.'

He tore at his neckscarf, waistcoat and shirt roughly, removed his breeches and in a matter of seconds was taking her in a wave of passion and tumultuous desire that held both longing and a bitter-sweet despair. Resistance died in her; she succumbed blindly, until the climax, like a dark swirling river, took her to momentary forgetfulness.

When it was over she lay quite still beside him, exhausted, but at peace. As memory slowly registered she turned to look at him. He was already half seated on the bed.

'I hope you enjoyed it,' he said cruelly, and could have bitten his own tongue for the unfeeling remark.

Hurt and stung, she said nothing.

He jerked his breeches on, gave a short laugh, and remarked, 'Well? Satisfied?'

'How *could* you?' she said with a vituperative sting in her voice like that of a young wild-cat enraged and at bay.

'I can do more, madam, if it's required,' he told her in equable tones, though his heart was racing and filled with an agony of loss. 'For your own sake, you'd better see to it that it's not. Now – cover yourself and get dressed. I shall expect to see you downstairs in the parlour within half an hour. There are matters to discuss with Clara and your aunt.'

Blinking away the tears of frustration from her eyes, and with a sullen belligerent thrust of her chin, she obeyed mutely, refusing to look at him again before he'd tidied himself and slammed out of the room.

During her first days at Blackstone Clara was careful to behave decorously, in every way doing her best to please Richard and cause her aunt no anxiety. Her manner to Lydia, though always gentle, was sometimes mildly reproachful, and for the first time in her life, Lydia found herself resentful of her younger sister's unfailing aptitude for playing the martyr so gracefully. Seething with emotional conflict inside, Clara might be. But she seldom showed it. Her ability to charm by her beauty, and through her physical frailty command compassion, remained unimpaired. Even Richard was touched. It had been easy enough to disregard the attractive qualities of the pathetic young creature when they so seldom met, but seeing her every day – which Clara skilfully contrived – was quite a different matter. Everything about her was subtly devised to arouse the male protective instinct, of which Fearnley had a wealth to give. He could never love her, but the knowledge that Clara liked and looked up to him was balm to his wounded feelings, and on her he bestowed every consideration possible.

Lydia was quick to notice it.

'You seem to find Clara quite irresistible,' she said to him once, smiling, but with a tart edge to her voice.

'Is there any reason why I shouldn't? You wanted her here, didn't you? Or can it be that you've become slightly envious?'

'Of what?'

His lips twitched.

'Your sister's capacity for facing her unhappy situation with such courage and docility. I must say she's become quite a restful influence in the house.'

'Oh?'

'Don't you agree?'

Lydia shrugged.

'If you want passiveness and flattery all the time – perhaps. But there's another side to her you don't know. Underneath she's edgy, I can feel it, I think she secretly blames me – partly – for what's happened.'

'How could she?'

'Well – if I'd – if I'd—'

'If you'd become Mrs Clarke, everything would have been different; he couldn't have married her,' Richard interrupted. 'Quite so. But then he *wouldn't* marry you, would he, Lydia? Because you hadn't the wherewithal. Oh, don't try and delude me. I'm quite aware of how things were. Clara was a means of getting his own back on a situation that had decidedly disgruntled him. Then again—' He paused before adding, 'She's quite a beauty in her porcelain way. No man could deny that.'

'Of course not.'

Knowing she was huffed, he continued, 'Still you must admit, that the outcome hasn't worked out too badly. It's unlikely Clarke will ever dare to show his face again in the vicinity, and your wish to have your sister ensconced in your own home has been granted.'

He made a pretence of rearranging his cravat through a mirror, noticing with gratification a momentary frown cross the lovely face reflected behind him.

'Well? Doesn't that please you?'

'Of course.' She spoke stiffly, knowing in one clear moment that she lied. There were times when she didn't want Clara at Blackstone at all – wished she'd never suggested it in the first place. But then, as things had worked out what *she* wished would have made no difference. However skilfully Richard might have placed the onus on her, it was *his* plan that had emerged and been put into effect. *Why?*

One afternoon, escaping the vigilance of Anne for a brief half hour, she took a short walk along the lane in the direction of the farm lying between Blackstone and the Dower House, and with a shock came suddenly upon Jess, carrying a basket with eggs in it in one hand, and a bundle of sticks under the other arm. The girl's face was sulky, with a sickly tinge, her underlip was thrust out, her prominent eyes heavy-rimmed and accusing. In those last few weeks any semblance to sensuous allure had disappeared. She looked what she was – a defeated light-o'-love who'd taken what she wanted and was now paying for it. Lydia felt uncomfortably that she might owe Charles's former fancy woman some sort of apology for the harsh way she'd treated her and turned her from the Dower House. After all, Clara's husband had been partly – if not mostly to blame.

So after a moment's hesitation, Lydia asked, trying to sound non-committal and dispassionate, 'How are you getting on, Jess?'

'How do you expect? With me as I am, and my dad not able to work?'

'What do you mean?'

The girl gave a contemptuous cough that could have been a mocking laugh.

'You haven't heard, o'course. He got a fork dug into his foot and it's gone wrong. Have to have it off most likely.'

'Oh,' Lydia was shocked. 'So you're short-handed on the farm.'

'There's the boy, and my brother that's all – and me of course.'

'But you're—'

'Expecting a kid. That's right. *His* – that stuck-up no-good man of your sister's. Took off he did, as soon as he heard. High-and-mighty lord and master Fearnley seen to that. At least, that's what Tom says.'

'Your brother?' Lydia knew him by sight – a rough looking handsome character, not too bright in the head, who had grown truculent during the years due to his father's strict discipline, and wages which amounted to practically nothing when his son's keep was deducted. The farmer himself was considered a pious man by natives of the district, appearing on Sundays regularly and impeccably clad in his black best suit, with Maureen, his downtrodden wisp of a wife by his side, accompanied by his son and daughter.

'I'm sorry for your – family's misfortune,' Lydia said hesitantly, while her mind searched this way and that for some solution that would ease matters.

'*You?* Sorry?'

'Yes.' Lydia's lips closed firmly against her teeth. 'I'm human, though you may not believe it. I—' She searched in her pocket and found a few coins. 'Here, take this. Perhaps it will help to get a few things you need. And I'll speak to my husband. If your father's in such a bad state something should be done about it.'

'So it should, but it won't be. And it'd be better to keep your mouth shut over this. If things got round, and Tom or my father knew I'd kept your gold to myself I'd be belted by one or the other – though Dad wouldn't find it that easy to catch me as he is now.' She smiled with unpleasant satisfaction.

'Very well,' Lydia agreed shortly. 'I'll say nothing about the money. But I shall certainly do what I can to get medical advice for your father.'

An hour later Lydia told Richard of the meeting.

He frowned.

'I don't want you immersing yourself in the affairs of people like the Treen family,' he said. 'I've already sent a doctor to call at the farm, and apparently the foot is turning gangrenous. The man's only chance of recovery is to have it amputated – I was willing to get him into hospital, but he won't hear of it. So there the matter ended.'

'You mean he'll die?'

'Most probably.'

'But it seems inhuman.'

'It's his own choice.'

'And then what will they do? That delicate wife, and – and Jess, as she is?'

'There's a son. He'll have to do double work. From what

I've heard, ever since the unpleasant accident he's made a point of spending valuable time that should keep the farm going, in riotous company at the Tinker's Retreat.'

'You sound very hard.'

'I am when I have to be. And see you remember what I've just told you, Lydia. Keep away from the Treens. Tom's an unpleasant character who could prove dangerous. If I have much further trouble from him they'll be evicted.'

'I didn't know you'd had trouble, and I didn't know Jess was—'

'Enceinte?' Richard's lips took a downward twist. 'They breed early, her type – which your former lover should have realised.'

'You don't know Charles is the – the father.'

'The father-to-be? Oh, I've no doubt of that at all.'

'Then you shouldn't have sent him away,' Lydia retorted. 'He should be here to help, and take responsibility.'

'For his bastard? Clara's husband? Your own brother-in-law?'

'There's no need to speak like that.'

'There's every need. Consider your sister's feelings.'

'I always have considered Clara, as you know. And anyway, when the child's born it will become common knowledge—'

'Not necessarily.' There was a pause, then Richard touched Lydia's hand lightly, and in gentler tones said, 'I'm not without feelings myself, Lydia. I've given quite a lot of thought to the matter and it's occurred to me that later on, after the baby's born, Jess might be sent away to some place where she could be trained domestically – as a cook perhaps – to take a position in a respectable household. There are some, catering for women in her circumstances. They might allow her to keep the child with her, or it could be sent to—'

'The workhouse?'

'No. I was going to say to an orphanage. It would have a better chance there than being dragged up in fear and trembling at the Treens. At the moment however all that is for the future. Not *your* future, though. You understand?'

'I'm trying to.'

'Perhaps it would be better not to. Just one more thing—'

'Yes?'

'Don't start giving presents to the family. And keep away from Tom Treen. I don't trust him.'

Giving orders again, Lydia thought, instantly on the defensive. Not that she had any wish at all to encounter Jess's unpleasant brother, but her independent spirit still chafed at the restraint her husband seemed determined to impose on her. He was quite aware of her irritation, and in an effort to persuade her – and himself incidentally – that he felt he could trust her – he opened a personal bank account for her in St Kerrick, where, if necessary, she could take out money for a considerable amount.

'I think I must be going off my head,' he told her with a whimsical grimace. 'So far your dealings in financial matters haven't been very encouraging. Still—'

'What do you mean? *What* financial matters?'

'The absurd clothes and ridiculous jewellery and perfume and heaven knows what else that you indulged yourself in, in Devon.'

She blushed faintly.

'I know you like to see me in conventional lady-like things,' she said. 'But you know very well I'm not actually a lady at heart. And Agatha brought out the worst in me. Anyway—' She lifted her chin, smiling brilliantly in that certain way which always enchanted him, though he tried not to show it. 'You have mining families on the estate who, I'm sure, could make good use of them. You say many of the children are poorly dressed. Most working mothers would be grateful of the material, and able to make suits and dresses for them.'

'I'm sure you're right, but don't get the wild fancy into your head that I'm prepared to feed and clothe willy-nilly any Tom, Dick or Harry's offspring just to give you something to do. In other words – grow up, Lydia. Money doesn't grow from trees.'

Lydia sighed.

'You do *lecture* so, Richard. And yet with – with Clara you're so indulgent.'

'How could I be anything else with anyone like her?'

'You mean because she's so beautiful?'

'Partly, and because life has dealt her one or two vastly unkind blows. Not that she's entirely defenceless,' he added quickly. 'Your sister has quite an artful mind when necessary. She knows how to charm blood out of a stone.'

'What a horrible expression.'

'But apt, I think.'

He walked away, leaving Lydia wondering reflectively what exactly his thoughts were about Clara. Obviously during the past weeks she'd wound herself very effectively round his little finger. Normally she would not have cared, would indeed have been grateful. But now, strangely, she resented the fact.

Nothing at all was heard of Charles during that period. And nobody superficially, cared. But as the days passed to early autumn, Clara became faintly piqued, and extremely resentful that he should not even have bothered to write a line to her. At first she had been too angry and distressed to feel anything but relief at his absence. But when the grey mists began to cloud the valleys below the moors, and visits to St Kerrick and other Cornish centres became rare, her mind frequently strayed to the past, shrouding her in long silences while her lovely violet eyes gazed absently through the windows across the moors, and her fingers lay still above the tapestry on her knee.

Her aunt, ever vigilant, was quick to notice, and generally managed to think up some practical task to occupy her. Lydia, also, was unable to escape for long from Anne Teague's observation. Anne, in fact, found her task an increasing strain, but was not prepared to admit it; she recognised however that a time would come when defiant opposition could easily rise between them. Lydia so far kept her quick temper under restraint. But there were occasions already when she reminded her aunt, gently, but with a hard glint in her eyes, that she was the rightful mistress of Blackstone, and Miss Teague merely a visitor in the house. The words were always carefully and subtly delivered. Anne, indeed, would rather have preferred a loss of dignity on Lydia's part. But at the moment the girl was careful. She had changed a great deal, Anne thought frequently, since the time before her marriage when she'd had to suffer Joseph's stern discipline. Wild at heart she must still be, but quickly learning the art of sophistication.

Even Richard at times seemed puzzled, regarding his wife speculatively, and wondering probably what went on in her lovely head. Anne noticed, then, the admiration on his handsome face, the look of ardour in his eyes which was unmistakable. However much he might openly appreciate Clara's beauty and winsome appeal, she could kindle merely compassion from him. He was 'besotted' – the only truly applicable word she could think of – by the wilful Lydia, and it would be better for all concerned if the emotional battle between them could be resolved as soon as possible. One day it would happen – Miss Teague was no fool. Two such fiery individuals must inevitably face the truth, or go their different ways. She sighed. 'The truth', she recognised, was really so simple. They needed each other with a passion seldom felt by ordinary mortals. In the meantime Blackstone remained a receptacle for hidden stormy emotions over which she was supposed to keep control.

As if she could.

One day, after an early dish of tea, Anne, feeling her age, and unduly tired, went to her room for an hour's rest. Clara was already lying in bed with a cloth soaked in cologne on her forehead, to allay a headache. The late afternoon sun was low in the sky, and a veil of mist filmed the grounds and brown moors beyond.

Lydia, on impulse, pulled on a pair of boots, and a cape over her orange gown. She had a sudden impulse to be away from Blackstone and wander as she had before her marriage. Richard had been called unexpectedly to Truro for a business meeting concerning the mine, Wheal Chance, shortly after lunch. This had flattened her spirits, because he'd promised to take her to Falmouth simply as recreation and the fun of an unnecessary spending excursion.

Now that harmless diversion had been spoiled because of the stupid old mine. Well, mines weren't actually stupid, of course, neither were the men who worked them, Lydia admitted to herself, as she made her way from the gardens towards the nearest ridge of hills. She had every sympathy with families at the moment out of work – those whom Richard was doing his best to get employed again. But the business side bored her. If he'd allowed her to go on her own, carrying baskets of goodies and other essentials to the poverty-stricken cottages – or even asked her advice, as a woman, concerning the priorities of mothers with young children to rear, she would have complied enthusiastically, pointing out that sanitation came first – the necessity of having cesspits as far away as practical from living quarters, then sufficient plain food to give strength for the future. Clothing, too, was important to withstand winter cold and the hard conditions imposed on youngsters sent at an early age for surface working and sorting.

Richard naturally recognised such things, but he refused to discuss them with her, or refer to such personal details, except by a chance comment requiring no answer from her. If she gave any, or made any suggestion, he might pretend agreement, with an ambiguous nod of the head, but she knew he really hadn't heard or considered it of any importance.

She was a *woman*. His wife; and as such, she often thought, irritably, supposed to be brainless – a mere chattel for his sensual pleasure.

It was in such a mood that she strode up the slope that afternoon, defiant and free, like a young captured creature released suddenly from bondage. The air was tangy, pungently sweet in her nostrils, heady with the nostalgic scents of sea, tumbled blackberries and fallen leaves. There was no wind. The frail mist brushed her cheeks, and impulsively she pushed the hood to the back of her shoulders, and loosened her wealth of dark hair from its combs.

Her spirit rejoiced as the chill touch of heather and bracken brushed her thighs. She removed her cape, let it fall for a few moments at her feet, then lifted her arms wide towards the ancient menhir which stood to her right by the track that eventually led to St Kerrick. It was only when a form emerged from behind the granite that she picked up the garment hastily, and placed it round her shoulders again.

The man was tall and broad, and had a slow, swaggering gait as he approached. She knew him at once. He was Thomas Treen, Jess's brother. They'd met briefly before, in the past, but had not been on speaking terms, except to say 'good morning', or 'afternoon', as the case might be, or merely pass with a nod of the head. Some said he was on the simple side, others that he was more shrewd than he looked; none could deny that he was a formidable figure physically, with a brutal look of strength that made other men wary of crossing him, and caused girls, mostly, to avoid his company, although inwardly admiring his handsome, aggressive countenance. He and his sister were not at all alike. Where Jess was fair, plump, with pale eyes and hair – Thomas had a thick crop of black curls above strongly carved features. His weakness was in the low forehead which receded above the thick brows.

That day, against the indefinite light, his form appeared more massive than usual, hunched and bull-like. Lydia had a curiously unpleasant impression of some macabre primitive being reborn from the past.

She paused involuntarily, as he approached. Then she forced herself to say in light false tones, 'Good afternoon, Tom,' and would have passed on. But he planted himself in front of her.

'Is et?' he answered, holding her with his stare.

'What?'

'Good afternoon, you said. Well, mebbe for you. But what about *her*, eh? My sister Jess, an' the one she's carryin' o' your smirkin' high-born lot?'

'Jess's affairs – her plight – are nothing to do with me.'

'Edn' et? They do say round St Kerrick way that you was matey enuff with the one as laid her, afore you caught richer fry—' He thrust his heavy-jawed face nearer hers. 'Ais! I'd say et was quite a bit to do with you an' your crook-backed sister. He married *her*, didn' he? But Jess! Sent off with a kick an' a sneer wasn' she? By *you* an' your kin—'

'How *dare* you?'

He laughed, thrust out a rough gigantic hand and clutched her shoulder.

'Doan' you act haughty-like with me, Missus High-an'-Mighty Fearnley. An' I c'n tell you one thing – ef you was my wumman, I'd take a belt to your back. That's what you need. I seen you carryins on all right. I seen an' know what you are. Tryppin' about with your fancy airs, an' your don' touch me look. Oh I'm not that daft! Not fool enough to bend a knee to you, or tek your – "marnin' Tom" an' "good day Tom" wi' a bow an' touch o' me cap. I doan' bow to you, not any other fancy bitch. An' I'm not lustin' for 'ee either.' He turned his head slightly and spat into the heather. 'Muck, you are to me. But Jess is different, and my dad, what about him?' The angry flow in the darkening eyes deepened.

Trying not to show fear, Lydia managed to free her shoulder.

'I'm sorry about your father, Tom. My husband told me. He did all he could to get him to hospital, but you know yourself he wouldn't go.'

'No. An' why should he? Some workuss place—'

'Not a work-house at all,' Lydia corrected quickly.

'Well, he didn't want et. No more would I. When 'ee goes et'll be in 'is own place with the moor round 'im, even if et's without a crumb in 'is belly—'

'That won't *happen*, Tom. My husband will see none of you go hungry. The farm is on Blackstone land—'

'Ais! An' that means we c'ld be turned off any moment, with nuthen to see him safely laid underground wi' a stone over 'is head. I tell you – tedn' right.'

'No. There's a lot wrong about the law,' Lydia admitted, sensing a slight relaxation in Tom's manner. 'But it wasn't *my* fault, *or* my husband's that your father got a fork in his foot, and there's no fear at all of you being evicted—'

'No? Wi' only *me* to work the place, an' a half baked lad, an' Jess carryin' a brat sired by that theer brother o' yours—?'

'Brother-in-*law* you mean.'

'What does it matter? Same thing. Do you know what I reckon, Missus?' His voice was once more avaricious, his expression ugly.

Lydia didn't answer.

'I reckon you owe us compensation. Edn' that what they do call et? A bit o' gold under my fist to help. That's what I'd say.'

Lydia hesitated before replying. Then, cautiously, she remarked, 'I myself gave your sister something secretly the other day, and I'm sure my husband—'

'Your rich man?' The words were a sneer. 'He's a sly one. I doan' mek no deals with one as haven' no mind to keep et.'

'Then what—?' Lydia's courage began to ebb. 'What *are* you asking, exactly, Tom?'

He smiled again nastily. 'Well now. I c'ld, say, tek off them things an' let me have yer in the heather all luscious an' helpless like the one as took Jess, couldn't I? An eye for an eye, a tooth for a tooth. Oh we're a fine religious lot, us Treens. But that wouldn't make sense to Jess, would et? No. I'd say a hundred gold sovereigns, wumman, to kip me content an' help get a new start—'

A *hundred*, in gold? Lydia's heart sank. How was that possible? She had her own bank account, true. But she was quite certain that Richard somehow would keep an eye on it, and be outraged at her drawing out such a sum. He'd question and poke, and eventually get the truth out of her. No, it was impossible. She told Tom so, with an enforced show of bravado. His face darkened. He approached again, grabbed her to him, and ran his hand forcefully and resolutely round her buttocks. Helplessly she struggled.

'So what's it to be? Money in me pocket, or my seed in your womb, eh?'

Her wild frightened eyes stared unblinkingly into his lascivious narrowed dark ones. 'All right,' she gasped.

'What? The gold?'

She nodded. 'I'll get it.'

He released her.

'When?'

She shook her head.

'I don't know. I—'

'You'd better. An' tell me quick.'

Recklessly she named the following Friday, which gave her three days clear in which to arrange things as unobtrusively as possible – finding some excuse to visit the town twice, so that the bank manager couldn't raise an eye, or play with the idea of confiding her withdrawals to Richard if he should by chance look in.

'And how shall I get it to you?' she asked in cold clear tones. 'And where?'

He smiled.

'In any way you care to, an' *here*. Under this rock. See?' He indicated a stone. 'An' I doan' care how. Mebbe you c'ld crawl up here on your belly like an adder through the bracken. Snakes is wily critters, so c'ld you be, I reckon. Anyways, that's your business – how to kip out o' your rich husband's way. Just doan' let on though – ef you do, an' he finds out I'll have you an' get my own back in my own way, sure as eggs is eggs. Understand?'

Fearful, but with a fierce rage burning in her she agreed, adding, 'There's one thing though that *you* can be sure of. If you pester me for more I'll see the whole area, *including* Mr Fearnley hears about it, and you'll end up in jail, Tom.'

He grabbed a grass and stuck it between his teeth.

'Suits me. A hundred'll do for me, an' help Jess through her trouble. After that I'll see she does *her* wack of work proper – an' the bastard too when he's old enough.' Lydia shuddered at the thought. Poor little thing: she didn't envy the life he'd be born to. Indeed, it was ironic he should be born at all. And if the unfortunate infant turned out to be a girl matters could be even worse for her.

A minute later, to her great relief, the unpleasant interlude with Thomas was over, and Lydia watched him striding, head thrust forward on his thick neck, in the direction of the farm.

She picked a few autumn leaves and berries and presently walked back sharply to Blackstone.

Richard, happily, was not back, but Anne had left her room and was lingering about the hall uneasily when Lydia came through a side door.

She eyed her niece disapprovingly. 'So you've been out again on your own. You know very well your husband doesn't like you tramping about the hills unaccompanied. Did you see anyone?' An impudent touch of humour lit Lydia's eyes. 'Let me think! – oh yes! – a fox in the distance, and a rabbit lolloping back to its hole. There were a few gulls too, and crows pecking in the fields.'

'You know I didn't mean that,' Anne snapped.

'Yes. But details of nature can be quite interesting,' Lydia remarked equably. Then she added in quite a different type of voice, 'Why must you always be watching me? And where's Clara?'

'She's still in her room. Fretting, naturally.'

'For *Charles*? After what he's done? Then she should forget him. He's not worth a fig.'

'Perhaps if you were in *her* position you'd think differently. Oh I know Richard has behaved admirably in having us here. But poor Clara had been so distressingly *humiliated*. And now she's heard about that – that trollop's condition her depression has deepened. She's demanding that Jess should be sent away somewhere before it's born, and I quite agree.'

'I don't.' The short statement was decisive.

'Why?'

'Richard suggested something like that the other day. I've thought about it, and it seems somehow – inhuman. Homes and orphanages can be cruel. I know that and you do – you visited, didn't you, when my father was alive? I went with you once or twice, and wasn't at all deceived. Poor little white-faced terrified things trying to appear happy and content because they were frightened of what would happen if they didn't – afterwards.'

'You're exaggerating. I just can't understand you, Lydia. It was *you* at first who was so enraged when you found Charles with that – baggage. Now you seem to have changed your mind, and want to do all you can to keep the girl in the district. Have you thought at all what a young thing's life would be like in the Treen household?'

'Oh yes. That too.'

'Well then!' Anne's thin arms enclosed her narrow chest in a self-satisfied manner.

'I think we should have the baby here,' Lydia stated loudly and firmly. 'Jess could be found a place somewhere, and sign a paper – document or something – renouncing any right to the child's future. I'm sure she'd be relieved and gladly agree.'

'Ridiculous.' Anne gasped, when she'd recovered from the shock. 'What would *people* say? And *Clara*!'

'Clara would come round. As for *people*! Who cares?'

'You should. Since your father died you seem to have lost all sense of decorum.'

'Aren't values more important?'

'If Joseph were alive. . . .'

'It wouldn't make a scrap of difference. I wish I could look back on him with affection, but I can't. He was a bully. You know it as well as I do. And because we were women under his command he took it out of us in every way possible. All except Clara of course. Beautiful Clara.'

Something in Lydia's manner disturbed Anne profoundly. 'I don't know what's come over you, Lydia.'

Lydia smiled faintly.

'I'm seeing life in rather different proportion than before.

Even Clara. I think it would be very good for her to have to take an interest in something and someone else beside herself. A young child about might help.'

'Her husband's *illegitimate* offspring? But how terribly hurtful, and when she was so passionately devoted to Charles.'

'*Was* she? I wonder. I don't really think so. She may have tried, at the beginning. But her main object was to have a husband and satisfy her vanity. A kind of compensation for her back.'

Anne shook her head slowly. 'You *have* changed, Lydia. You used to be so fond of your sister, so protective and warm-hearted.'

'I still am. But differently.'

And with this comment Anne had to be content, for the time being.

There was naturally an outburst from Clara when Lydia's suggestion eventually reached her ears.

'I wouldn't *dream* of it,' she declared fiercely, 'not Charles' and that woman's brat. You've no right to expect it. The idea's horrible. *Hateful*.' She was starting to sob.

Richard who heard the pandemonium, raced up to Clara's apartments, to find her lying face down on the bed, pounding it with her fists, and Lydia and Anne doing their best to restrain her.

When he heard the cause of the hysterical outburst, he forced Clara round, jerked her up and said firmly, 'Control yourself, Clara. Nothing has been decided yet, and on the whole I'm inclined to agree with you. In the meantime, behave. And please—' turning to Lydia and Anne, '—stop your feminine tongues wagging. For heaven's sake let us have a bit of peace in the house.'

His obvious anger magically silenced the distraught scene. Clara controlled herself, turning her woeful face to his with quivering lips, and eyes which despite their reddened lids were still beguilingly beautiful.

'I'm sorry Richard,' she apologised after a brief, stricken sob.

'It's all right.' His voice was gruff. 'Just try and be a little rational. Or aren't you happy here? Would you rather return to the Dower House?'

'Oh no.' There was a further rush of tears. He patted her cheek lightly. 'Very well then. Do your best to be happy and not upset everyone.'

The velvet lashes shadowed her damp cheeks demurely.

'I will, Richard,' she agreed in docile soft tones. 'I promise.'

Lydia, unfortunately, received the reaction of his irritation. 'You must have been talking too much,' he said afterwards, coldly. 'For once won't you make an effort to be discreet over this business?'

Lydia shrugged. '*Servants* talk. All the house must know about Jess and Charles now. That's why I think we should make an effort to have the baby here. It would be kind, and appear charitable.'

'And Jess?'

'Your suggestion for having her trained for service might be the answer. It would probably enhance your growing reputation for being a good landlord and squire.'

He was faintly amused by her perspicacity, and touched a curl nestling at her neck with a fleeting gesture.

'I can't see it working out, and the girl would have to agree; about the baby, I mean.'

'She'd grab the chance if she's any sense at all. Her father's a bullying invalid, and her brother's hateful.'

'You speak very convincingly. As though you *knew*.'

Turning her face away so he would not notice the tell-tale blush staining her skin, and with a pretence of fiddling with a flower on the table, she replied airily, '*Everyone* knows. I'd be dull not to. Apparently he's drunk most nights now, at that disreputable kiddleywink.'

With which explanation, Richard had to be content. Luckily for Lydia she managed to get the money safely to Tom without her husband's knowledge, but doubt and uncertainty gnawed at her. The future darkened her high spirits. A sense of doom seemed to linger about Blackstone.

By late October, rumour concerning the Treens and their unhappy existence had intensified and become accepted as fact in the district. The farmer's condition had worsened, and he could no longer move from his chair to get outside, even with the aid of sticks and crutches, to keep an eye on what was happening round him. His slave of a wife became sick with a cough, and Tom's addiction to bawdy nights at the local kiddleywink increased. More often than not he returned to the farm in the late hours raucously singing, in a drunken condition. Naturally the state of crops and livestock deteriorated. Richard got an extra hand to help, but the man soon left, unable to put up with Tom's daytime bullying. The heaviness of pregnancy and having to cope with such unpleasant and frequently frustrating circumstances, turned Jess into a resentful slattern.

Thomas jeered and openly accused her of bringing shame and poverty on the family. Yet habit had been so firmly embedded into him by his strict and pious upbringing that he made a show, on Sunday evenings, of listening with the rest of the family to his father's half hour reading extracts from the Bible aloud. At such times the old fear curdled Thomas's heart – fear of a wrathful fiery-eyed God rising in the shape of the old man from his chair, with a flashing sword to strike him dead. The next morning the swaggering, bullying Tom would be back again ready to lash out at anyone who crossed him.

Jess's only escape was to creep out of the house at odd moments and find some hidden spot on the moor where her heavy tired body could relax for a brief period, with her aching back against a stone, or thick tump of undergrowth.

She didn't want the child. At first, when there'd seemed to her just a chance that Charles might come back, she'd felt a queer stirring of comfort, knowing the seed in her was the fruit of them both. Now she realised he wouldn't return, and she hated him. She hated everything – the sordid quarrelling, endless work, and having to see herself day by day getting larger and plainer, feeling an encumbrance to everyone around her. Occasionally she made an attempt to tidy herself, and salvage something of the peasant sexual appeal that had once been hers. It was no use. And what was the point?

One day, unknown to Richard, Lydia called at the farm and found Jess in the dairy. Following a few sullen comments from the girl, she brought up the subject of the home, and a possible training for work in some large house. Jess, with a sudden renewal of vitality, wheeled round and exclaimed contemptuously, '*Train?* In one of them starchy preachin' places where all you say is "yes, ma'am", an' "no ma'am"?'

There was a short pause until she flung back her head, and as a bright flush stained her broad face continued, 'Who d'you think you're talkin' to? An' what d'you think I am? I'm no skivvy of yours any more Mrs High-an-mighty Fearnley. So you jes' get out, d'you hear? And don't go talkin' to me about homes again.' She was breathing heavily.

For a moment Lydia thought she was going to be ill; then a male voice behind her said, 'You heard what she said – get out.'

Startled, Lydia turned and saw Tom staring down at her. There was a sly sneer on his face. She could feel his hot eyes burning her – probing through her clothes to the flesh beneath. Lusting.

She drew the bodice of her riding jacket tightly to the neck against the white cravat, and said coldly, with her chin held up more boldly than she felt, 'I've no intention of staying. I was merely trying to help.'

'*Help? You?*' He laughed, uttered a coarse word, and with the smell of beer penetrating her nostrils, Lydia left as quickly as possible, not looking round, or pausing until she found the place where her horse was tethered to a thorn tree.

Jess stood watching until the slim figure, so handsomely clad in the fitting velvet, and plumed hat, had disappeared beyond a fold in the moor. Then she moved laboriously into the dairy. Tom followed. 'You just tell 'er ladyship where she gets off,' he said, 'Give her an earful. One day she'll get more 'n that from me.'

'What d'you mean?'

'Never mind. I've got plans all right.'

'Don't go making trouble, Tom,' Jess said wearily. 'Haven't we got enough as it is?'

'No. Not by a long chalk. An' I'm not talkin' of trouble – it's gold girl, *gold.*' He smacked his lips appreciatively. 'There's plenty where the first come from, an' there'll be more, you mark my words. I'll see to that.'

When Jess tried to dissuade him, he brought a hand against her face smartly.

'You shut up. I know what I'm doin'. No man's goin' to lay my sister without proper payin' for it.'

Desolation overcame Jess with such force, slow tears of hopeless exhaustion rolled from her eyes down her cheeks.

That night she disappeared.

Two thoughts were uppermost in her tired mind as she made her way willy-nilly through the undergrowth up the hill at the back of the farm, dragging her feet heavily over the soggy ground where withered heather creaked above dead wet leaves and decaying bracken. The thoughts reiterated in a ceaseless refrain like a macabre chorus from which somehow she had to escape. Had to. *Had* to. A home, or life with Thomas. Tom? Or the home? Which was worse? Tom probably. He'd been eyeing her lately in a new, queer kind of way. Furtive, as though at any moment his large strong hands would be upon her.

No one knew. And while her father was up and about to keep an eye on him, he wouldn't have dared. But things were different now. And after the child came – the child! The senseless echo started again – The home, or Tom? Homes were cruel wicked places, where you couldn't get enough to eat and had to work until you couldn't stand. Oh she'd heard all about them. And whatever the vicar said, she knew it was the truth. And she wasn't made for that sort of thing. Charles had liked her. Charles had said – what was it he'd whispered when they'd lain together? She couldn't remember exactly. It was all lies anyway. He didn't care. No one did. Only Tom, and Tom was a beast.

So she clawed her way blunderingly ahead, gasping, pausing intermittently to get the breath back into her lungs, with no goal ahead – no clear thoughts – no destination except the enclosing darkness that was already turning to mist and thin rain. On and on she went – what strength she had intensified by the deepening hatred in her – hatred of everything – the world, her brother, father, and the hungry life in her womb struggling for survival. God! How she hated it. She didn't want it. Self-rejection became a loathing, a sickness so intense she longed for extinction and death. Why couldn't she die and be rid of the burden? Why did the lonely moor so mock her? Tearing at her face, torn hands and feet, with a shiver of wind creeping slyly from the sea – whispering, whispering—? What was it the breeze sighed as she fell? She never knew.

But suddenly the earth rose to meet her, and she was on her back, staring up into the darkness. Her breathing had turned into sharp painful gasps now. Something tore at her stomach. Her mouth fell slightly open as she saw the face leering down upon her – a gigantic, evil, macabre face – that of a menhir carved by unknown hands in a far off ancient civilisation when the first Celts walked Cornwall's primitive hills.

Instinctively Jess's hands clutched her stomach beneath the heavy breasts. The granite entity appeared to sway towards her, and it seemed to her, in a surge of emotion, that the old gods called – called her to obeisance! She managed to struggle to her feet – lifted her arms wide, and gave a high scream, wilder than the gulls' crying, before she staggered and collapsed, striking her head against the hard ruthless surface of the stone. The impact was sharp and violent.

She fell to one side, with her head twisted at a curious angle, moaning fitfully, until gradually even the moans died away. A trickle of blood coursed from a temple down a cheek, to merge with the boggy ground. Her hands at length lay cold and still on either side of her slumped form. Rain thickened, and soon every trace of light from a thin climbing moon was blurred and taken into obscurity.

Her body was found two days later by Thomas Treen. He poked her with his foot, stared, bent down, and lifted an arm. Then, with a disgusted threatening look on his face, he drew himself up to his lumbering six feet two, and lifting a fist to the sky, said, 'I'll get 'ee for this, sure 'nuff I will. A life for a life. An' that's what it'll be yet, that's what.'

He pulled her down to the foot of the hill, and lightly buried her beneath brambles and decayed undergrowth.

Then, with revenge seething in him, he went for the law.

No one could get any sense out of him, except a repetitive accusation indicating that what wits he'd had before were now – temporarily, at least – crazed by shock.

'*They* did it,' he said, time after time. 'It was *them*. Murdered her they did, like as if she was a pauper's bitch. *They* did it.'

At last they got him back to the farm. He drank all that day and the next. When at last he came out of his drunken stupor he remained practically dumb for a week. Then he set to work with a savage zest he'd not shown for years, achieving with the help of the lad, more than the three of them had ever done when his father was active.

Meanwhile a verdict of accidental death was recorded on Jess.

Tom made no comment when he heard, but his expression was dark and unfathomable, and through his head the refrain still ran – 'a life for a life,' though no one guessed the macabre plan slowly evolving in his sick mind.

10

November was a cold month, and Clara's spirits as well as her body, were chilled by the grey skies and sense of isolation imposed on her by Charles's desertion. Both Richard and Lydia did their best to cheer her up, and any resentment Lydia had previously felt concerning Richard's attention to her died frequently into sympathy and a lingering sense of guilt. Anne was more acerbic. 'She should rouse herself,' she stated firmly. 'Make herself eat and do a few things about the house. Mooning after that no-good husband of hers is a waste of time. He'll never show his face again, and the sooner she realises it the better.'

Was she mooning? Clara herself didn't know. But it was dawning on her gradually that however much Richard Fearnley might admire her looks, his attitude to her was mostly sympathy. Pity, perhaps, would be a better word, and she wanted more than that. Obviously Lydia was and always would be – the only woman he desired, and Clara began to regret her decision to leave the Dower House where at least she had been mistress.

She spent hours in her room, pretending to occupy herself with sewing, or a little reading of the poets, sometimes leaving her chaise-longue to stare out of the window across the wind-blown hills towards the shadowed valley where The Hollies stood in its cluster of trees.

Occasionally, when leaden skies lifted to winter sunshine, she put on her boots, fur wrap and bonnet, and with her gloved hands in a muff, took a walk on her own beyond the grounds, following the lane bordered by holly, willow, and sloes, along which the chaise had brought her following Charles's departure.

Anne considered this extremely foolhardy. 'The air is too

cold for you,' she said on one occasion, 'and if you caught a chill in your back the results might be very serious indeed. Remember what the specialist said – spinal weakness and heart trouble often go together. You're not *strong*, Clara. You should not, in any case wander about on your own.'

Lydia who was arranging Christmas roses in a bowl, lifted her head sharply and said, 'I don't agree. If Clara wants exercise, it'll probably help her. She's not so weak and fragile as you're trying to pretend, are you, Clara dear?'

Clara smiled wanly. 'If I feel tired I come back. It's wearying being cooped up here all day long.'

'Cooped up?' The three women looked towards the door and saw that Richard had just entered. 'Now what's all this about? What's the trouble, Clara?'

Lydia began, 'I was just—' but was interrupted by Miss Teague explaining about Clara's brief spell of solitude and walking on her own.

He eyed Lydia for a moment, and said, 'I think your aunt's quite right. At the best of times the moor's not a suitable locality for any young lady strolling unaccompanied.'

Lydia's eyes turned to smouldering green. 'He *would*,' she thought. 'Anything to contradict *me*.'

'Thank you, Richard,' Anne said quietly. 'I knew that I should have your support.'

'I know I can rely on your good sense, Anne, as always. And I shall be able to leave tomorrow with a quieter mind knowing you're keeping watch on these two.'

Lydia's heart jerked.

'*Leaving?*'

'I have to go to Plymouth, and will be staying over the weekend.'

'Why?' Lydia's underlip took its characteristic stubborn thrust, her voice held a hint of petulance.

'That, my darling, is none of your concern. Just a matter of business.'

Lydia's quick temper drove her out of the room with a flurry of frills and skirts.

Smiling secretly, Richard followed her, and found her upstairs in their room.

'What was all that about?' he said, putting an arm round her waist. 'Are you going to miss me so much?'

She pulled herself free.

'That isn't the point.'

'Oh, but it is. A little flattery from you means a great deal to me.' His voice had softened.

'I wasn't flattering. I was just annoyed at the way you acted – treating Clara and me like children. What possible harm can there be in a short walk? Clara's moping. I'm sure she's fretting for Charles. She was more fond of him than she admitted. And I think—'

'What you *think* isn't important,' Richard said sharply. 'I've made things quite clear to both of you, and that's an end to it. Understand? An order.'

'Orders! *Orders* always orders. If I'd known how obstinate you were I'd never have—'

'Married me? No, probably not.'

'And you wish I hadn't, don't you?'

His eyes narrowed. '*I* married *you* Lydia. That's the difference.' Then he laughed. 'Oh Lydia, what an independent baggage you are. So wilful. Such a child. Why won't you give up?'

'Give up what?'

He kissed her, surprisingly gently, for him.

'Fighting me, love. Then maybe—' He released her and shrugged. 'Maybe we'll get a chance to really know each other.'

Richard left Blackstone the following day. With a niggling, curious sense of regret, Lydia watched his strong form astride his horse, take the turning of the drive towards the lane and St Kerrick, where he'd join the post-chaise for Plymouth.

'It'll be worse than ever now,' Clara remarked. She was sitting by the large garden window. 'He's nice. One of the nicest people I know. And his eyes can be so – so warm, and kind of—' her voice trailed off.

'What? Kind of what?' Lydia asked with a stab of jealousy rising in her.

'Oh, I don't know. Life-giving perhaps. Yes that's it – when he's near I feel more alive and that it's worth going on after all.'

'Don't be silly, Clara. Life's *always* worth while, whether Richard's here or not.'

'To you, yes. You've got him. But it's different for me.'

Lydia was stirred again by the tender compassion she'd always felt for her sister in the old days. She slipped an arm round the slender waist, and was a little shocked to feel how thin it was, below the frail ribs.

'Dear Clara,' she urged softly, 'some time you're going to be luckier than me. One day you'll find love – true love. Someone will appear who'll care for you properly, and look after you so that all your worries and anxiety will vanish. You'll grow stronger, and have an establishment of your own far pleasanter than this place, where you will be able to entertain without any dragon of an aunt always telling you what to do.'

Warmed by Lydia's words Clara looked up, smiling faintly. 'It *could* happen,' she thought dreamily, if the right person came along. But the prospect was still only a wish.

'Where will I ever meet him?' she asked. 'Not many people come to visit us here do they?'

'In the future they will,' Lydia assured her, 'when Richard is better known. You must remember that the Fearnley name's a new one in the district. People are cautious, especially the rich established families – the aristocrats, and those whose roots have been here for ages.'

'It's sure to take a long time though. *Too* long for me, probably.'

Realising the sad truth of the statement, Lydia's hand slipped from Clara's waist, and enclosed one of her sister's. 'Don't be so pessimistic. You're very young yet. That was the trouble when you married Charles. *Too* young.'

'No, it wasn't that. It was *you*. He only wanted you, Lydia.'

'What nonsense.' She hardened herself to add, 'Charles only cares for himself. You ought to accept it and stop dwelling on him. He's not worth a thought. You're well rid of him.'

'But I'm not, am I? I'm not rid of him. We're still married.'

'Yes; well – Richard's going to see what can be done about that. There can be a divorce. Your name won't have to be mentioned publicly. Up country the Fearnley name counts for a lot, and Richard has influential friends.' Oh, Lydia thought, as soon as she'd spoken, how prim she sounded – like some well-meaning elderly relative giving advice.

Clara freed her hand from her sister's, and walked to the window saying, 'I don't care about my name or what people say. And I don't want pity. It seems to me the happiest people are fashionable whores who find rich lovers to keep them in luxury. Do you think I'd make a successful mistress, Lydia? To a lord or someone? I *am* quite pretty, aren't I?' She cast a vain, coquettish glance into a mirror opposite, and smiled at herself beguilingly. Neither of the girls was aware that Anne stood the other side of the half open door.

When she burst into the room her face was outraged. 'You should be ashamed – both of you – for talking in such a disgraceful manner,' she gasped. 'In Richard's absence too. Clara – go to your room immediately. I have something to say to your sister.'

Clara shrugged. 'All right. Gossip as much as you like. I really don't care about anything.' She walked away apparently quite indifferent to the approaching scene.

After the door had closed Miss Teague rounded upon Lydia. 'If you were younger, and not Richard's wife, I would punish you severely in the good old-fashioned way,' she exclaimed. 'But that, now, is only Richard's prerogative; all I can say is – is—' Her face turned a sickly hue. She reached for the back of a chair, staggered to it and sat down.

'You're not well,' Lydia said coldly. 'Here—' She handed Anne a bottle of smelling salts. 'Take a good sniff. Would you like some brandy?'

'No – no. You know I don't drink. Your father objected – except – except—' she struggled to speak calmly, 'for medicinal and special purposes—'

'My father's dead,' Lydia remarked. 'So will you be soon if you make such ridiculous scenes for nothing.'

Colour returned to Miss Teague's face in a stain of purplish red. 'Nothing? With you putting such disgraceful ideas into that child's head?'

'The ideas were her own, which you'd have realised if you'd listened a little more carefully. And Clara's certainly not a child any more. In fact—' slight amusement touched her lips, 'in some matters she seems very well informed indeed.'

'And from what source? *You?*'

Lydia refused to respond in temper.

'She reads Richardson, and others far more worldly. Blackstone has quite an extensive library you know.'

'And to think—' Anne remarked, 'that when your dear papa was alive we never dreamed of considering any reading matter except the Bible.'

Lydia laughed shortly.

'The Song of Solomon's quite titillating in parts,' she said. 'Or haven't you noticed?'

Anne got up.

'You're disgusting,' she retorted. '*Quite* utterly disgusting.' She walked unsteadily from the room, refusing assistance from Lydia, and went shakily to her room.

The next day she developed a cold and a temperature, and was confined to bed. At first Anne herself wouldn't admit there was anything wrong. 'It's just reaction,' she said, forcing herself to stand up by clinging to a bed-post. 'Shock, from the scene we had yesterday.'

Lydia, who had been called by a servant who'd taken up Miss Teague's cup of tea and noticed her flushed colour, ignored the statement. 'You've got a fever. It's obvious.'

'Fever? Nonsense. If you hadn't upset me by your coarseness I should be perfectly all right.'

Lydia's mouth tightened.

'Very well. Only don't blame me if you develop something worse than a chill. Influenza – or perhaps pneumonia.'

In spite of her contemptuous words Anne was a little startled. Pneumonia? What an idea. Why should she? She had never been properly ill in her life. No one in Joseph Teague's house had been allowed to be ill, except Clara of course.

She made a further attempt to appear normal, but her head began to ache in a sickening giddy way. She fell back again on the quilt, and at length agreed that there was something wrong with her.

'I shall fetch the doctor,' Lydia said decisively. 'Richard would never forgive me if something happened in his absence.'

'Very well, but that will take time – you'd better get the apothecary, Henry Julian, first – then – then if it's necessary – he'll call Dr Sykes—' Lydia eased her aunt's legs upwards between the sheets, saying, 'I'll go myself, get the boy to drive me in the small carriage, just in case I have to bring something – collect any pills or potions from St Kerrick.'

'*No.*' Miss Teague's face turned a deeper colour. 'I need you here. I won't allow it. I—'

'What about me?' Clara's sweet tones issued from the doorway. 'I'd like a drive. I'm sure it would do me good – the weather's fine, and I'm just as capable as Lydia of calling at Mr Julian's?'

Anne was at first doubtful, then, as the room whirled round her, eventually agreed.

'But I insist on Johns – the man – driving you. Not that new under-servant.' She put a hand again to her head. 'Oh dear – why must everything be so distressing? This constant argument—' Her voice failed.

'That's all right,' Lydia remarked soothingly. 'Just try

and rest. I'll see a glass of hot milk and brandy's sent up to you. Clara's quite capable of fetching the apothecary, and Johns shall take her.'

So it was settled.

As soon as Clara had dressed in her warmest cape and boots, and with a list of informative details and questions dealing with Anne's condition safely folded in her pochette, she stepped into the waiting carriage, and following a flick of the whip, the vehicle was rattling away down the drive.

Clara suddenly felt important and free. Her spirits lifted, and a stab of curiosity rose in her as the carriage passed along the high lane overlooking a steep track that cut down abruptly towards the Dower House. She could just discern its huddled shape in the valley behind the shadowed belt of trees, and the memory of an incident that had happened recently returned with vivid clarity. Once, when she'd escaped secretly for a brief wander she'd gone further than she'd meant, and on her way back came upon Thomas Treen unexpectedly, with a bundle of wood on his back. He'd stopped, stood facing her for a moment, just staring, with a sly look on his face. Then he'd cocked a thumb in the direction of the Dower House.

'Bin there recent?' he'd queried.

Affronted by his familiarity, Clara had replied, 'No, why should I?' Her limbs had stiffened; there was something about him that had intimidated and frightened her, but she'd managed to say coldly, 'Do you mind allowing me to pass?'

He hadn't moved for a moment. Then he'd said, 'Might be worth et. Then you'd know for yourself. Some say '*ee*'s back: that – that greedy murderin' swine you married. There's light at night sometimes. Knowed that, did 'ee?'

'I – I—' Clara had been shocked into speechlessness. The man had given a guffaw.

'Oh, yes. Someone's there all right. Someone as keeps 'isself hid by day, an' does 'is dirty work o' night. I've heered it's 'im. If I was you I'd tek a look sometimes. Unless o' course you're scared o' seein' what fancy wumman e's a—' An obscene word left his lips. Clara, putting both hands to her ears, had swept past him, not looking back but aware he was still watching her until she'd turned a corner.

The confrontation could have lasted only seconds, and in time she'd managed to dispel the unpleasantness as just a coarse attempt of Thomas to scare her. But the meaning of his words had remained in her mind. Someone – Charles, he'd meant – was hanging about the Dower House. She'd persuaded herself it might be a caretaker, although Lydia had informed her that Richard had temporarily left the house without one, and was making plans to have part of it demolished and rebuilt. She hadn't cared at the time. All she'd wanted had been to forget the faithless sneaky Charles she'd married. Now curiosity overwhelmed her, and as the carriage continued on its course to the apothecary's a plan deepened in her mind.

The journey took under an hour, and luckily Henry Julian was in when she arrived.

He was a portly, bewhiskered pink-faced man, wearing a green velvet jacket and fawn breeches with buckled shoes and silk stockings. When Clara explained her mission he hummed and hawed a good deal, stroking his chin, with a thoughtful air that appeared somewhat bewildered. Clara noticed a curious smell about him suggesting a blending of herbs and alcohol. Then he said after a considerable pause:

'Poor lady! poor lady. Fever you say? And the megrims? I'll be along, m'dear, along so soon as you can say boo to a goose. Just let me get my good mare with a saddle on her back, and I'll be there.'

'I have the carriage waiting,' Clara told him. 'There's no need for you to ride yourself.'

He looked shocked.

'Oh, but there's every need, midear. Don't trust carriages – never did. Light rattly things with loose wheels. Don't you worry now. Trust me – as I trust old Dolly and my own shanks' ponies as they say—' He beamed benevolently.

'But – I was told to ask if anything be wanted – medicines, or something from St Kerrick perhaps.'

Mr Julian slapped a stout thigh smartly. 'All I want'll be here – in my pocket, midear, even little Billie, one of my pet leeches, in his bottle and waiting for a bite or two.'

Clara visibly shuddered. The large hand went to her shoulder. 'Don't you worry, young lady, you be off now to tell your Auntie don't fret, an' that Henry Julian's on his way.'

Realising that in spite of his apparent good humour Mr Julian was obstinate and wouldn't be hurried or change his mind, Clara went back, explained to the coachman, and after a grudging comment they started on the return journey.

The morning sun had pierced the veil of mist, sending silver shafts of light through the tracery of branches and undergrowth bordering the lanes. As they mounted the rising land more slowly, Clara, always sensitive to beauty, noticed the delicate filaments of cobwebs diamonded with dew, and in the distance the quivering rim of sea beyond the coast. At the point overlooking the shadowed valley of the Dower House a sudden idea occurred to her, an impulse so strong she knew she just *had* to get a closer view of her erstwhile home, and see for herself if there was any sign of habitation, or of Charles.

She told Johns to stop the carriage, as she wanted to pick a few branches of holly.

'There's lots of it down there,' she told him, although she'd never before taken that particular narrow route down. 'All these tiny lanes are thick with it. But of course the carriage couldn't possibly get there.'

The man demurred at first. ''Twouldn't be right, miss – ma'am—' he objected. 'Supposed to look after you I am, and if I let you go wandering I'll be in trouble.'

Clara laughed. 'Don't be stuffy, Johns. I'll only be a few moments. You can keep your eye on me all the time. Honest.'

The trouble was that he couldn't. Some yards down the path it took an abrupt turn. The trees thickened and hid her slim form completely.

Clara, in a kind of bemusement, wandered on, hurrying at times as shadows once more eclipsed the sun. She realised presently that the house, this way, was nearer than it had appeared, and that the thread of track must have been used merely as a short cut in the past, by a shepherd perhaps, or gypsies possibly, and poachers. At last she reached a clearing with a few cattle grazing in a stone-walled field. Beyond that was a proper lane taking an immediate curve to the back of The Hollies.

Forgetting time and that Johns would be getting worried and impatient waiting with the carriage on the high lane above, Clara quickened her pace, keeping close to the granite wall and hoping to escape the notice of the cows. She didn't like cattle and was always fearful they would suddenly stampede with their frightening horns towards her. That morning, having been milked, and then chewing the cud patiently, they appeared not to see her, and she passed through the gate at the far end of the enclosure without incident.

She crossed the lane, and with her heart bumping uncertainly made her way up the side of the building, which had a door leading into the kitchen quarters.

She waited, turning her head this way and that, eyes watchful and ears alert for any sign of movement. The place looked derelict; there was no sign at all of life, or that anyone had been there recently. The only sound to be heard was that of twigs beating against a broken pane of glass, and a very faint creaking of wood as though a door or window was disturbed by a rising of thin wind. Taking a closer look Clara saw that this was the explanation. The door was slightly ajar, its grating on stone combined with rusted hinges and the squelching of a few dead damp leaves, could account for the eerie echo in that silent place.

Automatically, she lifted an arm and pushed at the damp wood. It opened slowly, raspingly, letting out a stream of fusty air.

How dark everything appeared. As though no one could have lived there for years and years. And yet it was only a few short months since she and Charles had gone there following their wedding, and merely weeks since the ignominious incident that had driven him away and taken her to Blackstone. For one tense moment she had a wild impulse to turn and run back the way she'd come. If Charles was here she'd surely sense it – some sign – a footstep, tinkle of a tin or drip of a tap, the ticking of the old clock from the hall – but of course she wouldn't hear that, and Charles might not have ventured to the kitchen at all; he could be camping upstairs in his studio perhaps.

She poked her head further in, and looked up. There appeared nothing but the damp ceiling, and a few cobwebs brushing her face. She shuddered, wiped them away with a hand – how she hated spiders – and then firmly went inside, telling herself it was only a house – the house that had been hers. All these dead ghostly fears were merely imagination.

There were three steps leading from the outer door to the interior of the kitchen quarters. The cold intensified. The flagstones were damp; thin rivulets of water stained a wall near the window where rain had leaked in. Without heat from the old oven or kitchen range where a fire had always burned in the past, the interior was chillingly desolate. From somewhere ahead, on the right, near the entrance leading to the butler's pantry and dairy, there was a very faint patter as though a mouse had scuttled by. She waited until all was completely quiet again, then lifting her skirts to her ankles, half ran across the floor to the door of the back hall.

The shadow deepened there. It was a narrow corridor, with a hatch in the wall half way up, used in past days no doubt for the dining room, when richer company inhabited the Dower House, and there were more servants to deal with sumptuous meals. As Clara's eyes became more accustomed to the pervading gloom, she had a brief glimpse of a light ahead falling on an old marble statue at the foot of the main staircase. It was of some mythical Greek god, and had occasionally startled her when Charles and she moved into the house.

She stopped now, and after rubbing her eyes, kept them firmly fixed where the glimmer had appeared. Her heart was beating unevenly. What could it have been? Surely if anyone was there, there'd have been movement, a stirring, or momentary shadow flung across the floor. But there was nothing. Just nothing. Her pulses gradually steadied as she recalled a long gothic window half way up the stairs. Just a natural phenomenon she told herself encouragingly – a touch of light from outside or the sky clearing to give a fading ray of pale sun.

With a start, she realised it must be getting late. During the flood of mixed emotions and her own curiosity, she'd forgotten about Johns waiting with the carriage at the corner of the high lane. She put her hands to her mouth, and called softly, 'Charles – Charles – are you there?' Then more loudly, 'Is *anyone* there?' Her voice seemed to echo through the whole interior; the effect was frightening, as though the Dower House mocked her.

'I was stupid to come,' she thought, with disappointment and an uncanny sense of unease mounting in her. 'Charles isn't here. He's never been back, he won't be. He's left for good. And I don't want him either, or this gloomy dark old place—'

On sudden impulse she turned to rush back down the corridor the way she'd come. But suddenly something warm and stifling came from behind her, catching her head back, and smothering her mouth so she could neither scream or properly breathe. There was a pause while she struggled, and when she was able to look up, she saw him –a large mouth curved in a lopsided leering smile. Eyes screwed up, but watching her like those of a wily snake. His features drew nearer to hers while he whispered in more of a hiss than words, 'Gotcher, haven' I – Crookback?'

Thomas Treen!

His grasp loosened a little. A great lump of terror had welled up into Clara's throat, half choking her. She was trembling violently, and found it hard to speak. At last she managed to say, 'What do you want? Don't look like that. Don't—'

'Like what? Mistress Toffee-Nose-Humpy? Like that lustin' smart man o' yours who did my own sister in?' Any suggestion of a smile died suddenly. '*I'm* not that kind – not lay a girl an' then tek off like a frit hare. But them as does must pay. You an' yours, missis, that's it. An eye for an eye, a tooth for a tooth—'

His face was suddenly close up again, touching hers. She gave a muffled scream that was more of a gurgle. He slapped a cheek smartly, saying, 'You do that agen an' I'll screw y'r silly neck. Tedn' no good neither. There's no one here – nor will be till that fine lustin' sister o' yourn come looking' for 'ee, an' then she'll larn. You just wait – she'll larn who's master—'

Clara's weakness suddenly overcame her. She fell limply against his arm, with her eyes closed. Her shivers now had turned to violent trembling. He stared at her silently for some seconds, gave her a little shake, and remarked more quietly, 'Here now – doan' you do that on me, no faintin' trick. I edn' goin' to hurt you, s'long as you behave. That's it, do what I say, see? It's that other one – that proud and haughty bitch of a Fearnley. See her squirm I will as my sister did afore she died—'

He peered closer to see Clara's reaction. There was nothing on her face but sheer terror, the terror of a defenceless young wild thing trapped and ready for the slaughter. He laughed, pressed her face hard against his chest, so she could see nothing, *feel* nothing, but the smothering heat of his body beneath the rough jacket. They started moving. She made one more final effort to free herself, but failed.

She had no idea where he took her, only awareness of bumping, and a chilling of atmosphere, followed by a rush of cold air, a grating and thumping sound, and the sensation of being carried down steps.

Through a sickening daze of semi-consciousness she heard him say presently. 'There y'are then.'

She felt herself being eased on to a bundle of straw, or sacking, or maybe some kind of a rough bed – there was no way of knowing. As his grip released her she opened her eyes. The place was very dark – obviously some kind of basement or cellar, with a barrel in one corner and a relic or two of primitive furniture scattered about. There was a torn piece of matting on the stone floor. But to Clara, nothing properly registered. The only light, which was quickly dying, came from some sort of a grating or crack in the ceiling above.

She felt too weak to move, and was far too frightened to have made any further attempt. With a queer feeling of unreality, and numbed by fear, she saw his hulking form cross to the opposite side of her prison, where he lit an oil lamp, and kindled a wan fire in a recess. Distorted shadows flickered round the dark interior. Cobwebs and thin trickles of water streaked the granite walls which were green and slimy between the stones.

When he'd completed his tasks he returned and stood staring down on her – a large lump of humanity – no, a *beast*, to her frightened fancy, something out of a nightmare from which she must wake soon; she must – she *must*.

The shuddering started again. She managed to move a leg, and with one elbow propelled her body into a different position. The man thrust out a hand and jerked her to her feet. She was trembling so violently she could hardly stand.

He glowered.

'There edn' no need to look like that,' he said. 'I told you didn' I – I don't aim keepin' you here. Not *you*, Crookback—'

Even in her condition the jeer stung her. She flinched. His expression changed again, became twisted by a lascivious smile.

'You got a pretty face though,' he told her. 'If you didn' look so moony white. Come on now – let's see the rest of you—'

Her eyes widened. 'Don't touch me. Get away—' Her voice rose. 'What's the matter with you? What do you want? Let me *go* – let me *go*—'

'Hey now. No hysterics. No screamin' see, or I'll wallop

you well. You jus' keep your mouth shut, an' let's have a look. I on'y wanter see you *darlin'* – see what high-bred hunchies has beneath their clothes—'

Automatically, sensing that her only chance of survival was to obey, she undid her dress, petticoats, and corsets; discarding under his vicious scrutiny, all her garments, until she stood a waif-like pathetic thing, a pale ghostly naked shape, quivering with her back to the wall. He approached her firmly, touched one nipple with explorative fingers, then another, running a hand afterwards to her waist and thigh, with a curious stroking motion. Then he said roughly, 'Turn round.'

She did so.

He laughed, and turned away. 'That's enough. Crippled you are an' no mistake. I doan' want you, not me. Class you may have, but us Treens want more'n that. Get dressed. Go on. I don' want no invalid on me hands.'

With tears of exhaustion rolling from her eyes, Clara pulled on her clothes, relieved yet filled with humiliation. Thomas Treen was a bully and a brute. But her back had offended him. 'Crookback' he'd called her, and Humpy. Was that what Charles had felt?

The rest of the day passed in a nightmare of misery. She was given food – bread and cheese, and a hunk of meat she couldn't swallow. Thomas produced an extra blanket from an old chest, and rekindled the fire.

'You'll be all right here,' he told her before night properly set in, 's'long as you don't try'n get out, or shout if you hears anythin'. You're mine now, see? An' if they has you back they'll have ter pay. I'll see as they do.' His tones had become menacing. 'An eye fr'n eye – a tooth for a tooth. An' you'll call me master; see? Get up agin now, an' bow. Or curtsey – edn' that what they call it? Curtsey an' say – "Thank 'ee master, for y'r charity. I'm yours to do 'xactly as you says."'

She obeyed mutely, muttering in trembling tones what he directed, while he stood watching, hands on both hips.

Then he said, 'That'll do. Get some rest now, wench, afore I changes me mind, an' 'as ee, crookback or not.'

The night passed. She slept fitfully, and was aware at times of him creeping up on her from the shadows and peering into her face. She kept her eyes firmly shut, and he made no attempt to molest her. In the morning he brought her a bowl of tasteless gruel and primitive facilities for her toilet and washing.

Later she heard a faint commotion from somewhere above, thumping that could have been the sound of footsteps and distant murmur of male voices. Thomas was with her all the time, gripping her warningly, on the alert to see she made no attempt to cry out.

When the voices had finally subsided, he eyed her shrewdly. 'Good thing you kep' quiet,' he told her. 'Ef you hadn't you'd be real sorry now, girl. An' et wouldn't have done no good neither, 'cos no one knows where this is, an' wouldn' 've heard anyway. Oh peck up, for gawd's sake. I tell you, I want no truck with 'ee – except perhaps—' he grinned slyly, 'a letter later – jus' a little note for your grand sister Lady Muck – the one as did poor Jess in. An' that won't be too hard, will it? Not a few words written by one as has such high eddication?'

'What do you want me to say? And why? When?—' Her voice was rising.

He frowned. 'That's my affair. You'll know when the time comes. Jus' remember though, while you're here you'll do as I say, an' learn a bit what *she* went through, my own kin. A bit o' discipline won't hurt ye, I'm thinkin', an' if I wants a glimpse o' you now an' then, you'll show me, won't you darlin'?' His teeth gleamed. 'Or else!'

Clara's jaws began to chatter. Just for a moment he looked taken aback.

'Now, now—' he said in conciliatory tones, 'there's no need for that – to be frit. Don' you go havin' a fit or anythin'. No use to you, *or* me, *that* wouldn't be. You settle now, an' get calm. The letter you gotter write must be firm an' clear, understan'?'

Clara nodded weakly, and presently, when he was satisfied she'd be all right alone for a bit, he made his way to the far end of the cavernous interior, where it narrowed into a shadowed corridor of complete darkness. There was a grating noise similar to the sound of metal and wood scraping, a rattle, and further clanging.

Then silence.

For two more days and nights the tortuous routine continued, although Clara lost all count of time. Hope was gradually dying in her; she existed in a limbo of fear and numbed forgetfulness in which nothing properly registered but the darkness and discomfort, and regular visits of her kidnapper who subjected her intermittently to indignities of behaviour that made her wish to die. He was careful always though to see that she had sufficient warmth and food to sustain her physically. Once she refused to eat, shutting her mouth obstinately. He slapped her face, forced her jaws open, and shovelled the concoction between her lips, holding her small face in a tight grip until she had to swallow.

'There!' he said, 'that'll teach yer. Obey me I said didn' I? –then that's what you'll do or I'll have the hide off yer backside. See?' And he waved his belt at her.

On the second night Clara vomited. At intervals, during the day, she'd thought she heard sounds above, but nothing had come of them. When Thomas brought her evening gruel she accepted it lifelessly, but a thin trickle of it filtered from her mouth down her chin. He brought a small oil lamp and held it close to her face. The brilliant stare of her eyes, together with the flush of high colour suggested she had a fever. He didn't want that – not before she'd fulfilled her purpose.

'Here—' he said. 'Time's come for you to go home, darlin', so we'd better get on wi' et, hadn't we?'

He shook her shoulder, handed her a piece of crayon or charcoal, and putting it on a flat piece of slate said, 'Print it clear now, do as I says, an' look sharp about it. Put your sister's name at top, an' write this. "I'm at Dower House," you tells her, "Treen's got me. Come quick afore I hops it. You come alone and bring gold with 'ee,' *alone*, as I said,"' he emphasised. '"Understand that – *alone*, or you won't never see your luvin' sister agen. Hurry now. Clara!"' He paused, and when she didn't answer repeated, 'Got it? what I said?'

'I – I don't know. I—'

He went over the words twice more, and at last she managed to write the message to his satisfaction. He took the paper from her, studied it under the lamp's wan light with frowning screwed up eyes, then put it in his pocket. Although he couldn't write he could read sufficiently to make out the large printed words.

'That'll do,' he said. 'An' don' you get up to no tricks while I'm gone. Or there won't be no luvin' reunion with your high-an'-mighty sister milady Fearnley, nor anyone else. Know why, 'cos you'll be dead, Crookback.'

The night was shrouded with mist showing only intermittent quivers of wan light when a thin moon pierced the watery sky. No one saw the humped dark shape of a man making his way furtively through furze and undergrowth beneath the rim of the hill towards Blackstone. No one saw him crouching by bush and boulder, listening, head thrust forward like some wild beast on the alert for prey, or heard his large padded feet cut soundlessly across the grounds to the side of the large house, where he stood for a time perfectly motionless with his back against the wall. He waited. There was no sound from inside; no flicker of candle or lamp. He bent down, and slipped Clara's note under the wooden door. A gull screamed suddenly; he looked up, startled. A ray of light filtered weakly down from above.

He had a glimpse of a face staring into the night – a pale face surrounded by massed dark hair, like that of a phantom's quivering above a candle flame. She apparently saw nothing. A moment later the curtains were drawn again. But *he* – the watcher had seen – and a lust of hatred and desire rose in him, a dark swelling hunger to have her soft breasts in his grasp, while she screamed from his ravishing, shamed and defenceless. His dry tongue became moist, caressing his lips, savouring revenge.

Presently, almost on all fours, he moved cautiously causing only a faint rustling of twigs, through tangled branches and undergrowth towards the moor, cutting across the drive, with the speed of a panther. The moon now, had become completely dimmed. Mist thickened and took his form into obscurity as he made his way by instinct downwards, pausing at intervals to get his bearings, guided only by the denser darkness of the wooded valley where The Hollies stood. When its outline eventually emerged, he didn't go to the front of the building, but plunged into a holed recess of the moor that was covered by heather, weeds, and tangled briar. It had become unnoticed and indiscernible through the years, resembling that of some treacherous derelict mine-shaft long since abandoned. The interior, though, held deeper significance. It was a tunnel used for macabre purpose in former times – an escape-hole during wars for priests or enemies of the crown, at others for smuggling, and a hide-out for wreckers and breakers of the law.

For a quarter of a mile the passage curved tortuously this way and that until it reached the foundations of the Dower House. Through its existence many dark deeds had been perpetrated, and remained undiscovered. The confined space where Clara lay was situated under the cellars, entered only by an iron door cut deep into the rock. From there were two loose stones in the ceiling, forming part of the scullery floor above. Through the years moss had pushed through the walling. Thomas alone during his secret plotting and investigations had discovered the tunnel's existence. And good for him he had, he thought, with evil satisfaction, as he crawled through Nature's thorny camouflage into the ground. He went carefully, burrowing like a mole in places where stones and earth had fallen. At one spot he passed the skeleton of some animal – sheep probably, or dog – that had been caught there and buried alive.

When he reached the cavern where Clara lay he thought at first she was asleep; or dead – surely she hadn't done that on him, the silly little fool. It was alive he wanted her, cringing and waiting, and at his mercy to do what he wanted so his revenge could be complete. He bent down and prodded a breast with his finger.

'Hey you! No tricks, didn' I say? Wake up now.'

Her eyes opened, but she didn't speak.

'H'm!' he said. He picked up a bottle from nearby, put it to his mouth and forced it to hers. 'Drink it. Come on now – no argyfyin'.'

She let the spirit trickle down her throat, then coughed. A little colour had returned to her cheeks.

'That's better,' he said, taking a further swig himself. 'We doan' want no casualties, do we darlin'?' He gave a great laugh of relief, and went to the far wall where food was stored on a rough shelf. 'You'll eat now,' he said. 'Eat an' give thanks to me an' your maker that Thomas Treen has a spot o' mercy in him for weak critters an' crookbacks like you. 'Tis *her* I wants – *her*. Aye, an' before long she'll be here to know it.'

He grinned in anticipation – an evil leer spreading from ear to ear. Clara stared, magnetised by horror. He bent down and slapped her cheek viciously. His smile had died.

'Doan' you look like that. Doan' you dare – as though I was crazy. There's nuthin' crazy 'bout Thomas Treen. D'you hear? Say et then, say et – there's nuthin' crazy 'bout Thomas Treen.'

Mutely Clara in a weak voice obeyed. Then, suddenly, everything became too much for her, and she fainted.

When Lydia received the note and read it in the morning, her face whitened. She didn't doubt that Clara's note was genuine or that it had been written under duress. Clara was there, somewhere in that dark old house where she'd lived with Charles, held captive by the evil Treen man – a creature insane enough to kill her if she made a false move. Yet for two days The Hollies had been searched, and the surrounding moor combed. Even dogs had been used, and at one point it had seemed by excited barking that a track had been found. But the scent had faded out, and the clue lost. Somehow, somewhere – they had failed.

It was up to her, Lydia, to take the only possible chance of saving her sister. Up till the writing of the note, Clara had been alive. The letters, though printed in capitals, had certain small peculiarities about them that proved she had penned them. She was being used as a hostage; fear in a great tide reduced Lydia's thought for herself to a minimum. She must do as that madman – Thomas Treen – directed, arrive alone at the Dower House to deliver money and somehow ensure her sister's safety – if it was at all possible.

'Saddle my mare for me,' she told the stableman peremptorily. 'And find me a pair of breeches and a coat. The new youth may have a spare lot – if not, yours will do. I'll want a pistol too, and my own old black cape. I'll see to that while you attend to the rest. I'll be back in a few minutes.'

Ignoring protests she rushed back to the house. There were arguments from the housekeeper and male servants – it was pointed out that the master would never agree, and that they would all be blamed if harm came to her.

'The master isn't here,' Lydia said coldly and firmly, 'and won't be for two days. I'm mistress here, and am going to handle things in my own way. Two of you men can follow at a discreet distance, but only when I've been gone for a quarter of an hour. Don't worry, Johns—' her lips relaxed slightly as she regarded the elderly retainer. 'I know what I'm doing. And not *one* word to Miss Teague.'

Anne, however, who was recovering, was not entirely deluded. 'What's happening?' she demanded of the girl who attended her. 'There's something going on downstairs. I *know* it. And why hasn't Clara been up to see me?'

The maid, backed up by the doctor who had just arrived for a visit, soothed her down by saying, 'It's all right, ma'am – a bit of trouble with a – a—'

'A farm hand,' the doctor said helpfully. 'Maybe a cow or a sheep gone astray or something, and Mrs Clarke is – a trifle indisposed.' Turning away from Miss Teague's distrustful stare, he added, 'These chills can be catching you know, but don't worry, everything's going to be all right.'

He was not aware of the details of 'the trouble' himself, only that Clara was missing, and that it was up to him to keep his patient from getting over upset.

Not at all satisfied, but gradually succumbing to the laudanum potion and professional influence of the doctor's assurance Anne sighed and relaxed. She did not see Lydia's form cantering along the moor until it finally disappeared along the downward track to the valley. The galloping sound of horses' hooves when the two men followed minutes later, did not penetrate to her ears. All she heard was the sighing moan of the rising wind, and the muffled undertow of voices from the hall below. Presently she forced herself from her stupor, and managed to pull the hanging bell near her head.

When a servant appeared she said, 'Bring me something stimulating – a brandy, something to wake me up. That man's a fool. He's drugged me. Laudanum, I knew what it was – I didn't want it. I *told* him. *Doctors!* pah! in my brother's house we never had them, except for Clara.' Two bright spots of colour burned her cheeks; 'Go on, don't stand there, do what I say, and be quick about it,' the irate voice continued: 'Hurry.'

Frightened by the fierce glance of the old lady's eyes, the girl departed, and was told by the under-housekeeper that on no account must spirits be administered to Miss Teague. She had had specific instructions from the doctor, and the only thing to do was to leave the poor lady alone until her sick mood had worn off.

And so time passed. A period in which the weather deteriorated, bringing a spatter of hail and sleet from the sea. Lydia, astride her horse like a youth, rode determinedly with her cape and dark hair loose, flying in a wanton stream behind her. The bracken and undergrowth were beaten and brown now, interspersed with patches of black bog and lurking secret pools. When the tips of the

Dower House roof came into view she slackened her pace, and felt for the pistol huddled by her waist. She had seen it was fully loaded before she set off, and although not properly accustomed to fire-arms, knew, that under her steady hand, and with the protective confidence it gave she would – God willing – be able to protect herself and Clara if necessary.

Providing, of course, Clara was still alive.

She clenched her teeth firmly. Never had she felt so wildly dedicated or determined on any mission, never so bent on proving herself more than just a helpless female bought by a man for pleasurable indulgence when it suited him – a man, unfortunately, that she had grown to care for, but who would never love her that way in return. However, just then, such a fact didn't seem to matter. Only Clara counted. Clara, her frail young sister, whom she'd cherished so deeply during their childhood and their youthful days.

When she reached The Hollies, she skirted from the back of the house to the front, and reined her mare briefly, waiting to see if there was any sign of life. There was no movement visible – nothing but the grey cloud of desolate sleet lashing past walls and windows, stinging her cheeks and whipping her hair wild in a flurry of cold fury. The horse became restless. She patted the wet neck soothingly.

'It's all right, Melody. Quiet now – this way.'

She kicked her mount gently on again, taking a turn to the opposite side of the building. Like a scene from a distorted mirage, the wall rose, lit suddenly to quivering movement by a frail gleam of light thrown from above.

She looked up, and saw a face. Pale, blurred, a terrified semblance of a human countenance with features pressed against the dripping glass of a window.

Clara? Could *that* be Clara – the silver-haired disc of a face with something else behind her – something that emerged menacingly from the shadows, pushing to the fore, dark and snarling – a threatening vile countenance, warped and evil with lust and desire for revenge?

Thomas Treen.

For a second or two Lydia's heart missed several beats. Instinctively her hand tightened on the pistol under the cape. She said nothing, just stared, until the window was pushed up, and Treen's voice shouted, 'Door's open – come in – d'ye hear?'

Setting her chin stubbornly, and still without a word, Lydia jumped from the horse's back, tethered Melody to a tree, then made her way to the side door. Once inside, the thickened cold air seemed to enclose her like a shroud. She blinked and stared. Could this fetid dwelling have been such a comparatively short time ago lived in – the home of her sister and aunt? It was more like a morgue, a place of the dead.

She stepped forward, clutching the pistol tightly, eyes darting this way and that, waiting for the stillness and the grey shadows to explode. A tap was dripping somewhere, a rhythmic beat through the spattering of sleet against the window. Then there was a hollow tread of wood from the stairs above, and she saw Thomas's large form emerging stealthily down, with a limp form over his shoulder, making a shield for his body. Clara. Her pale hair fell loosely over an arm, hiding her face, but Treen's other arm was pointed directly towards Lydia, and she saw he held a gun. She waited rigidly, afraid to shoot first, or let him know she too had a weapon, in case he lost all restraint and killed them both.

When he'd reached the hall, he jerked the body of her sister upright and thrust it close for a moment. Clara's mouth opened in a terrified whisper, but no sound emerged. The haunted eyes searched Lydia's in wild appeal. Lydia swallowed, and forced herself to ask in harsh shrill tones, 'What do you want, Thomas? Put that gun down, or I'll—' She paused, controlled herself sufficiently to add more quietly, 'Think now, Treen. Acting like this is only going to harm you. Let Clara go, and we can talk. I've brought the gold.'

'So you have, have you? An' you'll give it, en' b'lieve I'm

such a fool as to let you both free to go runnin' back to high-an'-mighty Mr Fearnley?' He laughed. 'Oh *no* y'r ladyship. Not till I've had a good taste o' what I fancy—'

'And what's that?'

Still with his arm tight around Clara, he answered thickly, '*You*, wumman. The feel an' taste o' you, an' moren' that—' his large tongue came out, licked his thick lips. 'T'have you weak an' cryin' beneath me – you with y'r fine airs an' haughty ways as sent my sister packin', an' her with a bastard brat inside 'er. Knowed it, didn' ye?'

'I did what I could for her. I gave her gold—'

He threw back his head and laughed, 'Gold – *gold*! You *really* think I care 'bout y'r bloody gold?'

Wave after wave of fear chilled Lydia's spine. She would have to shoot, she thought. But if she did, Clara might become the fatal target. Oh where were the men? Why didn't they come? Involuntarily she glanced back at the door. Thomas, still holding Clara, lunged closer. 'Expectin' someone, are you? Didn' I warn you—'

'No, no,' Lydia told him desperately. 'I've done what you said. There's no one – *no* one. If there were they'd be here. Just let me think – only don't harm my sister. Let her go and we'll talk—'

'Talk? You trollop. It's not talk you'll give, it's—'

'All right, all right,' Lydia interrupted. 'Anything – *any*thing so long as Clara's free—'

She sensed a wave of doubt and mixed emotions run through him, and as temporary giddiness overcame her, heard him say, 'Down there – in front of me; you jus' do as I say – every inch of it, understan', an' no tricks mind.'

Something hard was pressed against her back; as her mind registered again, she chided herself momentarily for not having taken the risk and used her pistol first. Her thumb was still close to the trigger. It would have been a simple matter to shock him if nothing else. But after the shock? Her heart lurched as she envisaged the probable consequences. So she did as he said, went ahead, propelled by Clara's monstrous captor, along the corridor to the kitchens. At intervals she caught a whiff of something alien, yet familiar. Spirits? Or paraffin? Paraffin! but why—

Her thoughts were broken by Thomas saying behind her, close to her ear, 'Don't lag – on with you, wumman—' The hard thrust of a knee against her thigh made her lurch. 'Tha's right, gel,' she heard him saying gruffly, 'plenty o'that you'll have—' His chuckle was obscene, lecherous.

From that point Lydia's mind worked clearly. An opportunity must arise, in some unexpected moment, when the madman would be off his guard. And then, she'd shoot. To kill.

At first, when they reached the scullery, she could only stare, dazed, at the dark hole yawning from the slab floor where the stones had been removed. Was he so completely off his head that he meant to bury Clara and herself there? Was it a grave he'd been preparing? She moved ahead automatically and then she saw the steps.

'Down,' Treen commanded. 'An' doan' you try an' skip it or I'll flay ye. Go on – *serf*!'

With Thomas and the helpless Clara close on her heels, Lydia made her way down the primitive steps. She put on a pretence of staring round, while the giant figure dropped – almost threw – the frail figure of her sister on to a mouldy pile of sacking. Thomas drew a hand across his mouth, and stood facing Lydia, small eyes screwed up in satisfaction, a trickle of saliva running down his chin.

This was Lydia's chance, and she knew it.

Swift as lightening, she had her pistol out and fired. For a second he staggered, and she thought with a stab of horror she might have killed him. But she hadn't. The bullet had pierced his shoulder, sending a quick stream of blood coursing down his arm. He lifted his gun. She fired again, this time catching a temple, then a third, grazing his foot. With a scream of pain he lurched towards her; she stepped aside, but the gun in his right hand went off, time after time, while the air thickened, and gradually curdled into flame.

Then Lydia remembered. Paraffin. She'd smelled paraffin as they went down the hall. Was this Thomas's last resort? To set fire to the place? She was seized by a fit of choking, and heard above all other sounds of creaking wood and falling timber insane laughter flooding the small interior – echoing in hollow macabre persistence down the narrowed passage at the far end.

When she'd rubbed her smarting eyes she saw Clara dragging herself down the aperture. Lydia glanced momentarily towards the swaying bulk of Thomas Treen, and made a useless attempt to drag him from the flames. But his clothes were already alight and he was screaming frenziedly, 'Bitch! Whore! – I'll have yer hide – a life for a life!' He was beating the air, clutching his chest, and then, suddenly, he fell.

Lydia rushed to the narrowing passage where Clara had disappeared. With hair singed, body smarting, and a jagged burn staining her cheek she reached the opening at last, staggered, then pitched forward and collapsed before she'd seen Clara lying yards ahead by a clump of dying heather. Very steadily the circle of burning undergrowth encroached over the blackened earth. There was the thud of bricks tumbling, and the shrill screaming of birds as they rose and flew towards the sea.

11

Richard, who'd unexpectedly returned home two days before expected, saw, from St Kerrick, the reddened sky above the valley west of Blackstone. Instantly he was seized by a wild sense of doom and disaster ahead.

'What's happening over there?' he enquired at the hostelry where horses were stabled. 'That's no sunset – and the air—' he sniffed. 'Smoke. My God—' He broke off explosively.

'There's a fire sure—' the inkeeper remarked, trying to sound as casual as possible. 'Some say an old house, others that the moor's caught. I dunno sure – men've gone to see.' He paused, noting the tightening of Fearnley's jaw, the hard glitter of his eyes, which for a moment seemed to reflect the glare of the distant flames, then continued, 'Best not to think the worst, sir. Could be a barn p'raps. Old wood's quick to get alight, or mebbe just the usual moorland fire we get sometimes when the wind's high an' quick to fan a spark—'

'Get me a horse,' Richard said curtly. 'Go on, man, hurry. I'll settle with you later. D'you *hear*?' Startled by the harsh tone and aggressive thrust of chin, by the sudden fury of fear stiffening Fearnley's tall form, the man hurried to an ostler in the yard, and moments later Richard, astride a massively built black stallion, was galloping cross-country towards Blackstone, ignoring paths, fences, lanes, or stone walls – kicking his mount to a furious speed, while the pungent air gradually thickened, and a pall of grey smoke crept menacingly from the distance, drifting threateningly over humped ridges of rolling landscape, billowing and clearing intermittently, leaving the stark shapes of mine-tracks and menhirs briefly clear, then obscured again into the general curdling grey.

When he reached Blackstone, he was aware instantly of the

uncanny silence which was broken only by furtive undertones from the kitchen and moaning of the wind round the walls. There was no word of greeting – no sound of activity or welcoming word from family or servants. He knew, without having to be told, that disaster had erupted. And Lydia? Terror engulfed him, although he showed no sign of it, when he strode down the hall to the back quarters, after tethering the horse firmly to a gate-post.

He pushed the kitchen door open and stood for a moment staring. The scene confronting him held the macabre tenseness of a stage drama – of a scene about to break into dramatic activity heralding some fearful climax. The cook and kitchen-maid, Johns, and another girl were gathered round the static figure of Anne Teague, who was seated in a high backed chair near the fire, swathed in shawls, with a bottle of some draught or other on a table at her side. Her face was strained and set, deeply carved with lines in the grey flesh. She could have been a waxwork figure rather than one of flesh and blood.

'What's happened?' Richard asked. 'What the devil's going on?'

Anne's head moved then, in a negative gesture, turning automatically from side to side, but she said nothing. It was as though she'd been struck dumb.

'Well?' The sharp interrogation brought Johns to explain. His hoarse, tired old voice burst into a flood of words, sparing nothing, taking the blame on his own shoulders, for ever having allowed the young lady, Miss Clara, to go looking for berries.

Richard's face, at first condemnatory, gradually changed. 'It's not your fault,' he said gruffly. 'Dammit – this isn't the time for an inquest. I'll be off again—'

'But sir, Master Fearnley, wouldn't it be better to wait till you *knows* how many exactly there are there – at the Dower House? There's so many gone, it won't be long before—' The housekeeper's voice faltered.

'Be quiet, woman. And you—' to Anne, 'get back to bed and stay there until I get back.'

Anne didn't move. Richard strode out again, and in less than five minutes was galloping along the shortest, most dangerous route towards The Hollies.

The sight that confronted him when he arrived half blinded him. Rubbing his smarting eyes he could perceive at first, nothing but a blackened shape encircled still with a dying rim of flame and smoke. Dots of men were darting about with all the means at their disposal for finally extinguishing the fire. Neither Lydia or Clara was to be seen. Desolation – a terrible loneliness swept over him. Where was she? Lydia, his wife? Oh God, surely not there – in that blackened shell? He kicked the great animal suddenly to full speed, and ignoring shouts and the sudden searing heat rising from the hot ground, drove his mount mercilessly head on, only just skirting the scarred tumbled walls taking a semi-circle upwards to the higher part of the moor.

And there he found them.

Clara was already being revived from shock and was regaining consciousness. But Lydia! Lydia lay below her, covered by a blanket, her head to one side, showing the scarred side of her face crimson in the dying glow. A woman, Richard recognised her as a local midwife, was kneeling over her, placing bandages on the wound and scorched forehead.

Richard, pushing the figure away gently but firmly, knelt down.

'Lydia – my love – Lydia – Lydia—' He rested a hand on her shoulder, peering into the hurt, wounded face, his own eyes half blinded by heat and watering. She recovered slightly, moaned a little, then turned her head the other way, wincing as renewed pain registered. Then she relapsed into unconsciousness again.

He dragged himself to his feet, called a fire-fighter whom he recognised as a tenant smallholder on the estate.

'Get a cart,' he said, 'transport of some kind – anything, and blankets – I want my wife taken to Blackstone. And where are my own men?'

'Over there, sir – one on 'em – worked hard, 'ee 'as. All of them as come. But you can' do much with this 'ere smoke an' heat. An' earlier – a real inferno 'twas – Job Sterne – from Wheal Chance – 'ee went fer apothecary, but he 'edn' come yet. In 'is cups probably—'

In a frenzy of anxiety Richard at last managed to get Lydia in a cart, wrapped in shawls and blankets. He refused to lay her down, but cradled her in his own arms, so no jolting over rough ground should sting the burns and cuts of her exhausted body.

Clara was placed on rough straw bedding. Her beautiful countenance was unmarked, but glazed terror from her ordeal haunted the violet eyes. She didn't speak except to murmur, 'He caught me – he was going to kill me. Where is he? Where?'

Richard did not reply. No one did, and presently the mechanical refrain stopped, and the clumsy vehicle started off on its rough moorland journey to Blackstone.

The glowing sky had died when they got there, leaving only a leaden pall on the horizon dying into the dark grey of encroaching evening.

Lydia and Clara were both carried to their rooms, where they were tended as carefully as possible by the servants and Miss Teague, who had determinedly insisted she was quite well enough to look after both nieces. Richard meanwhile rode off to St Kerrick for the doctor.

Hours later, tortured and more wearied than he'd ever imagined possible, from anxiety and stress, Richard dragged himself to the dressing-room adjoining the room he'd shared with his wife.

The doctor had been sympathetic but direct in his verdict. None of Lydia's burns should prove fatal. On one side her face would undoubtedly bear a permanent scar, but time, and cosmetics eventually would do much to disguise the injury. Clara, who had suffered only a mild singeing of hair, from the fire, should soon be up and about again, 'provided,' the doctor added, 'she is able to cope emotionally and mentally with the memories of her frightening experience.'

'She's stronger than she looks,' Richard commented wrily. 'Clara can cope with anything she puts her mind to – and generally succeeds in getting what she wants.'

'Hm!' the other man regarded him speculatively, wondering what lay behind the abrupt remark.

'Yes, well – this time she may have her work cut out,' he said noncommittally. 'It might be advisable for you to have more than one nurse in attendance. Your wife will certainly demand more attention physically. But the other young lady may suffer severe mental reaction unless she's given optimistic company and devotion at all times.'

'Yes I understand,' Richard agreed rather curtly. 'See it is done then, get what attendants are required. Spare no expense. Incidentally, Miss Teague will always be at hand in case of a crisis.'

'Miss Teague is not a well woman,' came the quick reply. 'You will be wise sir, to see that no undue pressure is put on her. She needs complete rest, or you may find you have another invalid on your hands.'

With which statement Richard had to be content.

For a month Lydia lay inert and compliant in her room, getting up occasionally to wander to the window, where she stared out apathetically across the grounds and bleak moors towards the sea. Clara was allowed downstairs, but the effort of walking up and down exhausted her. Occasionally she went to see her sister and was distressed by the sight of Lydia's bandaged head and the puckering from temple to jaw of the burned flesh. All mirrors had been removed from the bedroom at Richard's command.

Anne had not agreed. 'She'll have to face herself one day,' she said. 'Better get it over with and save the shock later.'

Richard had rounded on her.

'What do you mean shock? There's nothing shocking about Lydia.'

'No? But she was beautiful – in her way – before,' Anne had pointed out. 'And now—'

'She's *still* beautiful. She always will be. The scar will go,' Richard had affirmed. 'Anyway, her curls will cover it—'

'*When* they grow again, if ever. And then there'll have to be careful arrangement and constant covering up. You've got to face things. Lydia will never look quite the same.'

Richard knew that, but, strangely, the fact of her appearance did not worry him unduly. It was Lydia herself he'd come to care for, yet as the days passed she appeared to resent any show of devotion from him, and obviously preferred to be alone.

Christmas came and went, with little show of seasonal festivity. In January one day when Clara was with her, Lydia, seeing through the window that snowdrops were already starring the brown earth below, said suddenly, 'Fetch me a mirror, Clara.'

'But—'

'I want to see myself.'

Clara hesitated. 'Oh Lydia, not quite yet. Richard said—'

'I don't care what Richard said, I'm going to dress and go downstairs, and I can't do that properly without a looking glass.'

Grudgingly Clara fetched Lydia's French gilt-framed mirror from her bedroom, where it had been placed, and put it upon the dressing table. Lydia turned and went purposefully towards it.

There was dead silence and no movement at all for some moments. Then an arm went slowly to the injured cheek, followed by the other which completely removed the remaining dressing.

The pause was absolute, allowing no sound to register except for the ticking of the clock. Then a little cry broke from Lydia's lips. She turned away. Her sudden dead pallor emphasised the reddened puckering line. Clara stood transfixed, watching as her sister walked past her and stood rigidly at the window staring at the grey sky. Both Lydia's hands were clenched at her sides.

'It doesn't show so much,' Clara ventured to say

hesitantly. 'In time the doctor said it would fade a lot and then—'

'It will always be there,' Lydia interrupted in a harsh voice completely unlike her own. 'Don't lie to me, don't pretend. I won't be pitied.'

'But Lydia—'

'Oh go away. *Go*. Please go. Can't you understand? I don't want to talk about it.'

Clara swallowed nervously. 'I was only trying to—'

'Comfort me. I don't want comfort, I've got eyes in my head.'

'But you can cover it with your curls—'

'If my curls ever grow again.'

'They will, I *know* they will. The doctor said—'

Lydia whirled round. Her eyes were blazing. 'Didn't you hear what I said? Get *out*!'

Like some frightened wounded creature, Clara rushed from the room, closing the door with a snap. Sympathy for her sister hardened into resentment. There had been no need for her to shout like that. Lydia's beauty might be partially marred, but she had a straight back still, a great house, money, and Richard, whereas she, Clara, had nothing but a pretty face, which no one seemed to notice any more. She'd tried hard to win Richard's attention, and so ease the humiliating loss of Charles, secretly envisaging a time when she might make up to the wealthy master of Blackstone for what had seemed to be a deepening rift between himself and his wife. But since the fire he had hardly appeared to notice *her* – Clara. All his concern was obviously for Lydia, though she was openly hostile to any overtures he made. In public at least. In private? Clara tried to picture them together, wondered if they made love, and imagined what it would be like to have Fearnley's strong arms round her. Occasionally she was seized with jealousy. What right had Lydia to have so much, when she had so little? Nothing but torturing memories of her abandonment by Charles, and the terrible events following. At nights, frequently, she had nightmares, waking up with her thin form drenched in perspiration and her heart racing. The doctor had prescribed potions, ordered her to rest much of the time, but to get out for a short walk when the weather was fine. Anne, who was almost recuperated frequently went with her, and saw that her pathetic young niece had the tonics and potions ordered.

For Lydia, Miss Teague found she could do nothing. An air of sullen pride and indifference to others' feelings alienated her from the rest of the household – even Richard, who was unfailingly patient at first, then, by degrees, tried to force her to reality by demanding a certain resumption of their marriage commitments. He had endeavoured constantly but unavailingly to reassure her that she was fretting needlessly over her looks.

'It's hardly noticeable,' he'd affirmed, thinking a white lie was justified if it shook her from such morbid brooding. 'Nothing can change you, Lydia. To me you are still beautiful – more lovely than ever—'

The contemptuous curl of her lip had disheartened him, and after a moment he'd added, 'Well? what of it? You've a scar, but so have many other people, and far worse. If I don't mind, why can't you forget it?'

'Because I can't.'

'Then—'

'And don't *pity* me.'

So that was it.

'I don't pity you any more, Lydia, although pity isn't always a crime. But obviously you don't need it. So shall we have a try at being man and wife again?'

Lydia's heart jerked. There was nothing she wanted more – but nothing, on the other hand, that filled her with such resentment.

She complied grudgingly, but insisted on having all the lights of the room extinguished, having no candle flame even to give him a glimpse of her lovely form. When his hands caressed her body, she lay acquiescent, not fighting him, but stiff, and emotionally unyielding. The experience held no joy for either. And following her first glimpse of her own reflection in the mirror, things became worse. In the house she wore her hair elaborately dressed, fixed by chignon and combs so that the injured temple and cheek were mostly hidden. Whenever she went out – even if it was only for a stroll in the gardens, her features were shrouded by her veil; sometimes in the house she wore it, held in place by a circlet round her head, which gave her the semblance of some Eastern princess or legendary maiden from a mediaeval fairy tale.

Richard became profoundly irritated. He tried everything he could think of to divert her from herself – pleas, outings in the chaise, imploring and scolding her in turn. It was simply no use. Nothing was of any avail. She seemed determined to make the worst of matters, discrediting and doubting his love for her.

Eventually, hurt and gnawed by resentment, he left her to herself, and moved back into his own small room. Making love to her was as sterile as holding a marble effigy in his arms.

The doctor remained optimistic. 'She'll come round in the end,' he said. 'She's shocked and unable to face the truth yet. But she will in time. You'll see, sir. Just wait, and you'll find I'm right. And the burn won't show much later. It's new yet. Tissue has a remarkable way of renewing itself. No! I'm not unduly concerned about your lady wife. She's strong; a survivor. But the other one—'

Richard's eyebrows rose. 'Her sister? Clara?'

The other man nodded. 'Her ways seem to me a little – exaggerated, unstable. That's to be expected of course, after her ordeal which was prolonged and terrifying. I'm afraid there may be a reaction.'

'In what way?'

'I can't say, sir. But my advice is to keep a close watch on her.'

Richard tried, but left the main task to Anne. After all, he told himself, justifiably, he had other things on his mind – other commitments which were not quite as well as he'd hoped and anticipated – especially where Wheal Chance was concerned. Although a new shaft had been sunk which in the beginning had promised good things in the production of copper, the yield was proving disappointing. A serious ground collapse, and one subterranean fire had further complicated matters. On the advice of engineers when 'adventurers' were showing signs of unrest, it had been decided to sink a deeper shaft more than two hunded fathoms below adit. Optimistic assurances that although hopes of a copper revival had not matured, there was undoubtedly tin beneath to be worked, had proved sufficient stimulus for continuation of the project. Minor accidents and setbacks, however, had caused a growing feeling of restlessness among the miners themselves.

Suppose the old mine in the end, had to be written off as a failure? Where would the workers be then? Unemployed again? Oh, everything had appeared very encouraging at first. Miners and their families had been given new heart by the strong, but kindly squire, Richard Fearnley. Still – even if the venture went wrong, *he*'d be all right. *He* was rich – one of the masters. It was the men, the pit workers chiefly, who'd suffer. There had also been signs of ill-omen, which the workers had been quick to notice. More than one miner on his walk to morning shift, had noticed snails – bullhorns – on the track at a time when they did not usually appear. The creatures had been provided with pieces of tallow from the men's candles as a peace offering, and gesture of good will, since it was the old belief that snails heralded disaster.

Richard was quite aware of the discomforting age-old tales going around; there was no point in openly writing them off as nonsense. Belief in superstitions was too firmly embedded in the native Cornish mind to be dislodged by words.

Clara's presence at Blackstone was also adding to the problem. There were periods when Anne could not always accompany her on her short walks. The sight of Clara's fey beauty on her lonely strolls, combined with her bent spine, and the scandal concerning Thomas Treen who had died in the fire, was gradually imbuing her with an aura of strangeness, a figure to be avoided when necessary.

Pigs had died in the district that winter, from a strange disease that could not be defined. A smallholder had lost his only cow, and then – there was Jess Treen's death, wasn't there? That crookbacked pale girl had been the cause of it; partly, anyway.

The word witch was not mentioned at first, but the suggestion was insidiously growing that Clara was either bewitched herself, or in fact was one possessing dark powers to do harm.

'Tedn' that I warn' sorry for her at first—' a local woman was overheard remarking to another in a small village shop. 'A pore bent young critter like her – well, what more could any God fearin' Christian soul think? But 'tes different now. All these wicked things happenin' – an' lyin' there in that big old house with Treen's son – the one as died – how does a body know she didn' trap him there? Eh?'

'Like they say Luke Pettigrew was lured to Bocca Pool by the mermaid. An' all torn an' bleedin' by the pool 'ee was next marnin'! Oh et doan' always do t'think the best. Nor to go doubtin' what Cornish folk knows is true.'

So the murmurings, secretly, went on, and meanwhile Clara received a letter from Charles.

After a few polite remarks wishing her well, and hoping her health had improved, he went on to say that he was quite agreeable to the dissolution of the marriage suggested by Richard Fearnley's solicitor.

> . . . although I think it is none of his concern, [the note continued] you are obviously better off without me and I feel I must comply. You were always far too good for me, Clara, and would never have been happy leading my kind of existence. You are still young enough to start a completely new life without me, and I hope very sincerely you'll find a suitable husband to share it with, once this legal how-d'ye-do is done with. And continue with your charming water-colours. I am painting constantly now. Incidentally you may be interested to hear that I am preparing an exhibition of my work – chiefly of

ballet dancers and the theatre – to be shown at a small reputable gallery in London next month. I don't expect you to be there, but am sure with your natural sensitivity of spirit you will wish me well—

Ever your friend and admirer,
Charles Clarke.

Friend! Admirer! Clara thought bitterly – just that, when he was still married to her. Well, she was not prepared to make things so easy for him as he obviously imagined. She glanced at the address given, and saw merely that of a solicitors' firm, in a particularly seedy part of London. Still, she could write there, when – and *if* she wished. Even when she practically discarded the idea, she knew, secretly, that she would, and the following day did so.

After courteously thanking him for the communication and complimenting him on his success, she added that perhaps, after all, it would be better for them to think a little more seriously concerning the ending of the marriage.

There is so much to consider [she wrote]. I don't *like* being apart from you Charles, although at the time, as you know, I could hardly have considered living with you under conditions as they were. But we are both older for the experience now, aren't we? And it might be pleasant to meet occasionally for a friendly chat. This would be easier if we were still married. Still, if you dislike the thought of that I wouldn't try and force you, but I *do* think we should *ruminate*.

The last word was a good one, she thought. Ambiguous, but holding a wealth of possibilities. She ended the letter by saying:

Don't be precipitate, Charles. Try to remember, as I do now, our happier times. Once you said I reminded you of a snowdrop swaying in the breeze, and wanted to paint me, all in white like that. It was just an idea of course, and didn't happen. But the snowdrops are out now again – whole patches of them. One day you could still do it, if you wanted. Of course you must have heard – or haven't you? – what a *terrible* time I had not so long ago. I was abducted by a dreadful man who kept me hostage in the Dower House for days. Then he set fire to the building. I was saved, but Lydia's face got burned. She has a scar, poor Lydia. She was so proud of her looks. Richard is very kind to her, but she isn't nice at all. Still, I expect things may work out for them in the end.

I shall wait to hear from you, and best wishes for the exhibition.

Your wife still,
Clara.

The letter was sent. Days and weeks passed, but Clara heard no word. She told herself that the reason was difficult postal communications, and to keep her spirits up, devoted what spare time and energy she had in practising dancing – sometimes in her bedroom, at others, when she escaped her aunt's vigilance – over the moors, where, thinking herself unobserved, she let her hair down and moved gracefully to and fro by copse and in small clearings. Prying eyes, however, were quick to notice, and soon spread tales about her strange antics. A glimpse of her was observed standing by an ancient stone, where she lifted her arms to the sky, then, with her cape held up by both hands encircled the relic in a swaying motion suggesting some ancient ritual. Country folk secretly crossed themselves when they passed her, turned and watched furtively as she made her way back towards Blackstone, commenting she was 'witch sure 'nuff'.

Richard was too concerned with his own problems to recognise the full implications of what was happening, although he asked Miss Teague twice to try and keep closer observation.

'Clara's nerves aren't yet properly recovered,' he said, 'and she and Lydia don't seem as close as they were. It's not wise for the girl to go walking too far – especially on her own.'

'Wisdom doesn't seem a characteristic of this household

just now,' Anne remarked drily. 'The atmosphere could be a great deal more amicable if Lydia made an effort to forget herself and act like a normal human being. That veil! And her concern over her looks! She's too vain by half. The mark isn't so obvious as she believes. I should have thought you could have influenced her in some way. I can understand Clara wishing to be on her own sometimes. Her sister's no help at all. And you should also remember I am not a young woman. I can't forever be steeling myself to have eyes everywhere.'

'No, no,' Richard agreed. 'You're quite right. Still – do what you can.'

Anne nodded. 'I'll try.'

She watched him walk away, noticing a heaviness in his step that was unusual. She sighed. An air of anxiety – almost of premonition, hovered in the atmosphere – almost as though thunder was brewing, although it was not yet the usual season for such storms.

As it happened the forebodings proved to be accurate, bringing disaster that no one could have anticipated. Although expert care had been taken over the Wheal Chance venture, tragedy struck one morning, when a wall between the old workings and the new collapsed, sending a cage hurtling to a level more than two hundred fathoms below adit. Two men were brought up dead, others, including a youth, were found to be badly injured. All day womenfolk and families stood at grass, faces strained and drawn, eyes dulled by distress, some crying, others simply statically watching, glancing accusingly towards Richard who was doing what he could, knowing his efforts to be ineffectual.

When the worst was known he assured families and those of the injured that all dependents would be cared for and given security. There was no point in trying to explain that the mishap was due to a freak of nature which no human calculation could have foreseen. Hearts and tongues were beyond reason. Grief was the accuser, and Richard recognised that time alone could ease it.

He was on the site until dark fell. When he returned to the house Anne and Lydia were in the front parlour waiting, and a group of servants was gathered at the far end of the hall.

Johns stepped forward.

'Is it very bad, master?'

'Yes,' Richard replied. 'Very. Several dead.'

Lydia's face had softened when he walked into the room, although she still had one hand to her cheek. The gesture was becoming habitual.

'I'm so sorry,' she said. 'I heard what you said – but it wasn't your fault—'

Richard gave her a brief glance. 'What difference does that make?'

Her expression tightened and hardened. 'Of course not. I'm sorry I spoke.'

He moved towards a cabinet, took out a decanter and poured himself a stiff brandy. He slumped down into a chair, drank it quickly, and got up again.

'Where are you going now?' Anne asked.

'To see the mother of that poor youth. The one who died.'

'But at this hour? So soon? Is it wise? Wouldn't it be better to leave them alone now until the morning?'

Richard stared at Miss Teague with a look in his eyes so hurt and yet so icy cold, she winced.

'They have no bread-winner in the family now,' he said. 'The father's an invalid suffering from miner's lung disease. Another son died from consumption two years ago, and the wife has two young children to support. The meeting isn't going to be pleasant. But just now a man is needed.' He paused before adding, 'Go to bed all of you. I've no idea when I shall be back.'

He picked up his coat, crossed the room in three strides, and almost bumped into Clara at the door. She was a fragile figure in a white wrap; her violet eyes glowed huge and dark in her pale face.

'What's happened?' she asked.

Richard brushed past her without a word. A moment later Lydia followed.

The door slammed.

'That wasn't very nice, was it?' Clara remarked.

'What?'

'The way he ignored me. He was *rude*. There was nothing wrong in what I said.'

'People in great distress don't always wish to be questioned, my dear,' Miss Teague pointed out, 'as you should know by now.'

'All I know is that everything's getting unpleasant here.' Clara's voice had a lump in it, threatening tears. 'Ever since that horrible experience I had people have changed, especially Richard. Sometimes I think—' She paused, to swallow.

'Yes?'

'I think it would have been better if I'd stayed with Charles. He didn't *ignore* me, at least.'

'No, it wouldn't,' Anne told her firmly. 'As you know, my dear, I'm a staunch believer in a couple being faithful to their marriage vows – if *at all possible*. But blatant vulgar behaviour like Charles Clarke's made a travesty of your union. So put him out of your mind and concentrate on a better future. Try to forget the bad things, Clara. So much that is good remains.'

'For *you* perhaps.' The young voice was uncharacteristically defiant. 'But I'm different. You've never been married, Aunt, so you can't really know how I feel. After being mistress of a household it's beastly having to stay in the background and be told what to do and what not. Charles never did *that* ever.'

'I wish you wouldn't dwell on him.'

'I don't,' Clara lied. 'But I've had a letter from him—'

'Oh?' the sharp interruption came before Clara could finish. 'And when was this? Why didn't you tell me?'

'Some time ago. And there was no point in saying anything about it. Richard would only have taken it and scolded, and you'd probably have torn it up.'

Anne sighed and thought for a moment, then she said, 'What did it say, my dear? Surely you can confide in me.'

A faint look of triumph momentarily lit Clara's lovely countenance. 'He's probably coming to see me,' she replied with an air of nonchalance. 'As a matter of fact, he had news about an exhibition of paintings. He's becoming quite well known now.'

'Indeed. Then perhaps he may feel it his duty to offer a little maintenance on your behalf,' Anne commented, adding cryptically, 'Though I doubt it.'

Clara flushed.

'Naturally. Everyone here is against Charles.'

'Now, Clara, to say such a thing is wrong of you and most unfair. No one could have condemned him so fiercely as you did after that disgraceful scene with Jess Treen, and you know it. Richard has behaved extremely generously, all things considered, and it's time now you made more of an effort to get things into proper proportion. We all know how you must have suffered during that dreadful ordeal with Tom Treen – indeed the doctor is most surprised that you have managed to survive as well as you have. It's a wonder your health wasn't permanently damaged. But—' she lifted a finger, '—now don't fly at me, my dear – a word of advice. Don't go out alone quite so much. It's not good for you – or for any of us – especially Richard.'

Clara's eyebrows lifted in surprise.

'Why on earth Richard? What have my walks to do with him?'

'Well – people get ideas, and then talk begins. I've heard that you've been seen behaving rather strangely by that old menhir on the moor. In the evening too—'

'Strangely?' Clara laughed. 'Behaving strangely? What do you mean?'

'Dancing – or something like it.'

'And if I have? What's wrong in that?'

'It's not seemly, my dear.'

'*Oh.* I see. Because Charles and I aren't together, I have

to shut myself away and never enjoy anything, even on my own. I might as well be a widow. It would be better.'

Anne sighed.

'I'm afraid you and Lydia are more alike in some ways that I'd thought. Rebellious and wayward, which means of course that I shall have to keep a strict eye on you.'

This being the last thing she wanted, Clara, appearing to soften and become contrite, moved to her aunt and took both thin hands in hers. Her lips were smiling faintly, her eyes were warm when she said, 'Dear Aunt Anne, don't worry. There's no need to. I'm sorry if I've upset you – truly. And I won't go out so much, if you don't want me to. I can always stroll about the grounds. I should feel dreadful if I thought I was tiring you. So please forgive me—'

Her manner was so winning and shy, so gentle that Miss Teague's doubts gradually began to fade. The child, after all, *had* undergone the most frightening experience possible to any human being. Naturally her nerves were on edge. But underneath the old Clara remained, sweet and docile; the Clara her father Joseph had loved.

Not so Lydia.

Following Richard's hasty departure she had gone to her room, waited a brief time wondering if he'd change his mind and come up to have a few words with her before he left the house.

When he didn't she'd undressed despondently, and in her white shift and wrap, stood at the window, looking out across the bleak landscape, filled with dull disappointment. This was a time, surely, when a wife should have been able to comfort a husband – when barriers could have been broken, and forgetting her own vanity and the long months of estrangement, she could have revealed her true feelings and given the help he needed. Obviously she had left things too late. His only concern now was for the miners and their plight. In the glance he had given her as he'd pushed by, it was as though she no longer existed.

How cold and eerie the scene was outside. Behind a veil of cloud and mist, a watery thin moon threw a wan light over the moors causing interlaced shadows to move fitfully in the wind against deeper darkness, lifting occasionally to emphasise the bleak outlines of distant mine stack and high moorland ridge where the ancient carns and standing stones stood static and menacing as sentinels of Cornwall's past.

Lydia shivered involuntarily. Her whole body craved for warmth and human love, but she knew herself, for that brief time, to be forever a part of that wild land, with something secret and indomitable – almost pagan, that could be hard as granite. Pride. Relentless and unyielding as the jagged coastline thrusting into the distant sea.

Presently she moved back to bed and lay there listening for a step, some slight movement or sign that Richard had come back and might still want a word with her. But except for natural creaking of the old house – of wind moaning slightly and tapping of twigs against walls and windows, all remained quiet.

Eventually, when hours had passed, Lydia slept.

During the week following the mining tragedy the weather became calm and grey, fine, but filled with an ominous waiting quality that hovered over the district like a heavy cloud about to break, more menacing because of the dull acceptance shown by workers – a sense of inevitability worse, to Richard, than protest and argument would have been.

Clara, sly in her manoeuvres to avoid the attention of her aunt, continued her meanderings and prancing in hidden spots about the moor. She had become obsessed by the importance of being able to flaunt her dancing before Charles's eyes, when he arrived. The snowdrops had long since died, but wild daffodils bloomed in a sheltered valley, and near the sea the thrift was thick and pink along the rocks. Gorse flamed, gulls wheeled, silvered through the morning and evening mists. Down the narrow curving lanes blackthorn was a foam of white in the hedgerows.

Clara, growing used to Charles's absence, refused to

believe he wouldn't appear one day, buoying herself up with the thought – which became fact in her mind – that he had been delayed through some important commission, and had not written in answer to her letter because he wished to surprise her, and would suddenly arrive at an unexpected moment, smiling and charming, to take her in his arms as he had done in his brief courtship. She would dance for him then – lead him to a grassy slope of short turf, curving to the headland, where she would raise her dress delicately, and in her tiny pointed shoes, reveal all her artistry and poetry of motion. Her wealth of shining silky hair would be loose and flowing down her back and over her shoulders, drifting in the soft air like a gentle golden cloud. There would be no sign of her rounded spine. Charles would be too enchanted, anyway, to notice.

Then, when it was over, they would stand for a moment looking at each other, hands linked, while he said, 'Oh Clara, you are so beautiful, I do love you,' or something like that.

He would take her in his arms and kiss her, and all would be perfect between them again. That horrid girl Jess who'd died would be erased like a bad dream. They'd make a home together, once more, and she would be his inspiration. Her name 'Clara' would become famous, as his model and his wife, her face a beautiful legend depicted in all the great galleries of the world.

Oh yes. She was sure everything was going to be wonderful in the future. At times her eyes were lit with the brilliance of a fanatic's. Frequently she sang as she moved about the sombre quietness of Blackstone.

Anne was puzzled, but kept her thoughts to herself. Richard had too much on his mind to be worried, and Lydia no longer seemed concerned with Clara's activities. Her main occupations were a morning ride on Melody, and at other times fiddling about with her appearance, forever trying new hairstyles that would hide the scarred cheek.

What a life! Miss Teague thought frequently. Existence in Joseph's house had been hard, but there had been rules, and one had known where one stood. Here, in this great mansion emotions had become so strained, inexplicable and mysterious, that day to day it seemed something would erupt destroying the very foundations of their life together. She was not a superstitious woman, but she well knew things could not go on indefinitely as they were. A crisis would come, and she had a feeling it was not so far ahead either.

She was right.

On an afternoon predictive of early summer, when no breath of wind stirred the undergrowth or moorland heather, Clara slipped out of the house knowing that Anne was already resting in her bedroom, and that Lydia, rather unwillingly, had consented at Richard's suggestion to be fitted for a new gown, by a dressmaker from St Kerrick. She already had a full wardrobe, but he'd pointed out that something greenish-blue perhaps, to suit her eyes, would bring a touch of brightness to the house, and lift her own spirits.

'Something feminine and frippery,' he'd said casually, 'lacy, with frills or something at the neck.'

'You mean to hide the mark.'

'Oh, for heaven's sake, Lydia, forget the mark! It hadn't been in my head at all!'

This wasn't strictly true. It had occurred to him that a fragile shadowed and ruffled effect could skilfully reduce the red line, which would be a boost to her vanity and self-esteem. Then, perhaps, in time she'd soften to something like her original self.

Eventually Lydia had agreed, realising that having the dressmaker to Blackstone would relieve boredom. And anyway Miss Polcarne was a friendly talkative little woman who generally had snippets of gossip to impart.

She had arrived early, shortly after lunch, and Richard's departure for the mine, so Clara was able to slip out unobserved through the door leading out of the house from the conservatory. Over her full white muslin gown she wore a brown cape, a shade calculated to blend with the landscape. By then her physical health had improved to a remarkable extent, and she felt quite capable of the walk towards the headland, and her favourite spot, which would take her approximately three quarters of an hour.

Her heart was light, her head swimming with the excitement so habitual to her at that time whenever she envisaged Charles's future shock and delight.

Oh she could dance now. Every gesture, every step and movement had been perfected. To watch her gracefully swaying against sea and sky would make him long and want her as he had never really wanted any of those mechanically trained ballet girls! The mere possibility that he might not, in fact ever return to Blackstone didn't occur to her. She would never have considered the suggestion. Charles was an artist. A country lover. Poor Charles, she told herself whenever the picture of his banishment returned to torment her – she had been cruel, and refused to understand. Instead of being warm and loving, and wooing him to her side again with sweet and flattering words, she had sent him straight into that hard sophisticated London world where the cheap dancers waited to ensnare him.

But he would come; he would return. As she made her way along the narrow track through heather, rocks and furze, treading daintily over glittering shallow streams and tiny pools, the refrain was a joyful echo in her mind. 'He will return – he will come – he will come.' So wrapt in her own fantasy was she, that she did not notice furtive movement on either side of her when she reached the springy patch of turf at the base of the headland. She was oblivious to the low-keyed murmuring of watchers behind boulders and bushes, of signals passed – the lift of a hand or finger, a shape pushing forward, running a few steps, then crouching again to pause briefly before others followed.

Wilf Goyne, a fisherman was one; then came Nat Pelter, a mine-manager, with several of his workers. Luke Carne who kept goats and lived but a short distance away from the Treen Farm was another. There were also a few women in the rear, including Polly Stracken, owner of a small shop in the hamlet of Zaren. All considered themselves God-fearing righteous folk, attending chapel regularly on Sundays and Feast days, and all were determined that day to beat the devil from their midst and avenge the harm done to them by the Fearnley witch – 'the pale wanton crookback critter as ill-wished animals till they took sick and died, an' who'd put a spell on poor Jess Treen an' her brother, Thomas, so both of 'em was in their graves in no time.'

Such had been Polly Stracken's opinion, and her announcement had gathered momentum with each adverse happening – however small – through the district. Like a smouldering fire driven by random winds, the flames had spread, until logic and good sense were forgotten or completely disregarded. The deed had to be done, whether it was against the law or not. The witch had to go, even if she died in the beating they meant to give her. Like hounds scenting blood, the crowd now moved cautiously, watchful of its prey until the moment came – the moment when the devil-woman started her prancing about by the old standing stone, uttering her magic, and calling the evil powers, with her arms waving 'for all the world like twin serpents', Luke Carne's description of Clara's antics.

Most of the attackers carried weapons of some kind – stones, sticks, clubs, forks and garden or domestic implements. One – a particularly vengeful character, at the instigation of Tom Treen's father, had a knife at his belt. When the plot was prepared knifing had been forbidden, but Abel Starke was not one to be ordered about, and had defied the ruling. So on they went, impelled by their sinister mission, while Clara's gown drifted dove-pale ahead through the grey spring light.

She skirted the tall standing stone, stood for a moment with the voluminous folds of her dress held out like a butterfly's wings. Then she loosened her shimmer of golden hair, lifted her head to the already fading sky, was outlined there for a moment, slim and ethereal as a lovely phantom creature, before the rhythmic movement started.

For seconds there was complete silence from the

crouched onlookers. Was it her beauty that suddenly scared them? Fear? Awe? Or did reason for a brief moment penetrate their troubled minds? There was no answer, nor could there be; for warped passion had taken too firm a control of the most ruthless among them, and suddenly, loud and harsh a man's voice shattered the brooding quiet:

'Come on now – on with 'ee – get 'er an string 'er alive – on – on – after the witch—'

His yell was joined by another, followed by a muttering, a growling and clamour for revenge, as arms were thrust upwards from bracken and furze, and the first shower of stones began. Like animals in a pack, burly figures rose from hiding places, plunging menacingly after the terrified girl. A rock caught her shoulder, sending her stumbling until she recovered her balance and ran on, to the left side of the headland, clutching at anything for support – the branch of a stunted tree, a spike of rock, or clump of pink thrift, and behind her she could hear the clamour drawing ever nearer, interspersed with male shouts, women's screaming, lewd threats and the constant words of 'Witch – witch – get 'er – the witch—'

Gasping and half-blinded by exhaustion she was unaware of the dangerous course she was taking. But her pursuers knew. 'That's right,' one called, 'Sen 'er over, into sea. Let the devil's spawn drown. Drown 'er – drown 'er—'

Clara didn't comprehend the words. Nothing was intelligible to her any more except that they were after her, wanting to kill her, and somehow she had to escape. But she couldn't – she couldn't. There was no breath left in her any more, and her heart was just a dull heavy lump in her breast. She glanced wildly round and down, involuntarily taking a step back. The sinister dark rocks were sheer, dropping hundreds of feet to the swirling sea below. Huge cascades of foam were flying upwards with each breaking wave. Before her was certain death if she went further, behind her the hungry maddened crowd. There was no retreat.

None.

She made a vain effort to turn, and claw her way up the slope to the rising ridge of land. There were a few rocks scattered there which could afford temporary refuge for hunted animal or human. But after the first few steps a piece of granite accompanied by a shower of smaller stones caught her temple, and she fell.

Then they were on her. Mercifully, she lost consciousness. The angry murmur lessened slightly. One of the women said, 'That's 'nuff. Let 'er be now. She'll not come back t'night nor any other night either. Leave 'er now. I'm not one for truck wi' murder. The Book says—'

'Shut your mouth, Sal Briane. She's got it comin' to 'er I say—'

'A witch she is—' another voice joined in. 'Tie 'er up – drown the besom—'

'No, no.' A man's voice again this time. 'Leave 'er be. She won't try any tricks agen. Look at her – she's naught but a wench – a poor skit crookback wi' a curse on 'er—'

'Aye, aye. Mebbe – mebbe—'

'A Fearnley too,' someone muttered more quietly. 'To kill a Fearnley'd put a rope round our own necks.'

Comprehension about their action slowly began to dawn, but was swiftly dispelled when one of the ringleaders took action again, and after a wildly worded command to the rest brought a stick down heavily over Clara's bruised and torn body, then grabbing a coil of rope from a companion started to tie her up. With heads thrust forward the crowd surged forward, avid for a sight of the witch's punishment, although a girl nearby shuddered and started to sob.

It was just at that moment that the sound of hooves thundering from the opposite side of the headland caused a momentary cessation of activity. All heads turned. Astride his stallion Richard Fearnley's form appeared, kicking his steed to a ferocious gallop, riding as though all the furies of the elements were driving him.

He rode straight into the crowd, reined abruptly and for a full minute, seeing Clara's prone and tortured form with her attackers bent over her, there was complete silence. Then he asked in cold clear tones, shouting, 'Who's responsible for this?' There was no answer, only a furtive drawing away by the less vengeful of the mob.

'Tell me,' he demanded, 'or by God, I'll see you all hang.'

Abel Starke, with the rope over his arm, and dagger firmly at his side jumped to his feet and lunged towards Richard. He'd been sacked from a mine a week earlier, and was in no mood to be threatened or for compromise.

'Oh you talk swell, master,' he sneered, grabbing the horse's bridle, 'you an' your high'n-mighty-airs, an' your fancy whores who works magic for the downfall of us workers.' He spat. 'Devil's spawn she was an' is, an' doan you go try tellin' us how we mus' live an' what we mus' do an' what not, 'cos we're not havin' it, see—'

He brought a clenched fist upwards. The stallion jibbed, snorted, and reared on its hind legs, pounding the air and throwing Richard to the ground. Then the great animal was free and away, leaving Fearnley only a few yards from Clara, with a bright stain of blood trickling from one temple.

Starke laughed, an ugly sound signifying contempt and hatred.

'So now we've *two* of 'em,' he yelled. 'Good work, an' a bad day for both of 'em. Shove 'em both over the side, shall we? Good food for the fishes, eh, Goyne? No one will know. Come on now.'

But there was no answering response.

One or two of the attackers were beginning slowly to move away. Richard, stunned briefly, recovered consciousness and tried to get up. He was thrust back by Starke.

'Oh no you doan', mister. There's no goin' back for 'ee now, to get us in jail an' wuss. No sneakin' bullyin' furriners from Devon goin' to do that to true Cornish folk. You've got it cummin' to 'ee, mister—'

'Aye, aye.'

'Ais! that's true, sure 'nuff,' one of Starke's supporters

said. Given fresh courage a number of men drew nearer again, closing in on Fearnley, while another took a curious glance at Clara, wondering if she was already dead. She wasn't. To his astonishment she opened her eyes. They were so large and pitiful, with a wounded look in them like that of a hunted animal's, half-filled with tears, that it was difficult to imagine she was what they said of her.

He turned away uncomfortably, staring broodingly towards the prone figure of Richard, who was helpless against such a number of captors. Starke's cronies were once more reinforcing their hatred and desire for revenge, while Richard using every argument in his power to bring reason and a halt to violence changed his tactics from threats to bribery. He knew that every minute gained was a minute on his side. Eventually hot blood cooled in all but the most desperate. If he could get the majority on his side, by whatever means necessary, Starke would fail and be brought to ultimate justice. But how long would that take? And could he do it? How long the confrontation lasted he never knew. Just as he thought a quieter atmosphere was brewing a piece of rock hit his head, and he knew no more.

12

Lydia found the dressmaker's visit wearying. Although the gown would be undoubtedly attractive when it was completed, being fussed over and remeasured time after time, having pins stuck in constantly while she had to stand still, then enduring the bothersome business of the hem being lifted, let down again and adjusted once more under the critical bird-like eyes, frustrated her to such an extent that at last she sighed and said:

'I'm sure the gown will be perfect. And I'm sorry, but I really can't spend any more time now. I have so many things to do, and an appointment later—' She smiled artificially. 'Do you mind? You're so expert I'm sure there won't be a thing wrong when it's finished. If there is it can always be put right, can't it?'

The thin lips took a downward curve, the voice was brittle when the dressmaker agreed grudgingly, 'Oh very well, madam – Mrs Fearnley. As you know I don't like any imperfections in my work. I shall certainly have to come for another fitting before the gown's completed. Then we shall see.'

'Yes.' Lydia, with relief, stepped out of the dress. 'Will you take a cup of chocolate or tea perhaps? Before you leave?'

'No thank you, madam. I must return to St Kerrick. At the moment I'm extremely busy.' Her voice sounded huffed, and Lydia guessed she was merely doing her best to sound important. A few moments later a Fearnley carriage was rattling down the drive, with the small black-clad figure sitting erectly inside, surrounded by a valise, sewing bag, and a number of boxes including one containing the half-finished gown between layers of tissue paper.

Lydia was about to don the grey everyday dress she'd been wearing before the dressmaker's arrival, when she caught a glimpse of herself in the mirror. She halted, staring, and wondering why she'd agreed to Richard's suggestion for the new gown. True, it would be a graceful and becoming gown when completed. But on her? With a scarred face? She moved back, a little further from her own reflection, and had to admit to herself, with some astonishment, that in the afternoon light the disfigurement really did appear to have faded slightly. The injured cheek was half in shadow, leaving the other side of her countenance perfect in form and outline. She lifted a hand automatically to the puckered line of skin.

Could it be her fancy? Or was it really a little less rough and lumpy? The apothecary and doctor had both tried to assure her that in time the burn would be hardly noticeable. Oh! pray God they could be right. Then Richard might come at last to want her as he once had, in passion and without pity. The fact he'd tried so hard to impress on her at the beginning, that to him her looks weren't all that important – he loved her just as much, even more, than when he'd married her – had only proved to her that he was sorry for her. And it was not compassion she sought, but to be desired with all the ardour he'd once shown. Oh well! what was the point of worrying? She always had the veil, she thought bitterly. When her face was covered she still found a measure of enjoyment in life.

She decided abruptly that she wouldn't wear the grey gown after all. She'd put on riding clothes, have Melody saddled, and go for a canter before Anne had roused from her afternoon siesta and came fussing downstairs for her cup of hot coffee.

She put on her velvet riding skirt and jacket, pulled on her boots and placed the plumed hat on her head, glanced at the veil lying casually on the dressing table, picked it up, then casually threw it down. 'Not today,' she thought. Today she'd be free of constriction and fretting – the fading afternoon, though grey, was filled with the exciting stimulus of spring. She would take the track up the hill, keeping away from hamlets and valleys. Maybe she'd meet Athern. It was the kind of day – windless, yet sweet-smelling with the fresh tang of young turf and bracken, of primroses and early bluebells in secret hollows of the moors – when the gypsy boy could be about gathering flowers to make posies for sale.

She hurried to the stables, and had the boy saddle the mare for her; then, in a few minutes, she was off. Through the thin veil of silvered mist gulls rose and dipped above the heather; Melody whinnied delightedly, and Lydia gave her full rein, only jerking the horse to a halt as she saw she'd been right about Athern. There he was – skipping – no, *running* surely? – and with a purpose, along the rim of the hill, indicating that someone was in pursuit. When he noticed her silhouette against a patch of yellow gorse, he cut down sharply to meet her.

She waited till they were face to face. His expression and torn breath told her something was very wrong. She jumped down, held Melody by the bridle, and asked, 'What is it, Athern? You look – you're upset. Come now – tell me.'

When he'd regained composure the words poured out. 'They've got him, doidi, him and the fair one – the rackli they call witch. Mochardi they are – unclean, with wicked thoughts in them. You must get the gavver – the law, or they'll be killed—'

'*Who?* You said my sister? Who else? And who are *they*? Where?' She caught him by the shoulder. 'Tell me, Athern – and what do you mean by *killed*?'

He did his best to explain, saying that he'd hoped to reach Blackstone before it was too late. 'But they be inflamed an' ugly with o-Bengh – the Devil one,' he gasped. 'Master's on the ground bleedin' an' cut, an' the Rawni—'

Lydia did not wait for more. 'Go to the house, Athern,' she commanded. 'Fast, as quick as you can and get help. I'm off now—'

'But, dordi—'

'Do what I say,' she shouted as she swung herself on Melody's back again. 'Don't argue – for Heaven's sake—'

She didn't wait to see Athern cut down by the side of the moor, but kicked the horse to a wild gallop in the direction of the headland.

As she rode, her hat broke free from her head, leaving her hair a gleaming pennon of dark auburn glory flying wildly against the grey sky. Forgetful of everything but the need to reach Richard, she forced the horse to ever-increasing speed, and as she spotted the dark crowd of distant figures about their evil work, fury mounted in her.

'On – on, Melody—' she urged. 'Quicker now – faster – faster—' The words died against the impact of salt air, sweat strained from her body and the mare's. When she reached the gathering her face was streaming, and rivulets poured down the horse's flanks and neck. But she did not dismount. She rode straight into the throng of astonished figures and halted there, staring contemptuously at their upturned faces. The muttering and murmuring abated suddenly, quelled by curiosity, and the shock of seeing her so proud and fierce-looking, sitting erectly on her steed like some warrior-goddess of the past about to pronounce judgement.

'Where are they?' she shouted, 'My husband and sister?'

There was an ugly growl of dissent from the men standing nearby. One lifted a stone to throw, but a woman grasped his arm suddenly, wrenching it back. 'Have done, Joe Simmons,' she shrieked. 'Enough's enough, and more harm's been done this day than should've—' She glared up at Lydia. The face was broad, and grimed from dirt. The small eyes glared with a wild anxiety, her jaw belligerently set. 'Over there—' she shrieked, pointing to a raised high mound of earth heaped with boulders. 'An' God save us ef they be dead. 'Tweren't me nor Joe here as done et. Like mad they was – the fools—' She crossed herself. 'The devil's roamin' sure 'nuff—'

Lydia's gaze followed the direction of the woman's lifted arm, and without a word she kicked Melody forward. When she turned the bend of cliff she saw Richard, with the blood still trickling from his head, struggling to his feet. A companion of Starke's was watching him, with both hands on his hips. Starke himself was about to roll the roped body of Clara over the cliff edge. Lydia, with horror, drove the mare at him, reined, dismounted, and cradled the terrified unconscious girl in her arms. Clara, she saw thankfully, was still breathing. Then she looked up. Her face was a mask of cold fury.

'Loosen her,' she cried, raising her riding crop. 'Loosen her, or God himself will strike you down.' There was a pause before she continued, 'Do you hear? Do you all want to hang?'

Something of her command must have reached the ears of the small crowd. They went furtively forward as growing realisation of what they'd done registered. Starke didn't move until a man sprang forward, shot an arm at his clumsy form and sent him reeling.

'No more violence,' Lydia shouted. 'Come here and tend my sister.'

Richard, now on his feet, walked painfully to Lydia's side, then he drew himself up and faced those of the assailants who remained. Though badly cut his expression was hard, condemning and strong – his form that of a ruler of men, symbolising power, and an indomitable quality of character that quelled them to silence.

'You heard what she said,' he called, and his voice rang clear through the air. 'Tend her. Bring her here, and someone get a horse – one is not enough for what you've done this eve.'

He glanced at Lydia. There was admiration in his eyes, passion, and a great pain, but most of all love and pride. Pride of her bold spirit and compassionate heart, at the mere sight of her so bravely defending her own, with her hair loose about her shoulders, and the brilliant eyes showing no flicker of fear or weakening.

'Get into your saddle,' he told her firmly. 'Ride to Blackstone for help. And you—' indicating the watchers '—don't dare lay a finger or try to stop her. Throw no pebble, or I'll have the rope round all your necks—'

'And how'll you do that, mister?' Starke sneered, lumbering again towards him, 'ef we says you go over the side?' He laughed, but a second later the grin died into an ugly snarl. 'You can't do anythin', can 'ee? Better for us all ef the fishes had y'r comp'ny 'stead of us?'

There was a rising murmur again from the handful of nearby men, but except for a small muscle jerking on his face, no sign of emotion from Richard.

Lydia swung herself on to Melody's back, and sensing the rise and fall, the uncertainty, and changing tempo of the crowd's mood, addressed the gathering.

'Be reasonable,' she urged, 'for your own sakes as well as my husband's and my poor sister. You've been misled and forced to terrible action through suggestion and wagging wicked tongues. What has my husband ever done for you but good? Think, before it's too late. He's given work to unemployed, bettered the condition of many derelict homes – he's given *care* and thought to you. Yet this is the way you'd pay him, with stones and abuse and murder in your hearts—'

'No – no—' a woman interrupted. ''Tisn' murder we was wantin' – only the witch – the witch as harmed our cattle and ill-wished folk—'

'Witch!' The scorn, the contempt in her voice and flashing eyes chilled them. 'A defenceless young girl, who has already suffered terribly at the ruthless act of one of your kind, Tom Treen, a bully and drunken madman? Look at her now – go on, *look* – if you dare. No one could treat a defenceless young animal worse. And she – with a weak spine and delicate health – you should be *ashamed*, and on your knees praying to God for forgiveness, though I doubt that even God will find it possible.'

She paused, while the men quietened, and the women muttered among themselves. Two had their heads bowed; one was crying. Another went to do what she could for Clara.

''Tes true,' a rough female voice agreed. 'We'm gone agen the good Lord,' a figure fell to her knees, head lifted heavenwards, hands clasped in a gesture of prayer. One by one others followed. Lydia felt her taut nerves relaxing and heard Richard saying, 'Go now, my love – we need help.'

But before she could do so, Starke, fearful for his own safety, shouted, 'An' ef we lets you free – what do we get? eh? Consideration an' pardon fer wantin' justice fer ourselves? Es that a promise? A bond? Eh?'

'No one's making bargains with you, Starke,' Richard answered bluntly, and his voice was stronger now. 'No one—'

There was a brief pause before something – a sound – penetrated the air. All heads turned slowly, and were static, as men from Blackstone came galloping towards them through the fading light.

Lydia glanced at Richard. 'There's no need for me to ride alone,' she said. 'They'll have pistols and guns. *Our* men.'

'But how—'

'I met Athern by chance on the moor, and he told me what had happened. I was out riding. That's how I knew. He was already on his way to the house.'

He stared at her long and hard. 'So you braved all this – for me – and Clara of course, knowing what you had to face? They could have had you as well.'

'No, Richard. Not me. Right was on my side, and they were already becoming afraid.'

'That's true—' one of the men, a miner who'd overheard the short conversation affirmed. 'I didn' hold with it proper in the fust place. But women's tongues get waggin' an' evil-minded ones like old Treen's an' afore you knows where you are y'r in it.'

'Not if there's a shred of bravery or loyalty in you,' Richard retorted. 'Still, settlements and arguments are for later. Right now you'll all be taken to the nearest gaol and kept there until the magistrates decide what to do.'

And so it was.

As the Blackstone men reached the scene, those of the rioters who could, had already made an attempt to scatter and disappear. One or two of the less dangerous were let go, but Starke and his ringleaders were taken, following a brief struggle, and clapped into handcuffs when the law arrived minutes later.

Richard, beginning to feel weak again through loss of blood and shock was persuaded to ride with one of his men to the nearest lane where a chaise was waiting.

Clara, who had still not recovered consciousness, was carried gently in the arms of another faithful servant in front, accompanied by Lydia leading Melody by the bridle. Her overwhelming wish was to be with her husband, but although Richard would be all right, Clara was a different matter. Could she possibly recover after the two terrible ordeals she'd endured? Her face was so white, her eyes closed. With her lovely hair loose and flowing in the now rising wind and her lips almost colourless except for the faint blueish tinge, she appeared like some drowned Ophelia more than a living human being.

There was little sound now from the grim procession they'd left behind. The captives were surly and downcast, the women filled with fear and blame for those who'd got them into such light. The cortège outlined for some way behind the family chaise, then took a different route in the direction of the nearest gaol. The wind was rising now, and twilight was falling when the Fearnley chaise reached Blackstone, but the mist had lifted. Around them the wild moors spread dark under a fading greenish sky. Dotted at intervals along the horizon, the pagan standing stones stood – grim relics of the far distant primitive past interspersed by mine stacks of a more recent date. An owl cried mournfully from the trees as Richard climbed wearily from the vehicle, and Clara was taken into the parlour to be laid on the chaise-longue.

Lydia stood staring at Richard, shaking her head sadly. Then she went forward, and before attending to Clara, lifted her hand and touched his wounded head tenderly, murmuring, 'Oh Richard – oh Richard—' before tension and strain in her broke. Tears flooded her eyes. 'The doctor should see you both,' she managed to say, in choked tones. 'Where is he? Why isn't he here?'

'He is, ma'am,' a maid said. 'Johns is bringing what is needed so he c'n look at the Master and poor Miss Clara before they're moved.'

Before she finished speaking the doctor entered.

His examination of Richard was brief, and after delivering a few directions and applying hot water and bandages, his verdict was that although a nasty wound it was mostly superficial, and should heal satisfactorily without complications.

Clara was a different matter altogether. Apart from physical exhaustion he could find no bones broken, and as far as he could tell, no internal injuries.

'Bruises and cuts of course,' he said. "Tis natural. But—'

'Yes?' Lydia enquired. 'But what? What are you trying to say?'

'I really don't know, madam,' the doctor admitted. 'We'll try stimulants first. Maybe a little bleeding, though I'm afraid as she's in such a sorry weak state the last mightn't be advisable. Has she had any spirits? Any pick-me-up at all?'

'She was given brandy before the journey back,' Lydia told him. 'Nothing since. It had no effect.'

'Then I have something here.' He opened his bag, produced a bottle, and asked for a glass. He filled it a quarter full, and placed it to the girl's lips, where it trickled, half spilled, into her mouth. She made no sound or movement. All devices were tried, and a further portion of the restorative placed in the spoon for Lydia to handle in an effort to get it down. But Clara remained unresponsive, as though indeed, she was dead.

However, her breathing, though shallow, remained rhythmical. At last the doctor gave up. 'She should be taken to her room and kept completely quiet in bed for the night,' he said, 'and I must add, watched all the time. I have to return briefly to St Kerrick. But if there is any change let me know immediately, and I'll return. I shall be back early in the morning anyway, please God. If she is still in the same state I shall ask your permission to call in a specialist—' He glanced at Richard briefly.

'Of course,' Richard agreed instantly. 'Everything possible must be done to bring my wife's sister back to health. The question of expense, as you must know, does not arise.'

The doctor nodded. 'So I thought.'

Anne appeared in a nightshift and wrap just as the doctor had left. By then she knew most of the details of the tragic events, and had assumed her old air of authority and self-sufficiency. When Lydia announced that she would spend the night hours herself by Clara's side, Anne forcefully refused to allow it.

'Nonsense. You must be thoroughly exhausted yourself. You certainly look it. Like a wild woman.' Her voice was stern, but her eyes were surprisingly soft as she regarded the tumbled hair, smudged nose, and dishevelled cravat of Lydia's riding habit.

'Now *no* argument,' she commanded, when Lydia started to protest. 'I may be old, but I'm not quite addled or senile yet. I've still my wits about me, thank God, and it's commonsense for you to be with Richard. You both of you need a little peace to recover and – other things.'

The hint was so obvious Lydia, despite her exhaustion couldn't fail to notice. Her aunt of course had long known of the estrangement between them, and this, she thought vaguely, was a chance for bringing them together again. But would it? *Could* it? Under such abnormal and terrible circumstances?

Lydia glanced at Richard tentatively. His expression told her nothing.

Suddenly she felt unendurably tired.

'Very well,' she agreed, 'if you think that's best.'

'I don't think. I *know*.'

So it was settled.

Clara, in Miss Teague's care, was taken up to bed, and when Richard's cuts and head wound had been re-washed and attended to once more, he and Lydia retired to their own room together.

She undressed lethargically, without coquetry or conscious desire to please. Love-making somehow seemed out-of-keeping, and in a mild way would have affronted her. Richard apparently felt the same – if he could feel anything much at all by then. He appeared suddenly so haggard and drawn; the injury, on top of the mining troubles had obviously sapped more of his strength than he – or anyone, even the physician – had realised at the time. He sat on the bed wearily pulling off his clothes, hardly glancing at her. She wouldn't have minded if he had. Her scarred cheek, for the first time, had ceased to matter, and when she caught a fleeting glance at herself through the mirror, after washing, carelessly running a comb through her hair, she hardly perceived the reddened line. Compared with Clara's tragedy her own troubles were reduced to a minimum. Tomorrow, perhaps, vanity would have returned to torment her. But for the moment she was content to be able to go to her bed, not even wondering that Richard for the first time for weeks, was naturally taking his place by her side.

They lay silently for a time, feeling the closeness and warmth of companionship, until Richard turned slightly and put an arm round her.

'You were splendid, out there, Lydia,' he said, forcing himself to observe her closely – the proud features, tumbled hair, and lovely modelling of facial bones – even the scar, which in those moments of awareness added to her beauty rather than despoiled it. His eyes, so utterly wearied from strain, observed no blemish, nor would have done, had he been fully awake and alert.

Lydia smiled faintly. 'Splendid? I didn't do anything except say what I thought; and anyway I couldn't have kept the words back. You know me. Reckless – wild—'

Richard kissed her shoulder. His lips lingered there, and she wondered for a second if he wanted something more passionate of her after all. If he had, she'd have given. But after the ordeal, this quiet and utter sweetness was surely best for both of them at that point in time.

He must have felt the same. Moments later he let his arm slip to her thigh gently, where it rested in peace. Presently they both slept.

They woke late the following morning. Lydia felt much revived, and Richard's head was already healing well under its bandage. It ached, but he said nothing. 'Superficial,' the physician had told him. But as for Clara – Clara still lay white and unconscious, and hardly able to move. Her condition remained the same for some days. She was carefully tended and fed by Anne and Lydia. A specialist was called, who pronounced somewhat gloomily that there was no way of saying when, and in what condition, she would regain consciousness – even supposing she did so, completely.

His doubts concerning the latter question proved wrong. After another week Clara emerged from her coma, apparently normal, and smiling sweetly at everyone.

The household was naturally delighted, until it was found that all memory of the terrible events on the headland seemed to have been completely blotted from her mind. She was docile and gentle, and when told she had been ill, asked with genuine concern, 'Have I been a dreadful trouble to you? I'm so *sorry*.'

Her brow puckered for a moment in bewilderment. Then she exclaimed with her old air of youthful charm and excitement, 'Of course, I remember. Poor Papa died, didn't he? And then Charles.' Her eyes became dreamy. 'Poor Charles! he was such a clever artist. It was a shame Papa couldn't like him. Still – it was nice for me that you married Richard, Lydia. It's kind of you to have had me so long with you. How long is it? I don't know. I can't remember much—' Her voice trailed off, her smile faded.

'Don't try, darling,' Lydia said. 'You had a fall you know—' This seemed the most reasonable explanation to give.

'Did I? Oh – I see. Papa—' her mind again travelled back to Joseph, '—always said I must be careful of myself. He was so right about many things. Very godly, wasn't he?'

Lydia didn't answer, she couldn't; but Clara didn't appear to notice, and continued dreamily, 'We used to talk about God. Once I thought I'd be a nun – you know – in St Catherine's, where they do such lovely needlework, and wear those lovely trailing coifs and robes. Papa hated the idea of convents, though. But he let me go to a bazaar once, where the nuns were selling things for charity, and now he's dead, he might like to think I was praying for him and saying those lovely – those lovely hymns and Hail Marys and Te deums – or what is it they call them – in their beautiful church. I went there a long, long time ago, Sister Winifred met me when I was painting, and showed me round; Papa didn't know, but—' Her voice faded, her eyes closed.

Lydia stared at Richard and Anne with consternation. 'She's still rambling, isn't she?' Lydia asked. 'She doesn't mean it?'

Miss Teague shook her head. 'How do we know yet, what she means or thinks? The convent idea may be an escape world she's forced herself into. Only time will tell if she's ever able to pull herself out of it.'

This was true. Time held the key, refusing to unlock the tired recess of Clara's shocked mind. Months passed and she still remembered nothing but her devotion to her father, and her compelling need for peace and prayer to show honour to his memory.

'It was the last thing he'd have wanted or allowed,' Anne said time after time. 'He was such a staunch puritan and averse to anything savouring of Catholicism. But perhaps after all it's for the best.'

'*Why?*'

'Because she's spared the horror of remembering that dreadful Treen and the suffering caused her by those murdering peasants,' Anne replied. 'Clara was spoiled perhaps in the past, poor child, but after what she's gone through, then it's my belief any peace she can find, is deserved. Perhaps it is ordained?'

'Things may come back to her yet,' Lydia prophesied. 'Time's young still.'

'Maybe, but I think not.'

Anne proved to be right, and as summer gradually passed into autumn, it became clear to all at Blackstone that Clara, not so far ahead, was destined to be accepted as a novice within the walls of St Catherine's Convent.

13

For a time following the riot, and criminal assault on Clara, an uneasy quiet hovered over Blackstone. Richard was preoccupied, divided in his mind concerning how to tackle mining affairs and bring better relations once again to the villages, workers, and the estate in general. He realised that it was women's tongues, allied to worry and uncertainty over their future, that had first set the dangerous fires alight. Yet it was the womenfolk that now had to suffer, more perhaps than the men concerned in the attack. The innocent as well as the guilty. Clara, too, though unaware of it – indeed it seemed as the days passed that she had become transformed into an image of saintly dedication – had been considerably to blame for the peculiar antics she'd been up to. Only Lydia – and this in defying him – had shown any measure of true responsibility. The knowledge made him diffident with her, and she, in her turn, was strangely sensitive to his moods, absenting herself whenever possible from his presence as though she feared to irritate him.

He attempted at odd moments to break the friendly but unspoken barrier between them – longed to have her as he once had – sweet and passionate in his arms. But passion seemed to have retreated into the limbo of things forever lost and best forgotten. She no longer bothered to hide her scar, or keep the injured cheek averted. It was as though his opinion had ceased to matter. Meanwhile he made a point of re-employing a few men who had been laid off at Wheal Fancy. At the moment, as a commercial venture the action was mere philanthropy, but Richard was reassured by a man from the North – one of the best mining engineers in the country, that in spite of recent difficulties and delays –

he was convinced a wealth of tin lay at a low level to be worked. A good deal more expense would be involved, but Fearnley could pay the price, couldn't he?

Yes, Richard grudgingly admitted, and was willing to if the end product proved worth it. But his pocket was not unlimited. He was already paying out more than he'd bargained for in compensation to any bereaved families in the district and to the unemployed. Good will somehow had to be won back, and be retained from natives and miners. Without an honourable and friendly working relationship, nothing worthwhile could be achieved. Richard, usually, was not one to buy a pig-in-a-poke, or squander his wealth carelessly. He could be hard-headed when necessary, and often had been. But there were occasions, especially recently, when his mind was at war with his heart, and he had a shrewd idea that Lydia would undoubtedly favour backing the latter. So he made a strong effort to ignore the watchful glances and grudging attitudes of the mining community, trying to establish friendliness instead of fear, and the promise of better things ahead.

The possible fate of the ringleaders of the violent attack, of course, hung heavily over the atmosphere. Of the dozen taken into custody, several of the minor followers had been given a severe warning, confined in the local jail for a brief sentence, with a fine, which unknown to all but the magistrate, was paid by Fearnley himself.

Starke and his two chief supporters were taken to Bodmin, there to a wait sentence at the Autumn Assizes.

'What do you think will happen to them?' Lydia asked Richard one day shortly before the event.

'They'll be hung.' His voice was so hard, so emotionless, Lydia gave an audible sound of distaste.

'Why? Don't you agree? It's what they deserve. Would you deprive sightseers of their pleasure?'

'An eye for an eye, a tooth for a tooth,' Lydia exclaimed, reiterating the favourite words of her father, Joseph, and of another – the madman Treen.

'Exactly.' The curt avowal belied the unconscious

doubts so uncharacteristically churning through Richard's brain.

'Well, I for one won't be there,' Lydia resumed. 'It's all so – barbaric.'

Richard glanced at her with a curious gleam in his eyes. '*You* – the strong, the rebellious one, so quick to defend a sister and husband – have you lost the fight in you, Lydia? Don't you want Clara's torture avenged?'

'Not really. Clara seems happier than she's ever been. That's the word *they* used – that awful crowd! – *avenge*. How can you avenge suffering? I know men like Starke have to be punished. They shouldn't be let loose on society. But – there's another thing, Richard. This may be selfish – is his death that way, sensationally hanging with a rope round his neck, going to help *you*? And his wife's rather a gentle woman. I met her once. They have six children.'

'Then he should have thought of them before,' Richard said curtly.

However, on the day of the trial, although a verdict of death by hanging had been taken for granted, Starke and his companions were given the lesser sentence of deportation for life to one of the colonies.

'This, through the sole efforts of one, Richard Fearnley, Squire of Blackstone, who had made a sincere and most charitable appeal on the men's behalf for clemency,' His Worship announced sternly.

When Richard returned to impart the news to the household, Lydia's features relaxed.

'Will his family be able to join him over there?'

'Possibly. After a time. We shall see.'

'Oh Richard, I'm so *glad*,' Clara said sweetly, although she remembered not a thing of what had happened. 'Poor men. But we must try to be kind as the good Lord wished us to be, mustn't we? I shall go and see Sister Catherine tomorrow, and say an extra Ave Maria for the poor things. It's such a pity dear Papa didn't understand about the nuns. They're so wonderful, *really*.'

Richard turned from her impatiently, thinking that the

convent idea, though to him entirely reprehensible, was really the best solution for the lovely pathetic docile creature Clara had become.

Lydia was less sanguine.

'To think of Clara, with her hair shorn off, saying prayers in eternal obeisance to some starchy old Abbess—'

'To God,' Richard corrected her.

'Well – the God *they* believe in. But I don't,' Lydia retorted defiantly. 'I believe in – in—'

'What?'

'I suppose I'm a sort of pagan. I believe in *giving* and running free, and loving animals and the warm, human, decent things. In loving I suppose.'

'No discipline of course.' Richard's tones were dry. He was not looking at her.

She laughed. Something of the old joy of life was in the sound. 'Not much,' she agreed.

'You really don't have to, I suppose,' she heard Richard remark, to her great surprise. 'You're so very much yourself. I doubt if there's a single thing in the world really essential to you.'

Was he probing? Or did he really mean it? It was on the tip of her tongue to ask, but she hesitated a fraction too long. With an abrupt gesture he had turned and left her. A second later she heard his footsteps echoing and finally disappearing down the hall.

Autumn came, turning the moors burnished brown, gold and copper. Gradually leaves fell from the trees, falling, on quiet days, almost unnoticed, one by one, drifting like small tired dancers to the earth; at other times, when the winds rose, blown in thin showers against the grey sky. Gradually the branches became bare and dark, beautifully networked over the bent bushes of furze and brown bracken. The old stones of the hills became bleak and commanding then, the humped boulders crouched like immense primeval beasts against the Cornish landscape.

On such a day in late October, Lydia accompanied Clara

to the convent, driven in the family chaise. The grey granite building had been added to during the centuries, and conformed to no particular period, being mostly simple in design except for the porch, and two towers. It stood partly hidden by woodland on a slope above a valley to the west of St Kerrick. On a mound at the rear was a tall statue depicting the Madonna and Child, and facing it on a still higher hillock, a shining crucifix. Walls confined acres of ground which was worked and utilised by the nuns themselves for produce. Some was sold in available villages and towns to imburse funds for upkeep and constant improvements.

'We're a working community,' the Mother Superior had told Lydia and Clara on their first visit. 'Except for visitors who come to stay for brief periods of peace and rest – we cater for a few acceptable guests you know – there's little time for idle hands. When a sister has proved herself she may possibly be asked to go abroad on some work of mercy. Our first prerogative, *always* – is to obey the wish of Christ. Not—' she added to Clara, after a brief pause '—that you would be required to follow any foreign course, child. For those who are not strong we have suitable work here – like sewing, needlework and making attractive gifts for charity and our own annual bazaar.'

'And what about leisure?' Lydia had enquired.

The kindly but severe face had softened under its mediaeval-looking coif. 'My dear, our blessed Lord Jesus never said one must have no spare hour during the day in which to enjoy His own gifts to us of sunshine, and the freedom to indulge in peaceful meditation. A considerable portion of time is naturally spent in prayer – but then I'm sure you must have already realised that.'

Clara's violet eyes had glowed. She had agreed with an impassioned sweet enthusiasm that had made Sister Catherine smile and rest her hand briefly on the girl's shoulder. After a pause the conversation – or eulogy – had continued, giving details of rules and the high quality of dutiful acceptance required of anyone wishing to become a permanent member of the order. In conclusion Clara was advised to return home and think the matter over very carefully.

'Girls sometimes turn to us merely to recover from some unfortunate love affair or tragedy,' the composed quiet voice pointed out. 'But this can never be a satisfactory basis for a dedicated religious life. I have been told something of your tragic experience, my dear, and I beg you not to be too influenced by what could be a mere temporary phase of unhappiness from which you may recover—'

'Oh *no*,' Clara had cried. 'I really and truly want to work for God. Please believe me. I *know* it's right and was meant from the beginning. I was married once, wasn't I, Lydia?' She turned her eyes innocently upon her sister. 'But Charles died.'

The Mother Superior had glanced at Lydia enquiringly. Lydia had said firmly, 'To Clara he is dead. I don't think her past will be any obstacle at all, Mother.'

'Well – in that case – the circumstances are still rather unusual. I'm sure it is very necessary great thought should be given to the matter on each side. Meanwhile I shall have to contact the Bishop—'

Somewhat vaguely the discussion had ended there. Lydia personally, though averse to the idea, had sensed such a *need* in her sister – such a pitiful desire to be safe and forever secure from the harsh realities of the world, that she'd found herself accepting the venture rather than producing the normal obstacles that under other circumstances would have occurred to her.

During the following weeks Clara had appeared more determined than ever to pursue her course.

So here they were, bound on a mission that for Clara, might endure for the rest of her life.

Clara sat for the most part, serenely with her hands encased in her muff, staring, with a pleasurable lift of the lips, across the wind-tossed countryside. Lydia wondered ironically how her father would have viewed the situation, and decided that had Joseph been alive, such an unheard of predicament would never have arisen. Anything savouring of Catholicism had been heresy to Master Teague. But then all the 'ifs' and 'whys' in the world couldn't alter facts as they were.

She sighed hopelessly, 'Are you *really* happy in what you're doing, Clara?'

Clara turned her lovely head in its pale blue bonnet that so soon now would be replaced by the unbecoming headgear of a nun.

'Oh yes,' Clara replied. 'I've never been so happy in my life, except when Papa was alive of course.'

'But how can you know? If you don't remember?'

Clara's expression became shadowed, veiled and empty-looking. 'I can remember a dark cloud, that's all. And wishing you wouldn't – you wouldn't—'

'Me?' Lydia interrupted. 'How do I come into it?'

Clara shook her head.

'I don't know. But you did. You were always so – so compelling I think.'

'But—'

'Please stop talking and bothering me, Lydia. I want to be quiet and at peace.'

Rebuffed, Lydia shrugged, and from that point remained silent.

The time at the convent following Clara's admission was brief. When a young novice had ushered the newcomer away, Sister Catherine spent a few more minutes with Lydia reaffirming times when visits were permitted and other domestic details, then polite farewells were said, and Lydia was accompanied by a nun, Sister Jeanne, to the gates of the convent where the chaise was waiting. To her, it was as though she had escaped from prison. Sinner she might be, with hidden impulses in her to be free and wild as the creatures of the moor; but she was as she was, born to live life to the full, to savour the fresh salt wind on her lips, to have a man's arms round her, and abandon herself fully to the rich dark claims of her woman's need. As the horses clippety-cloppeted smartly along the lanes towards

Blackstone, she lifted a hand involuntarily to her cheek. The raised line was already sinking – the red mark day by day growing fainter. Eventually, perhaps, she would really be beautiful again, for Richard's delight. Or was this just wishful thinking?

Anne Teague, who had been feeling ill that day, was in her bedroom when Lydia walked into the hall, but Richard appeared from the library to greet her.

'Well? How did it go? Any tears?'

'To the contrary. I think my sister was quite glad to see the back of me.' If there was hurt beneath the façade she tried not to show it.

'And you?'

'Oh, Richard! what a thing to ask. If that's what Clara wants I'm glad for her sake.'

'But you won't miss her.' A statement, more than a question.

'Of course I shall miss her. So will Aunt Anne.' There was a pause, then Lydia added, 'But to be honest it will be a relief in a way. It's all been so – so restless lately, thwarting and such terrible things happening – so many under-currents. And everything's seemed to revolve round Clara.'

'Do you mean you're jealous? Actually *jealous*?'

She turned away abruptly, and pulled the cape from her shoulders.

'Of course not. Don't be ridiculous. But it *would* be pleasant for once to be free of other people's problems and wars, and be able to enjoy things. Just *enjoy*.' She spoke more vehemently than she knew.

Richard politely took her cape and held it, but he did not put it down. Instead, after one intent look at the sudden lovely flush of colour staining her face, he replaced it round her shoulders, saying, 'I agree with you. Absolutely. There's been far too much misery and melodrama about lately, and far too little of – other things. Wear it, Lydia.'

'But—'

'Do as you're told. We're going out; I'm going to show you something.'

Bewildered, but quite agreeable – even eager to comply, she did as he said, and moments later he was taking her to the stables.

'We're going somewhere,' he said.

'Riding?'

'Yes.'

'But I'm not dressed for it. I must change into my habit.'

'There's no need, my love. For once we're going to ride as they did in the old days, on my stallion, with you before me – together.'

She smiled uncertainly; her heart had quickened.

'You're joking.'

'Oh no.'

'Why though?'

'You'll see,' he answered. 'In fact, you're really a bit of a ninny not to guess.'

She shook her head, slightly amused, titillated, and oddly excited. 'All right, only don't call me a ninny! I'm brighter than you think.'

As the boy was not about, and Johns was somewhere in the loft, Richard saddled the stallion himself, took the great animal by the bridle and led it round the back of the stables, along the shortest route possible from the paddock to the shadowed lane leading upwards to the moors. There he placed Lydia before him on the grey's back, and they started off at a brisk pace gathering speed as they reached the wild uncluttered spaces of the wild landscape. This time Richard took a path seldom used by riders because of treacherous bog pools, and the danger of meeting a lurking hidden mine shaft. But he knew every inch of the way, and the afternoon had lengthened, throwing a golden track of dying sunlight streaking down the slope.

In the ordinary way Lydia would have felt frustrated at being denied the opportunity to ride her own mare. But on this occasion it was different somehow. Everything was. Richard himself seemed to have changed and become younger – more reckless and unpredictable. Like the weather, like nature – calm and controlled one moment, the next bursting into a medley of changing moods – of alternating light and shade, of freshening winds and fleeting shadow heralding springtime chasing on winter's heels. And it was not even winter yet.

The air, so richly filled with the scents and pungent odours of damp earth, fallen leaves, late blackberries, and the subtle tang of brine from the sea – blew keen against them as they rode, taking Lydia's cape and flying molten hair into a russet cloud, whipping her face to a brilliant glow. The warmth of the steed and Richard's strong male body steamed close against her. Her heart sang. The further they went, the wilder grew her excitement. Past great boulders and menhirs they rode, until at the top of the ridge they turned abruptly, and on the skyline Lydia glimpsed the lonely outline of Castle Chynan-Tol – relic of an age thousands of years before Christ. It had been predicted that at some future time archaeological work might be started at the site, which would prove to be of tremendous historical value. But for the present the ancient remains stood as they had been for centuries – a large mound of massive boulders and tumbled relic of a wall, with a half-circle of standing stones below. Once it had been thought to be a burial ground, but more recent opinion veered to the assumption that at one period a castle had indeed stood there, at a later date than the circle itself which most probably held religious significance. Further on – to the other side, were indications of a primitive village. But so far any deductions were hypothetical. One fact superseded all speculations – Castle Chynan-Tol held a wild and savage atmosphere. It was a place of legend, a challenge itself to time and the elements. Some said ghosts walked there still at certain periods of the moon. Others that a dark phantom horseman rode whenever disaster threatened the district, with a pack of hounds at his heels.

Sensible people scoffed at such tales, but few went there, and the superstitious travelled many extra miles rather than put a foot there as evening fell.

Now, Lydia realised, Richard, for some strange reason of his own had that particular spot as his goal.

The fitful last ray of sunshine had quivered beyond the ridge of moor when they arrived, but as they paused at the highest point, a shaft of red gold broke into a myriad gleams of light before finally disappearing, lighting the tumbled stones and broken archway to brief rosy radiance. Then, suddenly, all was grey and hushed, except for the whining sound of wind through the sparse undergrowth.

Richard dismounted and opened his arms to Lydia. She sprang into them lightly. He held her for a few seconds, tight against him, then released her to tether the grey. The animal, after the miles of exercise, was amenable, and gave no trouble in being roped to one of the tallest stones, a giant slab of granite, considerably higher than the horse's head.

'He's contented at the moment,' Richard told Lydia. 'After his recent mating. I wouldn't have ridden him otherwise.'

But Lydia wasn't interested in the stallion's peccadilloes or love-life. She was standing with her arms out, chin lifted and head raised to the sky, her skirts, cape and hair swirling around her. How lovely life was! how wild, how sweet, how suddenly terribly, *terribly* exciting. She started to run – it was more of a dance – in and out of the stones, into the shadows and out again, laughing, singing, as though she was singing with the air, and streams, and flying clouds – a queen of that wanton elemental place.

'Hey!' she heard Richard call. 'Where are you—'

His feet went thudding after her; she eluded and mocked him, pausing in the shade of some rock or wind-blown bush as his eyes searched the quickly fading light. Then, fleet as a young deer, she sped on again; until suddenly she caught a toe in a bramble and fell. She wasn't hurt, but she was too late to elude Richard longer. He was on her in a second and was pulling her to her feet.

'Are you hurt?'

'*Hurt? Me?*' She laughed into his face, and he swept her up into his arms.

'You witch, you little devil.' His lips were hot against the soft hollow of her throat. 'Oh Lydia, how I love you—'

The smile died from her mouth. The green light of her blueish eyes deepened to darkest jade as they met the kindling flame in his own. Something she had never known before burned and took life between them – an awareness so mysterious and strong – so overpowering that they were both held transfixed – speechless, while the moments ticked into timelessness, and it was as though they were the first and only human beings in the world – man and woman, born of that force of which the universe itself first erupted into being.

'My queen,' he whispered. 'My wild sweet queen.'

He carried her a few strides to the broken arch of the ancient doorway, and stood inside the tumbled walls, holding her until he gently laid her down on the thin sweet smelling turf. Then he loosened her cape and clothes, and divested himself of his own, so they were both naked and trembling, feeling neither cold or the wind's brushing – knowing only the urgent compelling need and desire for unification – for belonging as they had never belonged before.

His lips traversed the perfect column of her body, reverently at first, adoring of her perfection. Then gradually, force and passion rose in a dark wave – a hunger so all-consuming that he took her blindly, senses reeling, and her flesh became his, swept to ecstasy on a wild tide in which they both drowned and were lost to the world – two rivers merged as one.

To Lydia the thrust of manhood was delight and thrilling forgetfulness, bringing purification and erasement of all former bitterness. Like a flower she opened to receive him, and from her upthrust breasts it was as though fountains of pure joy flowed.

When it was over he bent his head, and once more – only differently – with extreme gentleness – he caressed every curve and hollow of her perfect body.

She lay back, at peace smiling.

'I love you so much, Richard.' One by one he took the fingers of both her hands, and kissed each tip in turn.

'Oh, darling,' was all he said, time after time. Just the two words: nothing more.

But for her they were sufficient.

No doubt remained.

They belonged.

For the next few months Lydia felt happier and more fulfilled than she had believed any woman could be. There were occasional clashes of wills when Richard, as his male prerogative, asserted himself, and her temper briefly flared. But ultimately any difference was always resolved in his arms, and reconciliation was the sweeter for any slight tiff. Although he prided himself on being master, she knew her hidden power over him, and generally found subtle means of getting her way. Not always of course. But then she wouldn't have wanted that. She admired his strength and courage and capacity to dominate when necessary. They were a team, yet both were determined characters reigning each over their different spheres.

The only faint shadows clouding their mutual existence were Anne Teague's health which was failing, the mine that was still not progressing as quickly as Richard wished – and Clara.

Lydia, at times secretly worried that her sister who had undergone such distress should be confined to so unnatural a life.

'It seems so sad,' she said to Richard. 'And what will happen to her – how will she take it if she ever remembers? The physician did say she *might*. And then—'

'We must wait,' Richard said. 'I don't think it's very likely now.'

But he was wrong.

One afternoon in the following February a note was delivered to Lydia from the convent saying that Sister Annunciata – the name by which Clara was known there – had surprisingly revealed that morning that she recollected everything, and would like to see Mrs Fearnley.

I think it would be helpful and advisable if you could make a visit as soon as possible [the message concluded]. And please do not worry. Our novice is well and happy.

Yours sincerely,

Sister Catherine.

'There!' Lydia exclaimed, 'I said it might happen, and I was right. I *must* go immediately.'

Richard accompanied his wife in the chaise, but waited outside while the interview took place. Thinking it highly probable that Clara would wish to return with them, Lydia had packed a valise with some of her sister's most attractive clothes.

She was taken aback however when Clara, appearing serenely beautiful in her nun's habit, informed her they would not be needed.

They were sitting alone together in a small room specifically used for rare visits from friends or families. It was simply, almost austerely furnished in light oak, with a large silver crucifix hanging on a cream painted wall facing a small gothic-shaped window. Pale light filtered through the glass, falling directly upon Clara's angelic countenance. The sisters regarded each other over a small table, and Lydia noticed that Clara kept one hand reverently on a Bible.

'I don't want to leave,' the younger girl said quietly but firmly, following a short discussion. 'I'm happy here, Lydia – *really* happy. You see – it may be hard for you to believe, but I know it's true. I have a vocation, and all those dreadful things that happened to me in the past were just preparation – a way to finding Christ and loving Him.'

'But Clara—' Lydia tried in vain to put the situation differently. 'Don't you understand dear – can't you realise that you're still – well shocked? You're probably suffering from reaction. You *must* be. At least can't you wait a little before you decide to take any final vows. If you came home for a short rest – and I'm sure Sister Catherine would agree – you might change your mind—'

'No.' The denial was so firm, yet so softly spoken, Lydia was forced to realise that at the moment, anyway, there would be no compromise. After a short pause Clara continued, still quietly but with an underlying conviction that brooked no denial, 'And there's something else, Lydia. Something I must confess.'

Oh no, thought Lydia, please no religious confessional business. But Clara went on, 'In the past I was not a *good* person, Lydia. There were a lot of things about me you didn't know. It was because of my back, partly, I know. I was jealous. *Terribly*, of you. I didn't even love you all the time. Sometimes I even tried to hurt you. Did you know that—?'

'Oh, Clara! But—'

'It's true. I would have taken Richard from you if I could, but I hadn't any chance at all. I tried and tried. And that was wicked of me, wasn't it?'

Lydia sighed and shook her head. 'Clara, we're all human, and you've nothing to have a conscience over. Sometimes I didn't like you either.'

'You were always honest, Lydia. I wasn't. But living here has taught me that I can make amends – in loving God. And I do love Him. I *do*. In forgetting myself and becoming a Bride of Christ when I'm worthy, don't you *see*, Lydia? I shan't be wasting my life, as you seem to think? I shall be fulfilling it.'

Moments passed before Lydia asked, 'How did it happen? Your – your revelation? When did you remember?'

'During Mass, early today. I'd had a headache when I woke, and I suppose I must have looked ill or something. But I wasn't – just surprised and relieved. One of the sisters helped me from Chapel. I tried to explain, but she made me rest for a little in my cell, and then, later, Mother Superior came to see me. I told her everything, and she said it was her duty to inform you.'

'I see.'

'I wasn't unhappy though, Lydia, and gradually when

everything fitted into place – it was so wonderful the peace I felt. Oh please, *please* believe me. I shan't change. Really I won't. And—' her voice trembled very slightly, 'I'm sorry for what I tried to do to you.'

'Clara! My *dear*.'

The meeting ended quite soon after Clara's last impassioned plea.

The sisters parted, Clara with tears of gratitude and perhaps – Lydia conceded – real affection in her eyes. Lydia with a sense of tremendous relief to be out of such a highly charged emotional situation.

'I don't think she will change,' she told Richard later. 'It seems so unnatural.'

'It may be the best for Clara though,' Richard pointed out. 'She *is* someone there, she *counts*. And she's got something not very pleasant out of her mind in making that so called confession to you. I always knew the angelic Clara was no saint at heart. But perhaps, in the end—' he smiled, 'she may get half way to becoming one – which is more than you will ever be, my darling.'

Lydia was forced to smile.

'Talking about confessions,' she said, 'I've got one to make too – to you.'

'Oh?'

She touched his arm gently. 'Aren't you going to ask what it is?'

'Is it a very bad one?'

'Dramatic, I'd say.'

'Well, out with it.'

'I'm going to have a baby, Richard.'

Delight flooded his face. As he drew her to him he said, 'I'm not really surprised. I'd noticed a slight increase in weight, shall we say, lately. And when is this wonderful event to be?'

'July sometime.'

'Ah.' He thought back. 'That day at Chynan-Tol.'

'Yes.'

'So if it's a girl we'll call her Heather, because she was conceived where heather blows.'

'But it may be a boy.'

'If it is we'll have to think again. Meanwhile, my love, we must take a toast – to another Fearnley on the way, and to – love.'

He brought out a decanter and glasses, and with the blue-green eyes and the grey lost in mutual wonder, they drank to the unborn and the unknown future.

Epilogue

Heather Fearnley glared first at the sampler she was working upon, then turned her dark lashed eyes to the window. They were strange lovely eyes, neither grey nor green but holding the luminous quality of the ever-changing shades in quartz washed by the sea. At that moment they had a brilliant, almost defiant look. She hated needlework. She was nine years old, and it seemed stupid to be sitting in the stuffy parlour making patterns of birds and funny trees on canvas, when she could be wandering about the moors where the real ones were – racing with rabbits and gulls, clouds and wind-blown leaves. If it hadn't been for Great-Aunt Anne who was trying so hard to make her into 'a well-behaved little lady' she'd be free to do more of the things she wanted to. Her mama wouldn't have minded. Mama understood and Heather had a shrewd idea she'd been very like her when she was young. But Lydia, her mother, spent a great deal of time with Papa at the mine. It was as though they couldn't bear to be apart for long. Well, that was very nice, of course. Being so much in love must be wonderful. All the same – Heather's small chin took a mutinous thrust – it wasn't fair to leave her so often in Aunt Anne's charge.

'Be kind to her, darling,' Lydia said on such occasions, 'remember she's old and doesn't have many pleasures. She's so fond of you, Heather. So be a good girl – for her sake – and mine.'

Mama's smile was so dazzling that Heather generally complied. But today, somehow, was different. The old lady – and she must be *very* old – almost as old as God, Heather thought – wasn't even awake. She was sitting back in her favourite chair with her eyes closed, making funny little whistling noises between her teeth. Why then must Heather sit listening, and pricking her finger so that tiny spots of blood stained the pattern?

She stared at the thin countenance intently for a minute, then got up, leaving the canvas and embroidery box on a settle, with a jumble of threads, silk and fine wool, scattered untidily on the floor. She picked them up hastily and stuffed them into the box. Aunt Anne would have a fit if she saw such untidiness. When she was quite certain the old lady wasn't going to wake suddenly and start scolding, Heather tip-toed quietly across the floor, and opened the door as softly as she could. It creaked; the child's heart leapt into her throat. She waited, but nothing happened. The whistling noise had deepened into a snore, so everything was all right. She closed the door, holding the knob firmly until the latch had clicked into place almost soundlessly, then on light feet slipped down the hall and out of a side door into the grounds.

It was July. Her birthday had been the previous week, and she was wearing her new birthday dress, just because Mrs Carnley – the rector of St Kerrick's wife – was coming for a cup of tea with Aunt Anne and bringing her a jar of special honey, so everyone had to be looking nice, and on their best behaviour. But the afternoon was only just beginning. Mama wouldn't be back from the mine for ages – she had gone with Papa immediately after lunch, to deliver goodies in two baskets to cottages where some of the poorer miners lived. Papa liked her to be friendly with his workers, and most people loved Mama. Heather could understand that. She was so beautiful. What everyone didn't know was that Lydia also had a fiery temper, and could be strict when important people were coming to tea. So the little girl decided to be very careful of the new dress, and not get it torn or soiled. It was of pale green muslin, with a lace collar and a satin sash. Her lustrous dark curls were held back by a ribbon of the same shade. She wasn't, normally, a vain child – there were so many other lovely things to think about rather than appearances – but her governess, who had the afternoon to herself that day – had made her take a good look at herself in the long mirror of her bedroom before putting the final touches to her 'toilette' – what a funny word, and Heather had felt a strong stirring of pride.

'There now!' Miss Drake had said. 'You look almost handsome for once.'

'As pretty as the Queen?' Heather had asked, referring to the young Queen Victoria who had come to the throne the previous year in 1837.

'Now you're being stupid,' had come the sharp reply. '*No* one is comparable to the Queen. You should not be so conceited.'

'But she's not much bigger than me, is she? And Cook said she was *plump* – she said that—'

'What Cook said, or anyone else for that matter, is not your concern, and you shouldn't listen to gossip. Little girls should be—'

'Seen, and not heard, I know – sorry.'

Miss Drake gave a cross little tug to the sash, then said, 'Now go to the parlour, Miss Teague is waiting for you. And don't get up to any mischief, or I shall see you're punished.'

Well, Heather decided, as she hurried to the moors, keeping carefully in the shade of any available hedge or wall so she wouldn't be seen – there wasn't any mischief to get up to, just sitting with Great-Aunt Anne in the parlour – and she couldn't see there was anything wrong in wandering about outside for a bit. There was no wind, the sun was shining, and the air was so sweet with the scents of a hundred things – of bluebells, primroses, gorse and bracken and grass, and the faint tangy odour of brine from the sea. Gulls wheeled, silvery white against the sky, and the round tumbled stones glistened grey, green and shining darkest blue among the bracken.

She walked carefully, because on warm days in summer adders sometimes lay sleek and shining on the granite surfaces. Heather wasn't afraid of snakes. Their tiny glittering dark eyes fascinated her, but she knew if you trod on them or they became frightened they could bite, and the bites could be dangerous. Once, when she'd escaped from the house alone, she'd let an adder crawl over her arm. She'd waited for it to slither away, but before its sleek body had slipped down into the undergrowth, it had paused with neck arched, flat head reared, watching her with an unfathomable strange look that had momentarily puzzled her. It was as though some secret communion had been forged between them. An understanding that neither would wittingly harm the other. She had returned several times to the same spot, and generally the snake had appeared. Eventually she had come to regard it as a pet. Once a tip of her finger had touched its head and it hadn't moved. It had been the last time she'd seen it. Unthinkingly, she'd let out her secret to her father and he'd made a terrible fuss with Miss Drake. Heather had been forbidden ever to touch a snake, or even a slow-worm again. As it happened, she'd had no chance. She was watched more and when at last she'd managed to revisit the place, the adder didn't appear. Perhaps it was dead, she'd thought sadly, or had forgotten.

It didn't really matter, though. There were other creatures like birds and mice, and sometimes the burnished red-gold shape of a fox could be seen streaking across the moor.

Oh, there were so many lovely things in the world – things she wanted to touch, or find out about. She often wondered what it would feel like to be a bird, or a badger perhaps, with its home all cosy and clean in the moorland earth. People too. She had read legends about the ancient kings and queens of Cornwall, and sometimes pretended to be Guinevere or some other famous character when she stood by the old standing stones and menhirs of that wild area. That such territory was forbidden to her only made her 'escape adventures' more exciting. Then there were characters in plays by William Shakespeare. She had learned early to read – her governess had told the stories and plots of *A Midsummer Night's Dream*, *Macbeth* and *The*

Tempest, then made her read extracts aloud. Some of the long passages bored her terribly, but the magic of others had registered in her child mind, especially pictures conjured up of *The Dream* and excerpts out of *The Tempest*. When the weather was grey and mist crept down over the rugged Cornish moors and wild sea, she imagined herself as Miranda, and visioned a great rock or boulder as wild ugly Caliban.

Even *The Merchant of Venice* had engrossed her in places. Most of it she just repeated mechanically after her teacher, but she admired Portia, and could see herself in the role standing majestically in front of the horrible old Shylock, and telling him 'The quality of mercy is not strained. It falleth as the gentle rain from heaven upon the earth beneath.' Oh, those words were very splendid. Did she, Heather, look at all like Portia, she wondered? She had dark hair, of course, but her eyes were grey green, with violet shades, and somehow she thought Portia's would be brown. No matter. Quite a lot of people said she was 'a real handsome lil' maid' – old Dan the shepherd did. She would have liked, really, to be fair and pretty like Aunt Clara who was a nun in that queer convent place in the hills. But Heather knew the description 'handsome' suited her better, because she was tall and strong with red lips above a stubborn chin, and a creamy-golden skin with glowing cheeks that flushed vivid rosy pink in the wind.

'Like her father,' most people said; others, just a few, remarked, 'Oh, there's a lot of her mother in her.'

Well, of course, there must be. Because she'd come from both of them, hadn't she? And that was the wonderful thing about life – how everyone who was born was different – for instance there couldn't ever be another Heather Fearnley just like her in the world, could there? And this made her feel very important indeed. Just being unique, herself.

That afternoon, as she hurried up the moor, trying to remember not to catch her green muslin dress on a twig or thorn – scrambling a little, occasionally, clutching at undergrowth, then skipping ahead, almost dancing when she came to a clear patch of thin turf – or a fairy-ring – she was smiling. Terribly excited to be alive. There was an old menhir, with a kind of gnarled funny looking face that seemed to watch her as she passed. She touched it with a hand, wondering what she'd do if it suddenly heaved itself from the bracken and came towards her. Legend said it had once been a wicked knight who'd been turned into stone, but she didn't think so. Not really. It belonged to the earth – it had been there for millions of years; old Dan had said so. And Athern.

'It can't walk nor move, dordi, not like me or thee,' he'd said. 'But these old stones have a magic all the same. The oldest magic of all, rackli – that was there when O Del created the world. Put thy cheek against the granite an' feel its power an' a kind of o' singin' – the singin' of wind an' air, an' water o' the streams—'

Oh, Athern said wonderful things, and Heather had found out they were true – in a way. Papa didn't like her spending much time with him, but Mama understood; Mama's understanding was a great bond between them, although Heather loved her father more passionately.

She was thinking of Athern when he appeared suddenly from behind a cluster of wind-blown bushes. He looked wild and smiling, and gave a funny little bow when he saw her, lifting his cap from his head. It had a feather in it, and with his black eyes twinkling he reminded her of a grown-up Puck.

'Greetings, dordi,' he said, 'an' what's thee doin' up here at such a time? Won't theer be trouble?'

Heather nodded. 'If I'm late back. We've got someone coming to tea – the rector's wife. But I won't be late. I shall run, and be very careful of my dress. Do you like it? It was new, for my birthday.' She twirled round for him to see.

'A real little queen – a princess, you look,' Athern answered. 'It suits thee, dordi.'

'Like Titania, do you mean?'

'Like thyself,' he answered. 'An' that's what you should always remember – act what you like, but cling to what thou really are. If you can do that life will be rich for thee, princess.'

Heather studied him for moments before she said, 'You do say nice things, Athern. Where do your thoughts come from?'

'Ah.' He tapped his black curls, grinning. 'We folk have a way of knowin' things. There's a deal o' whisperin' in the wind, an' singin' when the fine rains beats the earth, that us gippos has a knowledge of afore we can properly walk. There's a bit o' that in thee too, rackli, and see it's not forgotten. Keep it close to thy heart, even if thy dukkerin is to marry a fine gentleman – a gorgeous gentleman in silks and satins, who'll give riches and a fine house to thee made all of marble.'

'Do you think I really *might*, Athern?' Heather's voice was awed.

'I reckon you could, dordi.'

'Perhaps,' her voice was dubious. Then, slowly, she shook her head. 'First of all though I'll want to know all the people in the world I can, and perhaps *be* them – just for a time. Oh, I won't forget what you said about always remembering I'm *me*, Athern. But—' her expression suddenly lifted, as a beam of sunlight caught her upturned face, lighting the bone structure and finely formed features to a sudden radiance.

'I know what I'm going to be when I'm grown up,' she said, in ringing tones, standing tall for her age, and erect against the Cornish landscape. 'I know *exactly*. I'm going to be an *actress*.'

For a moment or two even Athern was silenced by the conviction, pride, and beauty of the young form confronting him. Then, in a flash, she quickly became a child again, and the next minute had turned and left him – an elusive flying figure in delicate green disappearing down the hill in the direction of Blackstone.